Tempt Me, Trust Me

by

Renee Reeves

Tempt Me, Trust Me

COPYRIGHT © 2021 by Michelle Hiller Reeves

Cover Art by *Debbie Taylor*

The Wild Rose Press, Inc.
PO Box 708
Adams Basin, NY 14410-0708
Visit us at www.thewildrosepress.com

Publishing History
First Edition, 2021
Trade Paperback ISBN 978-1-5092-3881-1
Digital ISBN 978-1-5092-3880-4

Previously Published 2009 Black Velvet Seductions
Published in the United States of America

She was frowning, dark brows pulled down low over her eyes, staring at her car. Then the shaking started, first her hands, then her shoulders, even her chin wobbled. Tears spiked her lashes, making her eyes shine unnaturally bright. He knew delayed shock was setting in.

"Don't think about it," he said, "You're fine now."

She blinked at him, eyes huge and wet in her pale face. He wanted to grab her, hug her tight and never let go.

"I-I could have…I could have k-killed you. Or a f-family, or a—."

"Hush." He caught her chin firmly, shocking her silent. Ignoring her attempts to pull free he angled her head up, forcing her to look him straight in the eyes, "You didn't, and that's all that matters now."

The sirens were much, much louder now and Nick knew that rescue was only a few sharp curves away. Soon they would be surrounded by commotion and questions and police wanting reports. But for now, for just this moment in time, it was the two of them. They had an unspoken bond now, forced upon them by life's quirky nature.

She was watching him, like a wary doe would watch an approaching hunter. He let go of her chin, but brought his other hand up and stroked her cheek. Soft downy skin met the rough calloused tips of his fingers. She held still under his caress, holding her breath as if she were afraid to move.

"You're beautiful."

Dedication

To my mom. Again. You forever live in my memories and my heart.

Chapter 1

Keeping an eye on the sideview mirror and steady light pressure on the truck's gas pedal Nick smoothly backed the silver two-horse trailer into the small opening of the round pen. His brother, Jake, stood next to the corral fence, frowning and staring at the trailer. Each kick from the horse inside rocked the trailer side to side. Nick shifted the truck into park but kept this foot on the brake and then waved his arm out of the driver's side window to get his brother's attention.

"He's not tied so when you open the door be ready to get the hell out of the way," he shouted.

Jake nodded, then squeezed between the fence and the trailer and Nick heard the harsh clangs of numerous locks being thrown. A loud squealing of metal hinges sounded, combining with the clattering of sharp hooves. The horse let out a high-pitched scream before jolting the trailer up and down as the animal lunged out of the trailer. Nick heard the trailer door slam shut and put the truck into drive, pulling the rig quickly away so Jake could close the corral gate. He pulled the truck and trailer around to the side of the barn, then came back to stand beside Jake, who stood with his elbows and one booted foot propped on the corral railing, watching with narrowed eyes as the horse careened around the enclosure.

"Jesus Christ, Nick." Jake's usually level voice was

hard. "The bastard that did this should have been shot."

"Trust me, I was tempted."

"There's not an inch on him that's not scarred. Even his ears. How the hell did you get close enough to get the halter on him?"

Nick sighed, suddenly feeling very, very tired. "I tranqed him with the dart gun. Hated to do it, but it was the only way." He clucked and the big-boned quarter horse draft cross twitched his ears towards him. For a second Nick saw something soft flicker in the horse's eyes, but then it was gone and the madness was back. Lowering his head, the horse charged to the corner of the enclosure and struck out aggressively with both front legs.

"Looks like it's worn off though."

Jake snorted, watching the gelding's dramatic display. "Ya think?" He double checked the latch on the pen gate, "You've got your work cut out for you with this one, Nick, maybe more than you realize. I hope he's worth it."

Nick looked into huge brown eyes, seeing nothing but fear and distrust, but he also saw beneath the scars and misbehavior to the proud beauty the horse had probably been before he'd been bought and misused by a cruel owner.

"They're always worth it, Jake."

****

The hairs on the back of Nick's neck prickled and he reined to a halt just outside the hidden copse.

She was here again.

He exhaled silently, ignoring his now racing heart. Moving carefully, he dismounted and ground tied his horse, knowing the abundance of grass would keep the animal quiet and satisfied. Stepping off the path he moved quickly to the shelter of a huge Hemlock tree and relaxed against its trunk, crossing his arms over his chest. The moon was full overhead but shadows cast by enormous, low-hanging limbs would keep him hidden from her view. The low gurgling of the stream she sat beside would absorb any slight noise.

God she was beautiful.

Wrapped in a light-colored shawl because of the cool night she sat at the edge of his stream, knees drawn up to her chin, dangling a leafy vine in the water, completely oblivious to his presence. Thick dark hair trailed loosely down her back and Nick saw that a portion of it was trapped beneath her. Modern women just did not have hair like that, not without hundreds of dollars' worth of styling help. Gut instinct told him that the gorgeous mass cascading to the ground was real. Nick could almost feel the silky-smooth texture of it trailing over his jaw and across his chest as her mouth moved down to his stomach, his abs…

Shit…He shifted slightly, trying to ease the sudden heaviness in his groin.

She sighed. Turning her head slightly in his direction and resting her right cheek against her knees. Moonlight painted her skin translucent it appeared lit from within. She had a fragile bone structure, sweet, very delicate features; high forehead, dark arching brows and eyes a color he couldn't make out…Full, sensuous lips had him clenching his jaw against a groan of intense longing.

She shivered and wrapped her shawl more tightly around her, but her small shoulders continued to tremble. Nick frowned; the thought of her being cold bothered him, although why he should care was beyond him. After all, she was trespassing on his land, invading his private domain.

And he didn't give a shit.

He wanted to take her in his arms. Share his body heat until the both of them were burning.

The urge was insane. Coming out here in the middle of the night just to see her was insane.

She walks in beauty, like the night... The words popped into his mind, a poem he had heard once but damned if he remembered where or when. Most likely from a movie, since reading poetry was not high on his list of good times, although he had to admit that the line was certainly beautiful...like her. Nick rolled his eyes at himself; waxing poetic at his age wasn't a very good sign.

Soft undulations reached his ears. Humming. She was humming, for Christ's sake. Low, slightly husky, the soothing rhythm floated to him, vaguely foreign sounding. Sort of like a lullaby. Leaning towards the stream she plucked a blade of grass from between two rocks and ran the tip of it around her open palm, following the outline of each finger with the slender blade. Long, slow, stroking caresses. Up, down, and around. His throat tightened and his fingers clenched tightly against the waves of lust that gripped him. He imagined her hands upon his skin, slowly caressing...and then her lips following their path downward...

Suddenly she froze, her hum cut off in midstream. The blade of grass fell forgotten to the ground as she subtly cocked her head to one side, listening.

Muscle's tensing, Nick wrapped his palm around

the hilt of his knife. He stood tense, ready for trouble until she finally relaxed and focused her gaze on something near the water. Soon he was able to see what had her attention. A black-crowned Night Heron had landed in the stream about thirty feet from where she sat, an unlucky fish dangling from his wet beak. She smiled at the bird, a truly genuine smile that dimpled her cheek and flashed small white teeth. Nick caught his breath- He wanted her smiling at him that way, pure, open and trusting. *Jesus! What the hell is wrong with me?* Now I'm jealous of a damn bird!

Spreading its wings, the heron flew away to enjoy its prize and with childlike enthusiasm she busied herself digging in her pack, pulling out a sketchpad and pencil and beginning to draw by moonlight. The pencil moved quick and sure and Nick guessed she was capturing her memory of the bird while still fresh. He craned his neck, trying to get a glimpse of her drawing.

Oh Christ! His mouth went dry when in one of the most unintentionally seductive displays he had ever seen, she stood and used both hands to massage her butt, arching her back and causing her breasts to thrust out against her shawl. Full and natural, they were more than enough to fill his hands and more than made up for her lack of stature. She might be small but she had more than enough to satisfy him. Her wet-dream hair fell long and wavy down her back, past her thighs to almost touch the ground. Her soft appreciative sigh as the stretch loosened tight muscles reached him all the way across the clearing and he bit back a growl.

He wanted her now; soft and wet, stretched out naked in his bed, up against the wall; bent over a chair with her ass in the air, or hell, out here would do just fine too.

He sucked in a deep breath, knowing he was in deep shit when the flood gate of erotic images opened. When it came to her his body seriously outruled his brain, and if he had to endure much more of this torture he was definitely going to explode.

Chapter 2

Morgan stood slowly, balancing herself with a palm against a nearby tree. Sweat beaded on her forehead and she groaned, biting her lip as her cramped and kinked muscles gave and stretched. Seeing the bird had been so exciting that she had forgotten to massage and stretch her leg, and had been sitting, caught up in sketching for far too long. Hesitantly, afraid to move too suddenly, Morgan leaned back against the tree, glad for its rough support while she waited on her leg to relax and be able to take her weight. Finally, the cramping eased and she could stand on her own. The walk home would be slow, especially since she had to carry her full backpack, and she dreaded the night to come. She bent to grab her pack, gasping as a sharp pain jerked her back upright. After a moment she tried again, this time successfully.

"Well," she grumbled while adjusting the pack onto her shoulder, "you did it to yourself, Morgan. At least you have a few painkillers left." The tiny pills were in the bottle on the nightstand beside her bed. She hadn't taken one in over a week, preferring just to cope with the constant, dull ache in her hip and thigh, but tonight because of her overexertion she knew she would not be able to rest without them.

She sighed, absorbing the dark, glistening beauty of the stream and surrounding thicket of trees with their huge, weighted branches and thick egg-shaped cones. She loved it here. For some reason the place made her feel safe, protected…embraced. Nothing could hurt her here.

She liked to pretend she had entered a long-forgotten realm, one where time and reality ceased to exist and it was only her and the creatures of nature. It was a completely different world. One where her past did not matter and she was safe.

Safe. The word had been a mantra in her brain for a long time now. No more holding her breath and walking on tiptoes, dreading what would happen if that fourth stair squeaked and she woke him up. Finally, she was alone and safe.

She glanced around; taking in the crumbling, moss covered faded grey bricks of a long-abandoned wall behind her. Vines grew up the inside of it, reaching towards the bright moonlight overhead. It had been the first thing she had sketched when she had happened upon this place several nights ago during her walk. Everything had looked so beautiful that night, more…serene. She loved the quiet, the solitude, the moon's gentle light. Most people loved the sun, lived their lives in its shining rays and she had been no different…but that had been in her previous life. The life before her accident. Now…now she loved the night, with its concealing shadows and forgiving darkness.

Her cousin Lisa had been right in convincing her to find a new life for herself. Trying to escape the memories had caused her to move from Chicago to wide-open Montana. But leaving the memories behind had been impossible. There were still times when she woke up screaming from one of the nightmares, and the pain in her leg and hip were constant reminders. Not to mention her face. She had almost-but not quite-gotten over her hatred of mirrors. It was not their fault they told the truth. And one could never avoid the truth for long, no matter how hard they tried.

But at least she had her freedom and finally her own place.

Morgan smiled, remembering Lisa's excitement that night in Chicago when she had found the small cottage on the internet…

"It's absolutely perfect, Morgan! Look!"

"Just a second, the popcorn's almost ready." Morgan grabbed an ovenmit from the counter and then opened the microwave door, inhaling the strong aroma of freshly popped cheese popcorn.

"Come on!" Lisa called. "It even has a barn. You always wanted a horse."

Morgan rolled her eyes and set the steaming container on the stool next to her cousin. "Yes, when I was seven and still believed in Santa Clause. I've grown up since then." She sat down and watched as Lisa scrolled the mouse across the page, then clicked on a picture. At first all she saw were the mountains broadcast against a bright blue sky…and then the picture finished loading.

"Oh…" she breathed, "it's so beautiful…"

Lisa grinned, "Cheap too."

Situated on four acres of land and surrounded by forest the small cream-colored cottage looked like something out of a children's storybook. The three-rail wood fencing looked on the verge of falling down, but the old barn behind the house looked in reasonably good condition. Morgan closed her eyes, picturing newly planted flowers under each of the windows, and maybe a swing hung from the roof of the front porch…the isolating woods would be filled with singing birds and she could sit forever and just listen…and sketch…

Lisa grabbed the phone off its cradle beside the computer and shoved it at her. "Call the realtor, right now, before someone else grabs this."

Morgan glanced at the clock. Darn. "It's after midnight, Lisa."

"So? They have answering machines. Call and leave a message or I will." Lisa pushed the phone into her limp hand and dialed the number on the screen. "Don't let this pass you by Morgan, start living your dreams."

And so, after a long flight to see the property in person she had signed all of the paperwork. A week later she put her husband's glass and steel monstrosity on the market, hired a moving company, loaded her little Volvo station wagon to its limit and never looked back. Twelve-hundred miles and a load of worries and her dream had become reality.

A branch cracked, jerking Morgan back to the present. She glanced around but saw nothing but tree limbs moving with a slight breeze. She shivered, noticing that the temperature had dropped a few degrees and pulled her shawl more tightly around her shoulders.

She sighed deeply. Moving here had been her first grab at recovery, but she knew deep inside that she may never be fully healed; the trauma and humiliation ran way too deep. The knowledge that there were indeed evil people in the world had been made very clear to her, over and over again. And the things she had done…her throat tightened and she swiped at her eyes, wiping away the sudden tears that once started would go on until depression had her so weakened that she locked herself in her room, hiding away from her new life and letting him take control once more. She sucked in a big breath, held it for a moment and then exhaled slowly.

Wasted years, all of them.

Out of habit she pulled several thick pieces of hair over her shoulder until the right side of her face was covered then slowly limped to the path behind the stone wall and into the woods toward the trail home.

****

"Heard Eliza Ramsey's place was sold."

Nick glanced up from the bin of nails. Ben, the owner of Grenner's Feed and Hardware, the only hardware store in town, was standing beside him, an obvious question in his old blue eyes. He shrugged his shoulders, knowing the old man was one step away from talking his ear off. "I guess, saw a moving truck there last week or so."

"Come on, Nick. Ramsey's place is right behind yours. How can you not be interested in what's going on or who's going to live there?"

Nick sighed in irritation; he really did not need Ben hounding him this early in the morning. "First, it's none of my business; people come and go all the time and I could care less. Second, it's on the other side of my woods, completely out of view, so it's not like I'll have an immediate neighbor I have to associate with. And thank God for that." *Yeah right, Nick. Long dark hair, a 'take your sweet time and kiss me all over figure'…*One look from your new neighbor and you'd be standing on her front porch with roses in hand, hoping to do more than just 'associate'. Annoyed at his wayward thoughts Nick focused on the task at hand which was picking out the nails he would need to fix the board that Sultan had kicked out of the back wall of his stall. "You know as long as nobody messes with me I mind my own business."

"I know," Ben said, nodding, "I know. Too bad you moved to a town full of biddies and gossips." He shuffled out of Nick's way, using his cane to point down the aisle towards the back of the store. "By the way, got that new load of rubber pads if you need 'em."

"Yeah thanks. I'll take a couple, just in case. It'll save me a trip back if he tears one up again." And keep me from having to drive past the Ramsey place, he thought to himself.

Ben grinned, hobbling along beside Nick as they made their way back to the back wall. "Maybe you should put pads on that horse's hooves instead of the walls. I know they have somethin' like that out now, I saw one in a magazine. How's Jake doin? Ribs still botherin him?"

Nick nodded, "Yeah, it's called a 'hoof boot' and they're not meant for leaving on the hoof permanently. It's more for medicinal treatment." He bent down and examined the rubber pads, pressing his fingers into the material to judge thickness and durability. "Jake's doing better, back to helping with the barn some. He's staying away from the pony for a while though. He's convinced she's out to get him." Satisfied that the pads would do the trick Nick easily hefted one of the six-foot long, 75 pound bulk packages onto his shoulder. "These pads might work out better anyway. He only acts up when

I'm late feeding him."

They walked back to the front of the store where Ben rang up the purchases. "Okay, let's see. Fifty-five bags of horse feed, two bags of dog food, one carton of three-inch nails, one pack of rubber and a hose nozzle. Anythin' else?"

"Yeah, I almost forgot, throw in a bag of cat food. The barn cat finally had her kittens."

Ben shook his head, flashing gleaming dentures. "Total is two-hundred eighty-nine dollars and ninety-two cents. Nobody lookin' at you would ever believe you're such a softy."

Nick grimaced, giving the old man a pointed look. "Yeah, well do me a favor and keep it to yourself. I like my privacy. Keeps things smooth and quiet." He handed Ben three hundred dollars, then put the change in the back pocket of his blue jeans.

"I know that. You forget that I know your history, but too much privacy ain't good, Nick." Nick's whole body tensed, every fiber of his being hating that his history has been brought up, but then Ben had known him for almost ten years and while others barely had the courage to look him in the face, Ben had never once been intimidated. In fact, he was about the only person Nick would go so far as to call a friend.

"Get that look off your face, Nick," Ben said, "you know I didn't mean anythin' by that."

"Yeah well, in my opinion too many people are what's not good. I learned that lesson the hard way, and that's why I'm here."

Ben shook his head but kept his mouth shut, then just as quickly latched onto the previous topic. "Hey, let me know if you meet whoever bought the Ramsey place." Nick watched as Ben placed a gnarled hand over his heart in mock dismay. "That's about the most interesting news an old man like me has to look forward to right now."

Nick sighed and rolled his eyes, then pulled his truck keys out of his pocket. "I'll pull over to the loading dock. Tell Chris I'll need his help securing the tarp." He hoisted the bulk rubber onto his shoulder again, then gathered the bag of cat food under his arm to protect it from the rain. "Thanks Ben."

"No problem. Say 'hi' to that brother of yours for me."

"Will do."

Before the old man could say another word, he was out the door, striding quickly through the downpour.

Chapter 3

Morgan came awake by degrees, dread lying like a cold stone in her stomach. She was always tense for those first few seconds before she realized where she was. A blurry-eyed glance at her surroundings instantly reassured her. The aged white walls in desperate need of paint were becoming increasingly familiar and the yellow oversized armchair with burgundy floral pattern sitting in the far corner was immediately comforting. It had been her mother's as was the antique French dresser across the room. Morgan set up in bed, focusing on the two items and letting the well-loved pieces ground her to a past that only included her mother. A past that was warm and filled with loving memories. She stretched, letting the feelings of freedom and independence loosen her muscles and relax her mind. Relief settled in. She was in Montana, not Chicago, and had awakened in the bedroom of her new home, not in her husband's. She had waved goodbye to the movers two weeks ago.

The bedside clock read six forty-six A.M; she had a doctor's appointment at ten-thirty for a checkup on her leg, and to renew her pain prescription. Crap! She hated meeting new doctors; hated having to pretend she didn't see the suspicious looks at her face, or the way they murmured and gestured to their associates when they were in the hallway and thought she could couldn't see them. The worst was having to try to explain if they asked how she had been scarred…it never stopped and always managed to make her feel low, like her disfigurement somehow made her less of a person. Why couldn't they just look at her, examine her leg and hip, and give her their usual advice, but she already knew backwards and forwards. Stretches, massages, daily aspirin, use a cane if needed, more checkups and to take her pain meds only when the pain became more intense. That was all they could do for her and after months of painful physical therapy both she and the doctors knew it. There was no changing the fact that she would always be partially crippled.

But at least she had survived. Morgan constantly told herself that was all that mattered. Not looks, not material things, and definitely not men. No way. Not ever again. Men were sly, brutal animals…no, no, she shouldn't think that. Men were much worse than any animal could be.

Not that any would want her even if she was interested. By now she was used to 'the looks—' as she had come to think of them—and try not to let them hurt her. But it was definitely hard to deal with. People were naturally mean, critical and judgmental, especially when someone was different. The killer had been when people had started quickly looking the other way when she happened to look at them…and then she noticed that no one would look her in the eyes anymore. Several times she had toyed with the idea of putting a gun to her head just so she would no longer be in the world and those people—the ones that treated her like a sideshow freak—could get on with their lives. Luckily, Lisa had stepped in with the idea of her moving away from everything, hence the fresh start out here where there were fewer people and more open space. She had no direct neighbors except for the large farm across the woods, access to the internet and TV allowed her to shop from home if she preferred, and she only had to go out when she felt like it or when she had an appointment, such as today.

She sighed in resignation, knowing that she had to get her butt moving. The trip into the neighboring city would take at least an hour and a half, and then she had to allow herself time to find the doctor's office.

Throwing the sheet back she carefully swung her legs over the side of the bed and tentatively put weight on her bad leg. These first few minutes always told her how the day would go. When all she felt was a slight pull she let out a relieved sigh. Grabbing up her yellow robe from the back of the armchair she shrugged into it and moved to pull up the wooden blinds covering her huge picture window. Her reflection, all pale skin and shadowed eyes, stared back at her while rain splattered heavily against the glass and ran in rivulets along the pane.

Crying…Her fingers came up, trembling as they traced the tears on the glass. So much time spent crying…Thunder rumbled, shaking the small cottage and then lightning flashed, streaks of yellow and white striking deadly into the pond in her field; she jumped, startled back into the present.

Morgan dropped the blind back down, knowing that the storm was not going to let up anytime soon and dreading having to go out into it. Crawling back into bed, safe and snug under the cover sounded so much better, and she would have if she hadn't needed to renew her darn pain prescription.

Turning away from the window she moved slowly across her bedroom to the small adjoining bathroom. She was proud of her place, even though the walls were ugly and discolored and the who-knew-how-old wallpaper was peeling off in various rooms, it was still all hers. A pain of sorrow jolted her and she blinked back tears. Her mother would have loved it here, and Morgan would have loved having her here to help fix it up. More tears tightened her throat, the ache so bad she could barely swallow.

Not now, Morgan. Biting her lips, she hurried into her bathroom and started running water for a bath, adding a good amount of Epsom salt and fragrance to the warm water. The bathroom was next on her mile-long list of projects, and she couldn't wait to find time to go to the huge expo she has seen signs for. Her husband would have had a fit if she had tried to bring items from a flea market, or any second-hand store, into their home. It had been only the newest and most expensive modern furniture for him, hand-picked by an even more expensive designer.

Cold, hard furnishings that suited her husband's cold, hard to demeanor.

Morgan had hated every single piece in the house.

Shuddering, she looped her hair up on the top of her head and secured the heavy mass with several clips, then sank down into the almost full tub, sighing deeply as the warm water seeped into her muscles. Morgan loved taking long hot baths, but this morning was not the time to dally and so she scrubbed quickly and thoroughly before climbing out and toweling off. Spending as brief amount of time as possible looking at her reflection, she applied heavy concealer to her cheek and color to her eyes and lips. The camouflage wouldn't fool a close look by a doctor, but it did help her avoid being scrutinized by the unfailingly rude public.

Leaving the bathroom, she chose a white t-shirt and loose jeans from the closet, then pulled on her low-heeled supportive boots. The reinforced arches helped buffer the strain on her leg and she preferred them when she wasn't sure how much walking she would have to do. Making her way down the hall she tucked her shirt and grabbed an umbrella and light rain jacket out of the front hall closet, along with her purse. Taking her keys off the hook by the front door she stepped out onto her porch and locked the door behind her.

****

Dr. Bessick had been nice enough, and not easily fooled. Morgan had sat through the usual questioning; what types of exercises was she doing? How often did she need to take her pain medication? Had there been any worsening of pain? How long ago had the accident happened…and Morgan had answered them as she always did; with lies. Or, as she preferred to think of it, an altering of the truth. She was under no illusion that Dr. Bessick had believed her, but at least the female doctor had been less intrusive than most. She had simply examined her and seen no new injuries to be concerned about; only the older ones that had healed over as best they could and Morgan had honestly assured her that she now had nothing to worry about. She had left with a renewed prescription, an appointment for three months from today, and a special cream that the doctor said might help diminish her scarring a little.

There was always room for cautious hope.

Rain pelted her umbrella and soaked her boots as Morgan hurriedly unlocked her car and tossed her purse onto the passenger seat, then scrambled in, shaking and closing her umbrella after her. The storm had yet to diminish and she wanted nothing more than to get home and curl up in front of her TV or with a good book to wait out the remnants.

Pulling out of the parking lot she passed a McDonald's on her left and, as if on cue, her stomach rumbled, reminding her that it was half past one o'clock and she had yet to eat anything. Since her husbands 'lessons,' food had never been high on her priority list and she had a tendency to keep herself in a mild state of hunger. It was unconsciously habitual and something she was definitely trying to change, but her husband had been an effective teacher and she a very quick learner. He had made it clear in more ways than one that he wanted her thin and that she had damn well better get thin and stay that way. Or else.

A thin line of sweat broke out over her forehead. It had not taken her long to become extremely familiar with the 'or else' part.

Stop it. He can't hurt you now. He's dead, Morgan.

Her knuckles whitened on the steering wheel and she drew in a deep breath, releasing it very slowly. Yes, he was. She had claimed the body herself and made all of the funeral arrangements. But memories were powerful and at times it seemed that his hold was just as strong from the grave as it had been when he had lived. God knew she woke up in a cold sweat often enough.

Turning the wipers on high she slowly drove through town, slow enough that even with the rain she noticed things she hadn't before, like the buildings that were made of huge timber logs, just as they would have been back in the old west, situated amongst larger stone and brick structures. Trees lined the walkways and on sunny days would provide shade to people browsing the boardwalk storefronts. There were signs directing tourists to the local 'watering holes' and hotels, and signs for the upcoming rodeos. Festivals and annual celebrations of just about everything the population could think of.

Even on a thoroughly soaking day like today the town was quaint and beautiful. Stopping for a red light, Morgan sat nibbling her bottom lip. On green, she pulled her car into a parking area and grabbed her digital camera from the glove box, then locked her purse in the space vacated by the camera. Then she opened her car door and shook open her umbrella. Camera ready, she made her way through the rain and across the road, dodging puddles here and there until she reached the covered boardwalk. She leaned her umbrella against a wall and started snapping pictures.

An hour later the camera was full and she was feeling surprisingly revitalized. Her mind drifted back over some of the images she had captured, like the one she caught of a young cowboy dressed head to toe in a slicker, riding his soaked horse down the middle of Main Street. It would make a great subject for one of her paintings. She'd blushed when he caught her photographing him and tipped his hat. She had been half afraid that he would ride over to her and--coward that she was--she'd smiled shyly and turned away to start snapping shots of the cloud shrouded hills in the background. Her cousin would be thrilled with a series of paintings based on Montana. Lisa had been hounding her to start some new paintings for several upcoming gallery shows, and now Morgan had the perfect subject.

After putting away her camera, Morgan browsed several shops while waiting for the rain to lessen and ended up buying several unnecessary souvenirs, plus munching on two hamburgers. Finally, after two hours of waiting and wandering, Morgan was exhausted and her leg was starting to spasm. She could feel the dull prickling of pain starting in her hip; on top of that, she knew she still had the hour and a half drive home before she could relax in a warm tub. Limping slowly along the wooden walkway she sighed in relief when she spotted her car and was finally able to climb inside and relax against the supple leather seats. After starting the car, she turned the air on, letting it cool the humid interior while she massaged her aching muscles. Dealing with the small pinpricks was easy enough; it was the bigger, cramping spasms she knew were coming that were killers and she prayed to God she could make it home before those came.

Gritting her teeth, Morgan shifted the car into reverse and pulled out of the parking lot into traffic. Once hitting the highway she rolled the driver's side window down, letting in the sharp, crisp mountain air.

Even though pain was now dulling her pleasure, she had not felt this alive—this free—in over six years.

The wind brought in sharp droplets of rain and blew her hair in all directions, wildly whipping the long dark strands, almost making them seem alive, like Medusa with her tangled head of snakes. Morgan laughed at the image, feeling a kinship to the poor woman and on impulse rolled down all of the car's windows so that gusts of damp air came in from all directions.

This…this was living.

Chapter 4

You're beautiful.

Morgan sat on the edge of the hospital table after being poked and prodded for the second time that day, replaying his startling words over and over again. She felt hot and cold at the same time, unsure and off balance, all because of two unexpected words from a handsome stranger.

You're beautiful.

No, she wasn't. He had to have been lying, a simple attempt on his part to comfort a woman who had almost been killed. Morgan compressed her lips into a thin tight line, stilling their sudden quiver. She was ugly, inside and out. Richard had made sure of that. *I hit you because you drive me to it. I don't like it, but it's your fault. The broken bones are your fault, you know how clumsy you are, darling...you just need to learn to be more careful. I try my best to take care of you.*

A sharp knock on the door jerked Morgan out of her thoughts and back to the present. A middle-aged nurse walked into the room, smiling and carrying a clipboard along with a small white prescription bottle. "Mrs. Fletcher, you're free to go. Everything looks good, but the Doctor wants you take two of these pills each day for five days. They'll help keep the bump on your head from swelling, but its slight and not concussed so you'll probably only have a few headaches to deal with. If you start to feel nauseous, dizzy, weak or anything unusual at all, please come in immediately."

"I will, thank you."

Morgan gathered her purse and walked out of the cubicle into the busy hallway to check out at the nurse's station. Over the years she had become very well-versed in the procedure.

"Excuse me," she asked the nurses assistant taking care of the forms, "My car was wrecked and I need to call a cab, can you give me—" She stopped, puzzled by the sudden glazed slack-jawed expression on the woman's face.

"I'll drive you home." Deep and rich like the softest velvet his voice stroked up her back, caressed her spine and sent tiny sparks of awareness fluttering through her. Oh God…It was him. No wonder the woman looked like she would go into heat at any moment.

Her heart began to thud.

Morgan stood frozen in front of the nurse's station. She didn't want to turn around, but the weight of his gaze on the top of her head was making her skin feel tight and itchy. *'You're beautiful'*…She shivered once and closed her eyes, willing her heart to stop racing and her skin to stop tingling, but his image from the accident burned unwelcome behind her lids. He was easily several inches over six-feet tall with a long-limbed heavy, muscular build covered by a black long-sleeved shirt and worn jeans. Black hair shaved close to his skull framed a face that was fierce, strong, brutal… and handsome all at the same time. Darkly tanned skin stretched over high cheekbones and an angular jaw shadowed by dark beard stubble. His full mouth bordered on grim and his eyes…they were the most astonishing shade of icy blue. Morgan curled both hands into tight fists and drew in a long, slow breath, pushing back the insane urge to cup his jaw in both hands just to know what he felt like.

She wanted run, run far away from him and the chaos inside her—the sudden bodily urges of wanting, needing, and desiring that she had no control over. But politeness overcame anxiety and she turned, risking a glance up, way up. At five-foot two-and a half she was used to having to look up at most people, but this guy threatened to put a crick in her neck. And he was so close…his eyes stroking over her, staring at her with merciless intensity, making her utterly conscious of how small and vulnerable she was compared to him. Even so, as she stared up at him she was aware of her breasts becoming heavy…achy.

Stop. Just stop thinking about him!

But she couldn't stop the blush that stained her cheeks, or the niggling unease that came from knowing he knew she appreciated what she saw, even if she didn't want to.

She swallowed hard, pulling her eyes away. "I-um, appreciate your help earlier, but that's-that's not necessary."

There was a long silence during which he studied her, one raven-black brow raised consideringly. His perusal was so intense that Morgan began to feel like a bug under a microscope and her flush deepened. To her horror she felt a thin line of sweat break out on her forehead and raised a shaky hand to wipe it away. He grunted, apparently having made a decision, and then he stepped past her to the nurse's desk, took out his wallet and handed the woman a card. Morgan ignored the sudden and completely ridiculous sting of jealousy. Well, if that doesn't just prove that men are all pigs. Get turned down by one woman, move right on to the one waiting behind.

She turned away, preparing to move on and find a payphone while Goliath sexed it up with the assistant, only to stop when she heard him speak.

"I'm Nick Evanoff. Here's my license. Would you please make a copy of it so that everyone here knows I am the one who took Mrs. Fletcher home. I think it would make her much more comfortable about accepting my company."

The nurse winked conspiratorially at him and smiled at Morgan. Once the copying of the driver's license was accomplished he turned back to her, showed her the evidence and then handed it back to the nurse.

"Now will you trust me to take you home?"

The night air was cool when they stepped outside the hospital and walked across the parking lot to his truck, making Nick wish he had something to wrap around her shoulders, and then remembered she was *Mrs.* Morgan Fletcher. Shit.

"How long have you been here?" She asked quietly.

"About two hours."

She looked at him, suspicion tensing her small face. He ignored her unspoken question and pulled his keys out of his pocket, pressing a button. The truck lights flashed and there was an audible click as the locks let go.

She shivered and wrapped her arms around her stomach, stopping a few feet away from the truck. "Why are you doing this? You don't even know me."

He sighed; not really knowing the true reason other than to be near her was an impulse he could not ignore. "I just wanted to make sure you were okay. And then, when no one showed up at the hospital for you I figured you might need someone to take you home." An odd expression crossed her face, but then quickly passed, so quickly that he wondered if he had imagined it. "Which brings me to my next obvious question—where's your husband?"

She dipped her head, nibbling on her lower lip and plucking at the buttons on her blouse, studiously avoiding his eyes. Then, "He's...away." The words were mumbled and directed at the pavement beneath their feet.

Nick felt a spurt of irritation but pushed it firmly away. She was obviously lying, and doing it badly, but for right now he had no right to pry into her life. Choosing to let the moment pass he opened the passenger door. "I'll turn on the heat for you; it's not unusual for the nights to get chilly."

She nodded but moved no closer to the truck, just stood there watching him with big, wary eyes. A slight breeze lifted a few strands of her rich dark hair and Nick couldn't resist catching several of the wispy tendrils. Gently he let them slide through his fingers like the softest silk. Unconsciously he moved closer to Morgan until barely an inch separated them, then slid his hand through her hair to cup the back of her head. A small sob broke the silence and Nick stopped, realizing that she stood frozen against him in a type of desperate stillness and that his hand was wrapped in her hair, forcing her to arch her head back. Unshed tears made her hazel eyes glisten like burnished gold and Nick felt sick at himself for scaring her.

"Oh Christ, sweetheart, I'm sorry. Don't look at me like that." Carefully he untangled his hand and stepped back, giving her the space he knew she would need. "I didn't mean to do that, or to scare you."

Blinking rapidly, she wrapped her arms tightly around her stomach and occasional small shudders shook her frame. He could understand her being wary of him, but her reactions to an almost kiss seemed extreme, and the fear in her eyes had been very real. She had been…no, was still, terrified of him and what he might do to her.

"Morgan…I won't hurt you. Understand?"

She nodded but her lips were still trembling and she remained tense, belying the fact that she believed him. A cold fist clenched his stomach and a muscle in his jaw began to throb. Somewhere in her past someone had hurt her, and badly. Anger surged through him, and it wasn't because she was nervous or scared of him, but because this and her earlier freak-out when he had tried to pull her from the car, stemmed from something. Someone had hurt her, and the thought that some son-of-a-bitch had layed his hands on her in anger really fucked with his control. A shadowy, faceless image of her absent husband formed in his brain. Goddamn him…

Nick drew in a deep, calming breath. Now was not the time to go all protective male with her. "Look Morgan. I'm a stranger and I know that you're nervous, but everyone in the nurse's station knows you left with me. There were at least seven or eight witnesses. I made damn sure of that so you would feel more secure." He waved his hand at the open passenger door and stepped back, giving her space to get in without having to get to close to him. "I'm sorry about what almost happened a few minutes ago and it won't happen again. Nothing will happen. All I want to do to you is give you a ride home."

Before Morgan could open her mouth and force out some kind of reply Nick had turned on his heel and was heading around the back of the truck to the driver's side, leaving the passenger door open for her. Morgan stared at the open door for a minute, letting all of the reasons why she should not get into that truck with him roll through her mind. But then some long-buried instinct crept in, gently pushing aside the doubts…if he were planning to hurt you, he wouldn't have left his I.D. with everyone at the Nurse's station, much less waited over two hours for you to be released.

Morgan looked at him sitting comfortably behind the steering wheel. He was watching her with no hint of impatience on his face, one arm draped casually along the window-frame, the other resting in his lap, apparently willing to wait all night for her decision. Morgan got into the truck and set her purse down between her feet.

"Buckle up."

Even though the cab was large, it was also dark, with only the green glow of the dashboard illuminating his face. A wide console provided a barricade between them but Morgan still felt crowded and vulnerable—he was just so big. She fiddled with the seatbelt strap at her waist and then laced her fingers together. Fiddle, then lace…fiddle, then lace…finally she just grabbed her purse from the floor and sat it in her lap. At least her hands would be occupied by holding it and pressing it against her stomach helped ease the nervous cramping that had begun when he had almost kissed her. She just prayed that nothing would trigger a panic attack.

Silence stretched between them and Morgan sat trying to think of something to say. But she had never been any good at small talk and her mind was a blank, wiped clean of everything but the sharp edge of anxiety. She felt him looking at her and glanced over. He raised an eyebrow. The neon lights of the dash threw shadows onto his face, making him look harder, more menacing. Breathe, slow and easy. All he's doing is looking at me, nothing threatening about that.

He cleared his throat, tapped his fingers on the steering wheel, making her realize he had asked her a question.

"I'm sorry…what?"

He had beautiful hands, long fingered and strong looking.

"I said where to? I need to know where you live."

She forced herself to concentrate. "Oh, of course." After she told him he backed smoothly out of the parking lot, handling the huge truck as if it were an extension of himself. For some reason she got the feeling that it was like that with everything he did.

They drove in silence for awhile, each lost in their thoughts. Morgan watched the tree-line fly by, occasionally catching glimpses of glowing eyes in the woods lit by the headlights. "Are there a lot of deer out here?"

"Deer, possums, raccoons, bear…you need to be

really careful driving at night Morgan—do you mind if I call you Morgan? I know I already have been but it's polite to ask, and after today Mrs. Fletcher just seems a little…silly."

"Sure," she shrugged, "I hate being called Mrs. Fletcher anyway. Not only does it make me feel old but it—." That's right Morgan, you nitwit, tell him all the reasons you hate that name why don't you?

"But it what?"

"Nothing. Um, yes…calling me Morgan is fine."

Luckily more conversation was interrupted by him flicking the signal and turning onto her gravel road. Soon after her little cottage came into view. Morgan drew in a great breath of relief as he pulled into the driveway and stopped.

"You should have left some lights on," he said, his tone vaguely disapproving, "It's not safe for a woman to come home to a dark house."

Morgan looked at him, wondering whether she should be flattered or upset by his somewhat chauvinistic statement. She decided ignoring it was best and opened the passenger door. "Thank you again for everything." Clutching her purse she slid her legs over the seat and hopped out of the truck, ignoring the sharp jab of pain that shot through her leg when she landed. "Are you sure you don't want any gas money?"

He shook his head, watching her carefully out of heavy-lidded eyes, "I don't live far from here. Get your keys out; I'll wait until you've gone inside. Signal me that everything's okay by flicking the porch light and don't forget to lock up as soon as you're in."

Chapter 5

Strong hands, rough with calluses, smoothed across her stomach, tickling her naval. Morgan moaned, writhing on the bed, twisting and arching her hips in protest when he used his superior weight to subdue her. Her skin burned in a way she had never felt before, and a painful ache centered between her thighs. She felt hot, breathless, coiled with tension.

"Please…" Her neck arched and firm lips pressed against her rapidly beating pulse. She should hate her helplessness, but reveled in it instead.

"You want me." He whispered. It was not a question. His palms caressed the indentation of her waist, sliding up over her ribcage to the plump swells of her breasts.

Her ragged moan was answer enough.

His lips caressed her temple, his chin, rough with stubble, scratched her skin.

Gliding over peaks and bulges that formed rigid muscles her hands stroked his back; up to his strong shoulders… fingers skimmed the back of his neck, his throat, up to his darkly shadowed jawline. Imbued with feminine power she pulled his head down until their eyes met and she was staring directly into scorching blue depths…

"Nick…"

Morgan lurched upward, panting and struggling to

catch her breath. Moonlight filtering through her open bedroom window cast everything into an eerie blue haze. Sweat beaded her skin; her t-shirt was twisted around the tops of her thighs, plastered to her body. Using shaking hands she pulled it off, watching it flutter to the floor.

Her nipples were tight, throbbing peaks, aching for her dream lovers' touch. Feeling vulnerable and exposed she hesitantly covered them with her palms, embarrassed even though she was alone.

With a trembling hand she reached between her thighs, feeling the wetness, so natural yet so foreign. She was aroused. Her loins were tight and achingly empty, yearning for something more real than just an erotic dream. She had never felt desire before, never wanted the invasion of a man inside her, but now…now her body was on fire, the delicate entrance behind her labia was throbbing with unfulfilled need. She had never wanted to give herself to a man before but now that was exactly what her body wanted, and for the first time she wondered what it would be like.

Morgan pulled her hand away and looked at the wetness coating her fingers, frightened by her thoughts and shaken to the extreme by the strong urges rushing through her. She was used to nightmares of pain and helplessness and memories of being beaten until she was cowering and screaming. Waking up with her body in a state of unfulfilled sexual desire was shocking— frightening. Her heart was pounding, galloping out of control and banging hard against her chest, almost like when she had anxiety attacks. Morgan pulled the comforter over her body while gulping in several deep breaths, willing her body and emotions to calm down.

She had been a virgin before meeting Richard, and while they were dating he had never pressured her for sex, saying instead that he wanted to wait until they married so it would be special for her. Morgan squeezed her eyes shut and drew her knees up to her chest. Burying her chin deep into the comforter she remembered her Honeymoon night. Richard had made it special all right. The man who had promised to love and honor her, had left her on the bed, broken from his fists and bleeding from his use of her body. From then on she had hated having his body on top of hers and between her legs. Detested the feel of his penis, that weapon of invasion he had used to force himself inside of her body.

She had never felt anything but disgust.

But this dream…she shook her head, unwilling to examine the reason she was awake at four AM with her body in chaos because of an erotic dream about a stranger. A man she knew nothing about except that he had shown a little concern for her. Okay, putting his truck in front of her runaway car and then waiting at the hospital for over two hours just to take her home was showing a lot of concern.

And thinking about the possibilities of why made her heart race. He had an interest in her— a sexual interest. That much was obvious. The problem was that she just didn't know how to handle that the way a normal woman would.

Morgan sighed and clicked on the bedside lamp, then slid out from under the comforter and got up. Taking her robe from the foot of the bed she headed for the shower, knowing there was no way she would get back to sleep tonight.

****

"Sam Lindsey's coming by; he'll be here within thirty minutes." Jake's raised voice carried across the arena and Nick glanced up to see his brother standing by the gate. "Say's he wants to see you work his colt."

"Hell," Nick muttered, "I knew the day was going along too fine." Clucking softly to the horse he reined Nearctic, his grey Andalusian stallion, to a sliding halt mere feet from where his brother stood outside the riding ring holding an arm pressed to his ribs.

Jake slapped at the fine-grained dust floating around him. A layer settled onto the bill of his grey ball-cap. "He says he's been waiting over two months to see some real progress with his horse. Wants to make sure he's getting his moneys worth."

Stifling an irritated curse Nick swung down from the prancing stallion and patted the horses' thick sweaty neck. Dealing with Sam Lindsey was a guaranteed way to put him in a bad mood. "And I've told him I only go as fast as the horse wants to. If he wants to find another trainer he's more than welcome." Nick gathered the reins in one hand and led Nearctic to the water trough, letting the big animal take a few sips before leading him to the wash rack beside the barn.

Jake shrugged, following them. "That's what I told him. All he said was that your fees are too high for the horse to decide when real training begins."

Nick's curse was low and foul. He handed Jake the reins, then pulled the girth free and lifted the heavy Spanish saddle from the horses back. "I'll deal with Lindsey when he gets here. He either wants the colt trained correctly or he doesn't." Leaving Jake holding the stallion Nick walked over to the barn door and picked a black halter off of a hook, then turned on the water and began rolling out the hose. Handing Jake the halter Nick began removing the horses protective splint boots, then began spraying the stallions black stockinged legs. "I don't have the time or patience for his shit. That colt's coming along just fine and I'm not going to rush him based on the owner being a jackass."

Jake's whistle was long and low as he removed Nearctic's bridle and slipped the halter over the stallions lowered head. "Man, you're in a mood. What gives?" He snapped the cross-tie rings to the halter and stepped back so Nick could start washing the horse's body.

"None of your business."

"Does it have anything to do with the woman you played knight in a big shining truck to?"

Nick adjusted the force of the nozzle and lightly sprayed Nearctic's head and neck. The horses' wet dappled coat gleamed in the bright sunlight. "Don't you ever know when to not stick your damn nose into something?"

"I still think it was insane to just plant yourself in front of a runaway car."

"Yeah, well, I really didn't want to be hit head on." He snapped, in no mood to deal with Jake's teasing. "Make yourself useful and go grab that silver cooler sheet from inside the tack room." Nick ran the sweat scraper along the horse's belly in short, irritated swipes. The topic of the accident always brought the image of her, Mrs. Morgan Fletcher, to his mind. Not that she had ever been far from it. He exercised; she was there. He worked the horses; she was there. He picked a fight with his brother; she was there. He pissed; she was there.

"Here." Jake returned with the cooler and handed it to him. "You'll have to throw it on him; I can't raise my arms that high." Nick adjusted the sheet over the horse and they secured it under the animals' belly and around its chest.

Morgan.

The name fit her. Delicate and sleek she reminded him of the beautiful fine-boned breed of horse that shared her name.

"Nick…hey?"

Jakes voice cut through his dream-like haze. Nick blinked, clearing away the picture of thick mahogany hair, pale peach skin and bright gold eyes. "Yeah? What?"

"I asked if you wanted me to brush out the colt."

Nick unsnapped the cross-ties and led the grey stallion off of the washstand and over to the hot-walker beside the barn. "Yeah, thanks. Lunge him a little too if your ribs are up to it. I've got to rub some liniment on Raina's front legs. She was favoring a little yesterday. Hey, did you call that guy about getting a load of alfalfa brought in?"

"He said he can bring us three hundred bales Monday or Tuesday of next week. That's all he has right now."

Nick grunted in response.

Married.

Why the fuck did she have to be married?

****

Adjusting the lunge line Nick moved the sleek bay Thoroughbred colt out towards the center of the indoor training pen, using just his body posture as cues. The young horse responded beautifully, instantly breaking into a smooth lope while always keeping one ear turned in focus on Nick. At barely a year old the horse was already wearing a light bareback pad, pulling scary tarps around behind him without complaint, and responding to voice commands.

He demonstrated that now, asking the horse to 'whoa' right in front of its pompous owner. The horse stopped on a dime, head tucked, back legs sliding underneath him, billowing dust up into the owners sweating face. Nick smirked while Lindsey cursed and pulled a white handkerchief out of his back pocket.

He couldn't have asked for anything better from the animal.

"That's it for today, Lindsey." Nick turned his shoulder slightly in, the cue for the colt to come to him. He pulled a carrot from his back pocket and held it out to the eager youngster. "He's a good colt and performed very well, I'm not going to push him." Coiling the long lunge line in one hand he led the horse from the training arena. "You can judge for yourself if my time is worth your money."

Lindsey pushed off the rail he was leaning against, coming towards them with an its-good-to-be-me swagger. Nick almost had to shield his eyes from the mans blindingly bright yellow shirt. A banana couldn't have done any better. The Texan was nothing if not flamboyant and had a definite flare for gaudiness.

And bullshit.

Nick couldn't help but feel sorry for the colt he was leading. One day soon he was going to have to watch the horse leave with this clown.

"I know you're considered one of the best at what

you do Nick, but you have to admit that your monthly rate as a trainer is pretty high. Especially when you let the horse run things."

Nick tamped down his irritation, "You knew my rate when you brought the horse here two months ago. And you damn well know you're getting your money's worth." Lindsey's jaw went slack, evidence that the arrogant ass wasn't used to being talked to like that.

Tough shit.

He led the colt to the hitching post and began removing the tack. "If you're unhappy with my services, Lindsey, you are free to find another trainer. But you get what pay for, in everything."

"Now look here, Evanoff," Lindsey puffed up, reminding Nick of a disgruntled chicken, "you can't talk to me like that. That's my horse you're training and I have every right to say something about how it's being done."

"Not on my property you don't." Nick unsnapped the colt from the hitching post and headed for the barn, leaving Lindsey to stand there or follow.

Horses nickered in greeting as he led the colt into the dim coolness of the barn and to its stall. Leading the colt inside, Nick talked quietly and soothingly, knowing that the owners' raised voice was making the horse uneasy. Lindsey appeared in the doorway and leaned against the frame, twirling a piece of hay casually between his fingers.

"How many people do you think would trust you with their animals if they knew you're an ex-convict?" Lindsey ran his eyes up and down Nick and then one corner of his mouth tipped down. His voice lowered to a sneer, "A convicted murderer."

A red haze swam across Nick's vision, blurring and distorting everything in his line of sight and he slowly straightened from checking the colts' front hooves. He turned to Lindsey and could see the mans mouth moving, but the dull roaring in his ears blotted out whatever he was saying. Convicted murderer…ex-con… Nick's blood pounded, loud and fast in his ears, drowning out rational thought. How Lindsey knew Nick didn't know, all that mattered was that he did know and was threatening the farm and his livelihood with it. His fists clenched, aching with the need to smash something. Lindsey was now watching him with obvious calculation, expecting him to lose his temper. One frantic phone call to the police would be all it would take and the bastard knew it. Well, well, well, he thought, the smug-faced asshole actually had some balls.

A brief smile crossed his lips, then, deliberately he palmed the pointed hoof-pick, flashing the sharp tip. The cold steel pressed into his skin and sweet-smelling sawdust drifted up to his nostrils as he casually strolled across the large stall towards Lindsey. An uncertain expression crossed Lindsey's face and he slowly started backing away, stopping only when his back slammed into the stalls hard wooden wall.

At six-foot four and two-hundred forty plus pounds Nick towered over the other man. Using his size as intimidation he leaned down into Lindsey's rapidly paling face until their eyes were only inches apart and snarled, "Don't you ever, ever try to threaten me you arrogant son-of-a-bitch," he poked the sharp tip of the pick into the vee of Lindsey's yellow shirtfront, right below the pounding pulse in the man's neck, "or I'll show you exactly what prison can do to a man."

The barn was silent except for the ragged breathing of the cornered man, and then Nick was dimly aware that someone was clearing their throat. Jake's voice, low and tense, came from the stall doorway.

"Uh…Nick. Hey…Take it easy, bro."

The worry in Jake's voice managed to cut through some of the fury pulsing through him. Muttering an oath he shoved the hoof-pick at Lindsey's chest, brushed past him and slammed out of the barn.

Jake stared hard at the colt's owner who stood stock-still and gripping the hoof-pick as if it were a life-line.

"Your brother's insane!" Lindsey sputtered. Jake shrugged negligently and calmly held out the colts' red halter. Hands shaking Lindsey grabbed it from him, and then stood as if not knowing what to do next.

In a voice gone cold and hard Jake said, "I think you should make arrangements to have your horse picked up. But for now you can get your ass off our farm."

Chapter 6

Morgan pulled the rented Honda into a parking spot outside of Winnett's tiny convenience store and shut off the engine, relaxing back into the leather covered seat. One hand still clutched the steering wheel and she allowed it to drop heavily into her laps. She inhaled deeply, held the breath and then blew it out forcefully until her lungs felt sunken and empty. Getting behind the wheel again had, admittedly, scared her to death and she had driven most of the sixteen miles into town below the speed limit. Her knuckles were white and aching from the death grip she had had on the steering wheel.

But an almost empty refrigerator had convinced her to make the trip or starve to death.

A bell jingled as she entered the store. She smiled at the cashier, a bored-looking teenage girl with bright red hair. Her hopes died as she glanced around the small store and immediately realized that variety was pretty much nonexistent. Well, she supposed, with a population of only one hundred and sixty people variety was really not a necessity. Going up and down each aisle she selected a carton of eggs, several bottles of Diet Cola, some milk, bread, and several boxes of cereal to tide her over until she could get up the nerve to drive back to Lewistown, an hour and a half away.

"Excuse me," she waited until the cashier glanced

up, "is there another town nearby, one that's a little bit bigger?"

"Nope, just Winnett. Worlds End."

Morgan frowned, "Excuse me?"

The girl smiled a little and began ringing up her purchases. "World's end, that's what some people call Winnett. Or sometimes it's 'where you can see the end of the world'." She shrugged negligently, "To me it's just the town I want to get out of. Your total is twenty-two, seventeen. But you can always drive to Billings or Lewistown."

Morgan handed her the cash, "Yeah, I've been to Lewistown. It's pretty."

A stand of brochures by the register caught her eye and she pulled one out about the expo she planned to go to. Nerve dependent, of course. "Hey, have you ever—." A framed newspaper on the wall behind the cashiers head caught her eye. In bold black letters the headline read:

'EVANOFF FARM—A LAST CHANCE FOR MANY HORSES'

She couldn't make out any of the article, but there was no mistaking the man in the black and white photo leaning against a corral fence.

"Isn't he hot?" The cashier gushed breathlessly. "Trust me, that picture doesn't compare to real life, I get all flustered every time he comes in here." She shivered dramatically and made an odd sucking noise with her tongue, eyeing the man in the photo like he was a piece of prime rib. "Gerard Butler has nothing on him and I absolutely looove Gerard Butler. But…God, what I wouldn't give to have that in bed with me. His brother's not in the picture, but he's almost as hot, not to mention a lot friendlier."

Morgan blushed at the young girl's frank talk and wondered what her parents would say if they knew.

"So, he owns some kind of horse ranch?"

"Not exactly, it's more of a horse sanctuary. He takes in abused horses, works with them and then just lets them live out their lives there. A few of the horse ranchers around here think he's crazy and that he should just shoot all of those broken-down old nags. That's what they call them, not me. I think it's great what he does. He's also known for being a first-class horse trainer, one of the best. People bring their horses to him from all over the US. Maybe even farther."

She handed Morgan her change, then shot another dewy-eyed glance at the wall. "I'll bet he's as much of a stud as any of his horses."

Mumbling a choked thanks Morgan grabbed her bags and hurried outside into the cool, refreshing air.

****

"The gallery showing went great, sweetie. I'll be sending you a big, fat check next week!" Lisa said, her exuberance ringing in Morgan's ear.

"I wish I could have been there," Morgan smiled into the phone, "But I've already got some ideas for doing a series of paintings on Montana. I got a great shot of a cowboy riding his horse down Main Street, right in the middle of traffic!"

Lisa laughed, "You're kidding!"

"It's true; you'll never see that in Chicago. I can email you the picture once my internet is up."

Tucking the cordless phone tighter between her chin and shoulder she rummaged through her grocery bags, pulling out the cold items and putting them into the refrigerator. Cereal went in the cabinet above the stove.

"Right now I'm working on a painting of this great little copse I found in the woods behind my house, and I'm thinking I might base a series on how life has modernized out here while also staying the same. For instance, maybe showing a cattle drive in town when there were no cars and such, and in another painting show this cowboy riding amongst the cars, almost like he's herding them."

She was already picturing the scenes in her mind and added mental details here and there. It had been a long time since she was able to focus solely on her work and a thrill of anticipation ran through her. Years had passed since she was free to express herself as an artist. Lisa seemed pleased by the ideas and continued bringing her up-to-date on the showing.

"Wow, it does sound like that place is agreeing with you, at least from an artistic standpoint. I want to come see you soon, maybe in the next couple of months if I can manage it."

"Oh Lisa that would be great! Hopefully I'll have the cottage fixed up by then, at least painted and weeded. Of course, that might take awhile since I don't even own a lawnmower yet."

"Well, hon." Lisa said, "I can't very well pack one onto the plane, so that's your little problem." She cleared her throat, but not before Morgan heard a little breathy catch. "I-I'm really proud of you Morgan, really proud."

Morgan smiled, briefly closing her eyes against a pang of homesickness. "I know, Lisa. Thanks for making me do this. But I'd better go now, before both of us start to lose it."

Morgan hung up the phone, feeling more than a little guilty that she hadn't mentioned the accident to her cousin, but she knew it would have just worried Lisa.

With a start Morgan realized that there was no longer anyone she had to answer too, even Lisa. If she had been in Chicago when the accident occurred Morgan knew that she would have run crying to Lisa, expecting her cousin to help her pick up the pieces, but out here there was no one to rely on, and finally she was having to stand on her own two feet. She was no longer a Stepford Wife and had to learn how to function on her own without being told what to do, or wear, or how to act.

The cracked gilded cage she had lived in was gone.

****

That sorry son-of-a-bitch, Nick thought as he stormed out of the barn and got into his truck. Slamming the door shut he shoved the gear into drive and angled onto the main road. Lindsey was damn lucky he hadn't given into the urge to wrap his hand around the bastard's throat and squeeze until that self-satisfied smirk had been choked off the mans face. Ex-con, Lindsey had sneered, convicted murderer. Nick scrubbed his hand over his jaw and then slammed his palm down on the steering wheel. If Jake hadn't shown up Nick didn't really know how the episode would have ended. Lindsey had wanted him to lose his temper, wanted him to make a move that could have brought the police out to the farm. Ten years ago when he'd had nothing to lose he probably would have given into Lindsey's taunting and let loose on the man, but now being so stupid would cost him everything, especially with his criminal record. Nick pictured himself headed back to prison while his farm and horses went on the market with Jake struggling to save it.

The mental image was extremely frightening because it was a very real possibility.

Nick rubbed furiously at his eyes, refusing to acknowledge the burning in them or the choking tightness in his throat and sank back into the driver's seat, relaxing his head against the headrest. Nothing was worth losing his farm. Besides Jake, it was all he cared about, all he had ever cared about.

After being released and finding out that his grandfather had left him a little money he had put his whole focus, every ounce of himself and every penny to his name into getting the horse facility started. Nick sighed, remembering those long days and even longer nights of back-breaking plowing, tilling, cutting lumber and nailing thousands upon thousands of nails until he had the barn and corrals exactly the way he'd wanted. Love and anger had fused inside him, fueling his determination to succeed and to give as many hard-luck horses a second chance as he could. Four years after starting Evanoff Farm he had made a name for himself as an up-and-coming trainer which had brought in people from all over wanting their 'troubled' horses fixed. Ten times out of ten the horse's troubles had stemmed from a problem owner. Gradually, after many satisfied clients he had gained a reputation as a top trainer, and soon after that had his first international client.

Lost in thought Nick let instinct guide him and headed south for about a mile, not giving a fuck where he ended up. Soon raw frustration, both sexual and occupational made his decision and he turned down the thickly wooded side road towards the cottage.

Besides his ninety-two acre farm the little cottage was the only other residence within several miles and actually backed up to his woods, claiming four acres of partially fenced land. Since Eliza's departure to the nursing home two years ago, Nick had had the whole area to himself and had damn well liked it that way.

But now there was Morgan.

With a jolt Nick realized he had been stopped in front of the small cottage, just sitting there, idling, for ten minutes. He ran a hand over his face, and leaned his head back against the headrest and sat there, listening to the deep, rhythmic vibrations of the trucks heavy duty engine while staring at the cottage through the windshield.

Abandoned for two years the place was in desperate need of help, but still looked almost like he remembered from his visits with Eliza. The yellow painted wood needed a fresh coat of paint and he saw where some of the boards had warped, coming loose from the house. White shutters hung loosely from the windows, and the screen around the front porch needed re-tacking in several spots. The yard was overgrown, and for some reason that irritated him. Weren't the real estate agents supposed to take care of stuff like that?

But whereas before the place had looked abandoned, there were now obvious signs of life. The two large circular beveled glass windows situated on either side of the porch now had burgundy curtains showing behind them. Gone were the cream lace one's Eliza had favored. The front porch with its arched overhang was small and he remembered it had been just big enough for two of Eliza's metal lawn chairs and a tiny table decorated with plastic flowers between. Now, in place of the ugly green lawn chairs sat a pretty, white, very delicate looking wicker armchair. A matching table sat off to the side. Two huge pots of colorful pansies sat on the bottom step and vines growing amongst the flowers trailed from the pots to run down the steps. Both the outer screen door and the dark wooden inner door were shut tight. So far the impression he was getting was one of strict femininity…daintiness.

A fairly new red Honda sat under the attached carport. A rental…or her husbands?

What the hell are you doing? — Besides letting your dick rule you. You know she's married.

"Damnit!" Nick grabbed the gear shift, gripping it until his knuckles turned white, then muttered a foul curse and let go, leaving the truck in 'Park'. Hell, maybe subconsciously he was looking for more trouble. Funny, he had never thought of himself as the self-destructive type, although many would argue the fact that going to prison at eighteen was about as self-destructive as one could get.

A movement at the rear of the house near the barn caught his eye and he looked up. There she was, long dark hair tied back in a high ponytail, struggling to lift a heavy board from underneath a brown tarp. He watched, frowning as giving up on lifting the board she pulled it along behind her, head down and small form bent forward at the waist with effort. She was limping noticeably and Nick looked around, expecting to see someone come to help her.

Nick unbuckled his seatbelt and put his hand on the door handle, every nerve in his body wanting to help her, but then he sat back, forcing himself to watch and wait a few more minutes.

Once she got to the barn's big double doors she stopped, dropped the board and used her arm to wipe sweat from her brow. Her shoulders drooped and he could see each labored breath she took.

"Hell, I can't stand this much longer." He muttered to himself, gripping the door handle again. Once more he looked around, wondering where the hell her husband was and why she was hauling heavy boards around trying to do repairs herself. She should be in the house, resting, not out here doing this shit work. Back in action she struggled to lift the board back up and place it over a gap at the front of the barn just below the window. Nick saw a hammer in her back pocket and a box of nails at her feet.

Don't get involved, don't get involved, don't get invol—aw… fuck it.

Calling himself all kinds of a fool he opened the door, wondering if he was about to give up another six years of his life.

Chapter 7

Crap, Morgan thought as she lifted the board, struggled to hold it in place and reach down for nails at the same time. She jumped at the sound of a vehicle's door slamming, but in the position she was in, with one arm and a shoulder bracing the board and her body bent to grab the nails, she couldn't turn to look at whoever had pulled up. Uneasiness made her clumsy and her fingers slipped on the board. The far end tilted and then slid down. The end she was holding became deadweight and pushed her off-balance, making her stumble back and drop it.

"Damn it!" She never cursed, but the words gave her some satisfaction.

"Need some help?" The low male drawl was serious and instantly familiar.

Startled Morgan spun around. The movement was too sudden and her bad leg, incapable of such limber moves, cramped at the hip. Sudden tight fingers of pain slid up her thigh and into her side. She yelped, grabbed at her hip with both hands and stumbled backwards over the board, ending up flat on her butt. An unintelligible shout came from Nick and she heard him rushing towards her. Humiliated she stayed as she was, on her butt with her legs sprawled across the board as she desperately rubbed the now-easing muscles.

"Shit. Are you okay?" he said, hunkering down in

front of her and grasping her shoulder with one big hand. Morgan grabbed his wrist, but he ignored her attempts to remove his hand. There was no laughter in the question or in his voice, which she had partly expected. "I'm sorry I startled you."

Morgan shook her head, still clutching his thick wrist with one hand, acutely aware that her fingers only reached half-way around it. She used her other hand to rub until her leg began to loosen up. "I'm fine now…please…" she pushed lightly on his arm, "let me go so I can get up."

Nick withdrew his hand and rose, but didn't step back and she could see by the intense way he watched her that he was ready to catch her if she collapsed again. Morgan shoved away the silly spurt of pleasure and carefully pulled herself up off the ground. She busied herself with brushing bits of grass and dirt off her jeans, hoping that the motions hid her nervous tremors.

"You're sure you're okay?" His eyebrows lowered in a frown and he was looking her over like he was expecting her to buckle at any moment. "Do you want me to go get that chair for you?" He pointed in the direction of her green lawn chair across the yard. "You should be sitting down, resting that leg."

"No, really…it's alright. I'm used to moments like this. It's nothing new." She smiled slightly, hoping to erase the lines of concern between his thick black brows. "Although I don't usually have episodes in front of an audience."

Morgan got the feeling that that little revelation hadn't helped because his dark brows lowered even more and the muscles in his jaw clenched. Thick cords in his neck bunched as he looked around, surveying her property. His mouth formed a tight line, drawing her gaze. Her breath caught and she couldn't look away, her eyes glued to his face. Dark stubble shadowed his jawline and she wondered what it would be like to smooth her palm across it, to feel those short bristles scuffing her skin. Like in her dream…

"Why the hell are you trying to do this by yourself?"

Jarred out of her musings by the ferocity in his voice and the fact that he had stepped close enough to intrude into her space, she backed up a step, suddenly reminded that she was alone and he was very big.

"Where's your husband, Morgan?" he continued, seemingly unaware of her discomfort, "He should be out here helping you." He glanced towards her house, eyes narrowed as if trying to see inside. "In fact you should be inside, in bed and off that leg, while he does this shit."

Morgan swallowed tightly, the words almost choking her, "I'm not married."

"What?" His head swung back around to her. Nothing in his face had changed, but the penetrating intensity in his blue eyes seared her, so scorching hot that she almost recoiled from it, except that her whole body felt heavy, unwilling to move away from him. His voice, so hard with anger a moment ago, now lowered into a mild drawl, the sound brushing like velvet along her nerves, sending tingles of responsiveness coursing through her, tightening her nipples and flushing her skin. Even her mouth felt fuller than normal, plumper.

"You're not married?" He moved closer, crowding her, letting mere inches separate their bodies.

She shivered, feeling hot and cold at the same time. Her heart thudded and she fought the natural instinct to back away. She shook her head, unnerved by the force of his gaze; the fierceness of it and the overwhelming maleness of him. She swallowed, then stammered, "W-Widowed…"

Her breath caught, she was sure he was going to touch her. She braced herself. No need to panic, she told herself firmly, he hasn't done anything to hurt me and he put himself in danger to save my life. A prickling of awareness rushed up her spine and she glanced up, looking directly into ice blue eyes shuddered beneath half-lowered lids and thick black lashes. His gaze was hot, piercing, and suddenly she felt like a mouse being cornered by a big hungry hawk.

Her lips parted, her body softened. Temptation peaked, but just as quickly she slammed the door on it, mentally berating herself for her momentary weakness. Sexual attraction was something she couldn't deal with, didn't want to deal with, especially not with the man standing before her. She had been fooled once before. Richard had never hurt her until the honeymoon, and this man could do so much more damage.

The image flashed again in her mind—her underneath Nick while his hips thrust forcefully against hers, driving his flesh into hers, again and again… She shuddered, willing herself not to go there.

"Widowed. So when you said your husband was away you really meant he was dead and you just didn't want me to know." He crossed his arms over his chest; drawing her attention and making his biceps bulge under his tan shirt.

She chewed her bottom lip for a moment, feeling

strained and tired for some reason and then nodded, forcing her voice to work, "Yes."

He was studying her again, giving her that hunter versus hunted feeling that, combined with the intimate vision she had just had, made her even more uncomfortable. The blush that stained her skin felt like a five-alarm fire. She curled her fingers together, desperately trying to think of something, anything but him. Against her will her eyes were drawn to his arms and she noticed that on both of biceps shaded grey edges of tattoos peeked out from under his short sleeves. Intrigued she wondered what they were and, blaming her artistic nature, she fought the insane urge to touch them.

He tilted his head and looked her up and down, then stated, "I suppose I can see your reasoning."

Morgan had opened her mouth to reply with an automatic 'thank you', but snapped it shut when the expected "I'm sorry about your husband" never came. Not that she cared. She had never really known how to answer expressions of condolences because she had hated her husband.

But just coming out and saying how much of a sadistic bastard he had been and that she was glad he was dead would have shocked most people and probably made her look loony. After all, in circumstances like hers nobody ever believed the victim because the abuser always put up such a good front.

Exactly as Richard had.

Wide-eyed and feeling a little unbalanced with the way the conversation had gone she wondered if the man in front of her would believe her or if he would side with his own gender and blame her for what Richard

Tempt me, Trust me

had done. Would he see her as willful and as disappointing as Richard had? In need of constant obedience lessons?

The sharp acid taste of bile rose in her throat and Morgan swallowed tightly, fighting against the swelling sickness. A single candle slivered the darkness; shadowy flames danced and swirled on the bedroom walls. Morgan hurried to smooth every crease out of the freshly made bed. He would be home soon and everything had to be perfect, exactly the way he wanted. He liked the darkness, said it hid her true self, her ugly self that he had to constantly discipline... 'If you weren't so mouthy, Morgan', his voice would whisper from the dark, 'I wouldn't have to discipline you. Now look, you made me bruise my knuckles. Get down on your knees and show me how sorry you are...'

Something touched her cheek.

"No!' Startled she lashed out with her hand, hitting warm, hard flesh and then jerked back, stumbling like she'd been poked with an electric prod. Her back came up against something hard and rough. Trapped she stood there, chest heaving and sweat clinging to her forehead. Slowly she became conscious of bright sunlight, heat, and the large man standing very close to her, calling her name over and over again. Nick...not Richard. Nick. Relieved tears trembled on her lashes and Morgan squeezed her eyes shut, willing them not to fall.

"Oh God..." she whispered, taking big gulping breaths, "I'm so sorry Nick."

Silence stretched long and loud between them. Finally he sighed, cursing under his breath.

"No, I'm sorry. I knew better...But you looked

so…hell, I don't know. Lost…vulnerable." Slowly he raised his hand again, letting her see every move he was making and giving her ample time to protest or stop him. The rough pad of his finger touched her skin, stroked softly down her cheek. Morgan drew her breath in, then quieted when he did nothing more than caress her skin. Her lashes fluttered and she made a helpless little choking noise. It felt so good…His finger was hard, callused, but his touch was gentle— the touch of a man who knew his own strength and when not to use it. Morgan raised her eyes up, gold meeting cool blue. Unbidden came the dream again, of his body on top of hers, skin to hot skin pressing her down, of his hands touching her, his lips kissing her…the image was so potent that it cleared her brain of everything else, wiping out Richards malicious voice and replacing it with Nick's roughly sexual one.

'You want me…'

Oh God…heat infused her face; she could feel it spreading all the way from her chest to the roots of her hair. Her skin burned where he touched. Her heart skittered in her chest, racing and pulsing as her brain fast-clicked through the erotic imagery.

Nick let his hand drop and moved slightly away from her, apparently taking sudden interest in the barn behind them.

Morgan cleared her throat and struggled to return their conversation to something more mundane. Something safe that she could handle, wimp that she was.

"Thank you for helping me the other day."

He smiled, or rather, one corner of his mouth quirked up. "You're welcome. But you've thanked me several times already and I've told you it was no problem, though it was quite an introduction to my new neighbor."

She choked, then stammered, "Ex-excuse me?"

Neighbor? She blinked in disbelief as he raised his hand and gestured around the perimeter of her acreage, "Those woods are mine, and beyond them is my farm."

His farm. The horse sanctuary. Out of all the land she could have picked in Montana, she had chosen a plot next to trouble with a capital 'T'. Absorbing that bit of news she glanced back at his face. He was watching her closely, almost predatorily and there was something in his eyes that she couldn't discern.

She frowned at him, "But…But why didn't you mention it when you brought me home the other night?"

Nick knew she had been scared of him, but until now he had not realized she was scared of him as a man, and not just because he was a stranger.

He shrugged, "You'd been through a lot, and you were tired and scared."

The fear of him as a man had been obvious in those big gold eyes, and in the shaking of her small form, especially when he had almost lost control of himself and almost kissed her that night at the hospital. Christ, had he really wrapped her hair in his hand and forced her head back like that?

Nick wished he could kick his own ass for that one.

Wincing inwardly he glanced towards the woods, and then looked back at her, knowing he was about to take a huge risk and wishing he had never brought the subject up. At least not yet.

Oh hell, just spit it out.

"You, uh, should probably also know that I've seen you before—before the accident that is—you like to sit near the stream. My stream." He smiled at her to let her know it was okay. "I didn't say anything because you looked so peaceful and I didn't want to scare you. Plus," he hastily added, "there's really no good way for a man to approach a lone woman, especially in the woods. I recognized you at the accident."

Her eyes widened briefly, large pools of sunlit gold, and then she went utterly still, staring at him.

"Morgan…" He said her name clearly and deliberately, "No…don't look at me like that, I'm not stalking you, Morgan."

She blinked and cleared her throat, then glanced past him towards the wood line. "You, you should have said something, I didn't realize I was trespassing, if I had known…I just thought the woods were…" she shrugged, then finished lamely, "…free."

"Forget it," he shrugged, then strode purposely over to the barn and knelt down in front of the hole she had been working on, pulling away some of the crumbling pieces. "I didn't mind. I still don't." Grunting he yanked another piece away, cursing when several more came down on top of it. "Termites have really done a job on this. It's going to take more than just some patchwork to make it safe again."

He'd rebuild the whole damn barn if it meant spending more time with her.

Aware that she was watching every move he made Nick winked at her, grinning at her sudden blush, then wiped his hands on his jeans and stood up. "If I remember right Dalton kept his tools in here. Let me see what I can find."

"No, wait!" Morgan called, but he had already disappeared behind the huge double doors. Unused for years they swung slowly back on their hinges, creaking and groaning in protest. Concerned for his safety she hurried over and peered into the dark entrance. Murky sunlight drifted through numerous cracks in the walls, highlighting dust and cobwebs but also the boards that formed several open stalls. Straw, old and musty smelling still littered the floor. Morgan hesitated, then, hearing movement at the back of the barn, stepped just inside the doorway.

"Nick?" She leaned forward, straining to see and gripping one of the old doors for support.

"Back here." he called, "Don't come in, the floors littered with debris. You might step on something." There was more noise, then rustling as if he were moving a tarp or something similar. "I knew Dalton had several sawhorses."

Morgan saw a vague movement, then heard a low crash and muttered curses. She flinched, backing up a step. You bitch, I told you to pick this shit up! A shoe flew past her head, shattering the bathroom mirror. Glass, glittering like minuscule diamonds flew everywhere. She screamed and covered her head with her arms, ducking away from the mirror. Tiny shards cut into her feet as she tried to move away from him. Heart racing Morgan stumbled backwards out of the barn, dimly aware that a huge dark shape was moving quickly towards her, closer and closer, stalking towards her from the gloom.

Hide and Seek. Oh God.

Morgan gasped for breath. Fear gripped her stomach, churning like the beginnings of a violent storm. Hide and seek had been one of Richard's favorite games. A black fog swirled through her mind, clouding her vision until all she could see was a pitch-black hallway and all she could hear was her husbands laughing, mocking voice: I'll find you, Morgan, and then the fun will begin…you know what fun we always have together.

She whimpered, covered her ears and dropped to the ground, trying to make as little noise as possible so he wouldn't find her this time. Have to hide, hide, hide…Oh God; don't let him find me again!

The shadow closed around her, trapping her. No escape…the fun will begin…

Hard fingers closed on her shoulders.

I've found you again…

"No," she moaned "please no."

"Morgan!"

No, it wasn't going to stop. She had tried to hide but—

"Morgan!" The voice was urgent, almost bullying. "Morgan, its Nick. Come on sweetheart! Snap out of it."

Fighting was futile, she knew that. Morgan went limp but something was bracing her, keeping her from collapsing.

"Morgan, honey…nothings hurting you. It's all over. I'm not letting anyone hurt you." She rocking, back and forth, back and forth, engulfed in hard arms. Slowly she raised her eyelids, blinking in confusion. Dark skin engulfed her vision. Her head was pressed into the base of his neck and he was rocking her and stroking her hair back from her face.

Nick. It had happened…again, and he had stayed

through the whole nasty thing. Richard had won. He had made her look like a fool, a loon. She wanted Nick to leave her alone, but even more she wanted to stay in the security of his arms.

She wanted everything and nothing.

She was used to nothing. Nothing was safe. When a person had nothing, especially emotionally, then they could never be hurt, could never be used and had no reason to be afraid. Emotional nothingness was safe and Morgan had longed for it for years. Loving a man meant she would have to give up every ounce of self she had, would have to identify herself as his, and Morgan knew she would never, never, be that stupid again.

Ignoring the pain in her heart Morgan shoved her palms hard into Nick's chest and, surprised by the sudden attack, he loosened his grip. Immediately she sprang to her feet and half limped, half ran across the yard towards her house, stumbling up the steps and slamming the door behind her.

Chapter 8

"Okay bro, you going to tell me when your head will be free of your ass?" Jake asked as he walked into Nick's kitchen at six AM the next morning and grabbed a plastic bowl and a cup out of the cabinet.

Nick arched a brow, sat back in his chair and watched his brother rummage through his refrigerator until he came out with a jug of milk. "Excuse me?"

"You missed your appointment yesterday." Jake scowled at Nick's blank look and resumed his search of the cupboard. He set a box of Frosted Flakes next to the milk, then strolled over to the coffee maker. "With Mr. Porter? The guy from Arizona who wants you to train his two Appaloosa fillies."

Nick scrubbed his hand down his face. The cup of coffee he had been holding landed on the table with a thump, sloshing some of the tepid brown liquid on the table. "Shit."

He had totally forgotten. Of course, he hadn't thought of a damn thing except the episode with Morgan, which had left him cold, chilled all the way to his bones. And he still hadn't recovered, not if the fine trembling in his hands was anything to go by.

Not a whole lot rattled him, but Morgan in the throes of a flashback or whatever the hell it was called, that sure as fuck did.

He had to focus, get his mind on the here and now.

The horses, the training. He couldn't let his emotions affect his business; it was all he had, all he was good at.

But Christ he wished he knew what had happened to her. He had his suspicions, and all of them were ugly. He saw her in his minds eye, trying to fight him away the day of the accident, batting at him with her small fists, even though both of their lives had been at risk. Then, just the other day she had cowered on the ground at his feet, clearly expecting him to beat her. Maybe even kill her. Acid burned his throat and Nick swallowed convulsively, feeling as if his insides had been scraped raw.

Jake was still standing at the counter, munching his cereal and staring at him like he was a bug under a microscope. "Well?"

Nick looked up, having forgotten that his brother was still in the room. "Well what?"

Jake rolled his eyes, "Jeez, Nick! The owner of the two Appaloosas? Wants you to train them? Remember?"

Nick scrubbed a hand down his face, weariness setting in even though he had a full day ahead of him, "Yeah…Damnit. That was my fault. I'll call him today and apologize." Shit. He hated apologizing to anyone no matter the reason.

Jake set his cereal on the table, pulled out a chair and straddled it backwards, then folded his arms over the curved oak back. Nick leaned back in his chair and groaned, recognizing that Jake was getting into therapist mode.

"No need. I told him you had gotten sick and just to bring the horses on over in the next few days."

Jake contemplated him another moment and his

tone was much softer when he spoke, "You know, you either need to make a move on her or forget it. She's messing with you, and you never let anyone mess with you."

Nick threw a glare at his younger brother. "Stay out of it, Jake. You don't know what you're talking about. Besides, you don't need to worry; I seriously doubt she wants to see me again, not that she did before."

"Well, something needs to give. I've never seen you like this Nick. You're…mopey."

Nick rolled his eyes and shoved his chair back. Jake was like a gossipy old woman sometimes, always putting his nose where it didn't belong.

It was damn tiring.

Grumpily he growled, "I'm not," and stalked over to the sink, dumping the remains of his coffee inside. Going over to the laundry room he yanked his pullover from the rack beside the back door and jerked it on over his head. Shoving his arms into the sleeves he sent Jake a sharp look. "You weren't there yesterday; you didn't see her reaction to me. I walked towards her, and for no reason that I could see, she dropped and cowered down on the ground, covering her head like I was coming at her swinging an axe. You tell me what that means? Besides the obvious, that I scared the shit out of her. Talk about a major fuck-up."

Jake stood and made as if to follow him. "But you said—."

"Jake. Not now." Nick shoved open the screen door, but hesitated before stepping outside, "Look, I'm sorry for acting like an ass. I'm not…I'm just not used to this type of shit and it's got me—," he ran a hand over his hair in frustration, wishing he had his brother's easy way with words and feelings, "hell, I don't know what I'm trying to say. Anyway, I need you to do me a favor. I was going to handle it myself but I don't think that's a good idea right now. Besides," he glanced outside, watching the ever-brightening sky behind the barn, "I need to put some time on the Draft cross."

****

Lisa's voice hesitated over the phone line. "Is there something you're not telling me? Did something happen down there?"

"No." Morgan crossed her fingers, hating the lie. "Why?"

"I feel like you're keeping something from me."

Morgan bit the inside of her lip and twirled a strand of hair around her index finger. Several of the dark tips were fuzzy and broken. She had neglected getting a trim since before her move and now it was showing. "It's just stress. The move and being alone in a new place. I can't tell you how hard it is having to start your whole life over. I guess I'm just feeling a little lonely."

At least that was true. She had called her cousin just to hear a friendly voice and also with the intention of telling her about the accident and the man she now lived near, but at the moment it didn't seem like such a good idea. For some strange reason, which she didn't want to inspect too closely, she wanted to keep her six-foot-plus neighbor to herself.

Why? He almost certainly thinks you're psycho now, she thought to herself, the crazy neighbor across the woods. It almost sounded like a title for a nursery rhyme.

According to the girl at the convenience store and

the newspaper article Nick Evanoff was considered a local celebrity, world famous even. Morgan pictured the small-town gossips sitting on their sidewalk chairs and talking about their famous resident's insane female neighbor and closed her eyes as shame washed over her in a great wave, making her stomach churn and her throat burn with the urge to vomit.

Shaking, Morgan pressed the phone into her shoulder and covered her nose and mouth with her palms, breathing deeply. In...out...In...out...

Groaning, she sank into the comfort of her living room sofa and curled up against the padded arm, closed her eyes and went limp, sapped of energy. She couldn't help her reactions, they just...happened.

"I'm tired Lisa...this change has been really, really hard for me." She didn't want to tell Lisa about how she had cowered behind the door for about twenty minutes after she had run screaming into her house. And why? Because his shadow had scared her, for God's sake. "Sometimes I feel so out of control of my life."

There was no getting away from the fact that Richard still controlled her, even from the grave, and she couldn't bear to hear the pity she knew would creep into her cousin's voice.

Lisa sighed into the phone. "I know sweetie. But at least you have a life now."

Morgan nodded before remembering that Lisa couldn't see her. "Yeah, true. I guess I have to remind myself how lucky I am...all things considered."

"You know you always have the option of plastic surgery."

Immediately her hand went up to her cheek, one finger tracing the line of scars no longer hidden by cosmetics. "That costs a fortune, Lisa. I can't afford it right now." Morgan snuggled deeper into the sofa cushions. "Maybe in a couple of years, if I can free up some of Richard's money...or if my work sells really well."

"Maybe is right. I'm still shocked that the bastard left you anything. I mean with the way he treated you." Lisa's anger was palpable over the phone line. "I hope he's rotting right now."

"Lisa!" Morgan chastised.

"What? It's true! We both know what he did. Hell, if I could pin a medal on the drunk driver that killed him I would!"

Morgan dropped her forehead into her palm, letting the warmth of her skin soothe her sudden headache. "Please don't ever let anyone hear you say that, Lisa. Drunk drivers kill innocent people too, not just ones like Richard."

Her cousin's deep, indrawn breath was loud over the phone. "Jeez...I know that Morgan. I only meant that—."

"I know what you meant," Morgan interrupted, "believe me, I do. I'm the one living with what he did to me. But I have to go now. There are a million things that I need to be doing besides getting you riled up over the phone."

Lisa laughed lightly, "I'm sure there are. You'll call me anytime? No matter what?"

Morgan smiled, warmed by the obvious concern, "You know I will."

Feeling better she hung up the receiver and looked around her small kitchen. Dull, pea-green walls stared back at her. "Yuck." She really had to do something about that soon.

But for now, the day would be best spent with her canvas and paints.

****

Several hours later Morgan stood back from the painting, assessing it. Tilting her head she studied it, trying to figure out exactly what was wrong. What was bothering her.

Then it hit her. The cowboys' face— it was too young, too fresh looking. Out of place. She wanted a tougher face, one that was rugged and belonged to the outdoors.

She grabbed her palette knife and scraped at the canvas, carefully removing the young man's just-out-of-high-school-innocence and replacing it with strong, arrogant features and ice blue eyes.

"Perfect." She breathed. Satisfied, she took the canvas off of the easel and placed it on the drying rack near the window.

At half past ten in the morning she was pleased with the progress she had made on the start of her new series, tentatively titled 'Majestic Montana'. Once the painting was thoroughly dry she would pack it up and ship it to Lisa for display in the gallery.

Or maybe you'll keep it, and in the years to come, when you're old and lonely and kids are throwing rocks at your window trying to scare each other, you can gaze at it and remember the gorgeous man that told you you were beautiful. And you can wonder what it would have been like to meet him first, when you were normal and still had something left that was worth giving.

The knowledge that she was damaged goods settled over her while cleaning up her painting supplies, there was nothing left of her but damaged muscles, scarred features, anxiety attacks, nightmares, and fear. Oh, and the occasional bout of depression.

Satisfied that her paints and canvases were in order Morgan took a seat at her desk and started arranging papers and various odd items. Pens and paper on the left-hand corner just beside the stapler, yellow sticky pad conveniently next to the phone, pretty note cards decorated with baby animals in the top drawer. Her hand lingered briefly on the drawer handle, and then slid slowly down the polished wood to land on her stomach.

She would never have a baby, would never feel the seed of a man she loved growing inside of her or experience the pain of childbirth. She would never be called mommy or organize birthday parties. No watching her child grow up and start a life of their own…and no grandchildren to spoil.

Nick would make beautiful children…

Morgan shook her head, trying to not let the clawing depression find its way inside. Going into her bedroom and sleeping for days on end was so tempting, and would be so easy to do. In the past Nyquil had always been a big help, but now…now she had her own home and was reasonably successful with her artwork. Certainly successful enough to support herself. She had no reason to be depressed and no time for self-pity. No right to feel self-pity. She knew there were many women in the world that were still in abusive relationships and had no way out, no one to help them and nowhere to go. They would never get out and would most likely die because of that relationship. You're one of the lucky ones, Morgan. So quit whining.

She had escaped, certainly not by her own willpower, but that didn't matter. She was free. She would have good days and bad days just like everyone else, and like everyone else she would deal with the emotions and move on. Live day by day was all she could do.

The sudden distant sound of a door slamming jerked her around in her chair, making her heart stutter and clasping the edge of the desk for support she stood up. Visions of Nick and the last time she had seen him flashed through her mind and clutching a fist to her chest Morgan hurried from her office to the kitchen window. A red and white older model Ford truck was parked in her driveway. A tall man with light brown hair was bent over the bed, his back to her. She let the curtain flutter back into place and, fishing for courage, went to the front door.

"Hi." She called uncertainly from the relative safety of her steps. "Can I—Can I help you?"

The stranger turned and smiled, openly friendly and Morgan found herself hesitantly smiling back.

"Hey there. You must be Morgan." He started towards her, long legs covering the ground quickly, signaling speed and strength. Morgan interlaced her hands, squeezing them in front of her. Richard's hobby had been running and every morning he ran, trying to keep himself in shape. She remembered his pounding footsteps …pounding, running her down and easily catching her…and broke out in a sweat, squeezing her eyes shut Her back bumped into something hard, startling a squeak out of her and she opened her eyes, realizing that she was plastered against the side of her house and that the stranger stood stock still, watching her, an odd expression on his face.

"I'm Jake," he spoke slowly and distinctly, watching her carefully as if expecting her to bolt at any time, "Nick's brother."

"Oh." Oh God…First she made a fool of herself in front of Nick and now again in front of his brother. Could she feel any more ridiculous? Morgan looked closely and saw a few familial resemblances, namely the height and build, and she could already tell that Jake was the more amicable of the two. "I'm sorry, I-I'm Morgan." She relaxed, easing herself away from the house. "Morgan Fletcher."

He grinned, instantly charming again, "Nick's working horses today, he's been getting a little behind and needed to catch up," he said apologetically, spreading his hands wide as if to say 'and here I am'. "Anyway, he asked me to take a look at the barn, measure some boards and cut them for you."

"Oh, uh…okay." Disappointment wedged in her gut; obviously she had scared Nick off with her loony reaction yesterday, and now she had given his brother a taste of it. She stepped off the porch and held out her hand to him, embarrassed by her reaction.

Again.

"It's nice to meet you."

Chapter 9

His grip was firm, his fingers calloused and strong, but she felt nothing. There was no doubting that he was a handsome guy, gorgeous in fact, as tall as Nick with thick wavy brown hair and almost the same build as his brother. There were definitely some very good genes running in that family. But there was absolutely nothing. No tingles, no goosebumps, no lightning bolts, and no insane urges to touch him just for the sake of touching him.

She breathed a sigh of relief. This, she could deal with. This was safe.

"The boards are under a tarp beside the barn. You know, you really don't have to do this." She glanced up at Jake who was keeping pace beside her. "It's neither of your responsibilities."

Tools clanged together as they walked and he adjusted the belt slung over his shoulder. She noticed him wince slightly when he lifted his arm to adjust them. He gave her a wide eyed, incredulous glance, "Are you kidding, Nick would bite my head off if I went back without doing this. He told me you didn't have anyone to help you," he grinned again and winked at her, making her blush, "so let us help you."

"You said he's working with horses? I saw an article about him on the wall in Winnett's convenience store."

Jake snickered, "Yeah, he gets grumpy every time he sees it. He's not much for attention."

"But it's wonderful what you two do. I can't stand the thought of people abusing their animals, they're so helpless." Morgan glanced up at him and smiled, then. Here she was, relaxed and easily having a normal conversation— small talk— with a man. It was so totally unlike her that unconsciously her back straightened and she moved to stand closer to him.

"Yeah, we get some, like the one he's working with today, that have really been messed up. This one had to be shot with a tranquilizer dart just to get close enough to get a halter on him in order to bring him home."

Morgan gasped, feeling a sudden kinship with the unknown animal. "What happened to him?"

Jake shrugged, "Just a plain mean-ass—excuse my language—owner. He starved and beat the horse when it couldn't work anymore. Nick heard about the horse from some people and the next thing I knew he had gone and gotten him. Threatened to hand the owner over to the police if he didn't give up the horse." Jake grinned down at her, showing a dimple in his left cheek. Morgan could clearly see that he was proud of what his older brother had done. "Nick can be pretty persuasive."

Oh, yes. She could imagine. The horse's owner had probably taken one look at the towering, savagely angry Nick Evanoff and handed the horse right over.

"Who's Dalton?" She asked, changing the subject. "Nick mentioned him while searching around in my barn."

He looked down at her and she realized he had

green eyes. Not bright green, but more subtle, mossy. Funny, she had never met a man with greens eyes before.

"Dalton Ramsey was Eliza's husband. He died about five years ago and then Eliza was moved to a nursing home two years ago. You must have bought this place from their son."

Morgan smiled, "Yeah, the real estate agent said the son was tired of the up-keep."

Jake snorted and glanced around at the yard, "Yeah, I can see how much effort he put into it."

The derision in his voice made Morgan look around, seeing through his eyes the unkempt yard, the peeling paint, and the numerous repairs that were needed. The obvious carelessness of neglect was what had made her so determined to turn the place around.

A wrench fell out of the toolbelt, landing with a heavy thud on the grass, and she bent down to pick it up. A big hand flashed by her temple and the wrench was snatched up. The world blurred and with a little cry Morgan sank to her knees on the ground, throwing up her hands to protect her face as nausea burned in her throat and she waited for the first hit from that big fist to land.

"Jesus Christ."

Jake's voice, low and harsh came from way above her. Chest heaving Morgan lowered her trembling hands to the ground, gripping the short stalks of grass as if they were a lifeline. She didn't need to look up at his face; the short expletive told her everything.

He knew.

****

"Why didn't you tell me your woman's been

abused? I mean, Jesus Christ Nick, judging by her knee-jerk reaction to my hand it would have been a damned important bit of information."

Nick straightened slowly from his crouch in the middle of the small pen and stared hard at his brother. "What the hell are you talking about?"

The gelding, alarmed by the large creature now standing near him, snorted and stomped, then began pushing his chest against the bars to escape.

Jakes face was set in tight lines, a sure sign he wasn't joking. "Morgan. Someone's abused her."

Nick turned his attention back to the horse, knowing he had only a short time before the animal went berserk. The gelding had put up with his presence in the pen enough for today. Holding Jakes gaze with his own he let himself out of the enclosure and leaned back against the bars, crossing his arms over his chest. Keeping his voice level he asked, "I already suspected that. Want to tell me what the fuck happened since I seem to recall telling you not to scare her?"

Anger spiked Jake's voice, "Shit Nick, you're acting like I did it on purpose."

Nick kicked a clod of dirt, watching as it exploded and the remaining dust settled a few feet away. "Yeah, hell…you're right. I'm sorry." Apparently this was his week for acting like an ass. Nick ran a hand over his hair, "It just pisses me off that my suspicions were right."

His brother's worried green eyes met his, then fell away to watch the horse behind him.

"So," Nick turned and wrapped the lead line he was holding around one of the metal bars, then faced his brother again, "spit it out."

Nick watched as Jake sighed, still looking a little put out. His younger brother had always been a softy and easily got his feelings hurt, a trait Jake had inherited from their mother, along with her brown hair and green eyes.

"Well, when I first got there she seemed overly apprehensive, but I just figured it was because she was alone and didn't know who I was. But then she relaxed and we were walking and talking, heading for the barn. I was telling her about the horse and she asked who Dalton was. One of my tools fell onto the ground. We both reached for it and I guess I moved too fast or…something and she just freaked out, thought I was about to plant her a facer."

Nick stared off into the distance, picturing her slight figure in his mind as she had struggled with the board, and she had cowered against the side of the barn. She would be no match for any man wanting to take his fists to her. He drew in a deep breath, looking hard at Jake. "How was she when you left?"

Jake shrugged, sliding a hand through his brown hair, "She seemed to be alright. When she realized what she had done I thought she was going to cry. I think she did, because she pointed me to the boards and then ran into the house. I didn't see her again until I knocked on the door about two hours later to tell her I was leaving." He stopped; glancing at the horse behind them, then slowly shook his head. "It's a shame, she seems really sweet. Pretty too with all that hair." Jake ignored his brothers' scowl and clenched his fist, studying it, "I'm having a really hard time picturing some bastard using her for a punching bag. He must have been some mean SOB."

Nick rubbed a hand over his jaw, then his hair, then his jaw again, wishing for a shower and a shave, but the horses would keep him busy for at least another few hours. "Yeah, I wish I'd had the chance to meet the fucker. I'm thinking it was her husband."

Jake's head snapped up, "Shit Nick. What the hell are you doing trying to get into her pants if she has a husband?"

Nick rolled his eyes and pushed off the wall, giving Jake a dark look. "He's dead. She's a widow. I found out yesterday when she was trying to repair the whole fucking barn by herself."

"He would seem the most logical suspect then. Wonder how he died."

"Don't give a shit. When's Lindsey picking him up?" Nick asked, throwing a hand in the direction of the Thoroughbred colt, who was watching them over his stall door, ears pricked in expectation of a treat.

Jake walked over to pet the animal, rubbing between the youngsters' ears and around his muzzle. "Should be gone by Friday. Lindsey was in a fit after you left. Threatened to call the cops."

"He was damn lucky I left without breaking his nose." It was said without heat, just a statement of fact. "Did you get the boards cut up?" he asked as Jake disappeared into the feed room and then reappeared with the oat cart. Instantly the barn was filled with frenzied whinnies and banging oat buckets with Sultan leading the chaos.

Jake raised his voice to a near shout, "Yeah, I marked each one so you'd know where it goes, but now my ribs are aching like crazy. You owe me."

Nick winced as Sultan slammed a hoof against his

stall door, making the iron and wood rattle on its hinges. "I'll get him." Nick scooped up a can full of grain and headed down the aisle, ignoring the outstretched heads of several pleading horses. "Sorry. You guys will have to wait on Jake."

He entered the stall and immediately the old horse quieted, politely waiting until Nick had dumped every last oat into his feeder before beginning to eat. Nick grinned, moving slightly to the side so the Arabians silky muzzle could disappear into the feeder. Holding the oat can by his side Nick leaned one shoulder against the wall and stroked the old horse's neck, running his fingers along the muscles flexing under his touch. At twenty-seven years old the Arabian gelding was still beautiful, slightly sway-backed now, but with a shining chestnut coat and the extremely delicate dished profile characteristic of the breed. Nick stroked the horses glistening hide, carefully inspecting him for injuries.

"It's been ten years old guy, and you still think I'd forget to feed you." He smoothed his hand over the gleaming coat, remembering when it had been dull and stretched tightly over visible bones. After being almost starved to death by his previous owner it was no wonder that the horse got impatient at every feeding time. "And look at you now." Nick grinned at the quietly munching horse, knowing he was being completely ignored as Sultan lost himself in the seventh heaven of sweet oats.

Patting the horse one last time he rolled the heavy door open and stepped into the aisle way. He saw Jake giving oats to Raina, Sultan's girlfriend and a slight twinge of guilt beat at him as he walked up to the front of the barn. He'd had plans to move Sultan into one of the empty first stalls near the barn entrance so he was always first in the feed line and also closer to Raina, but distractions in numerous forms had occurred the past couple of days and he had yet to get the padded rubber in place on the walls.

Definitely a job for this weekend.

"Hey. Nick." There was a note in his brothers' voice that pulled him up short. "Did you notice her scars?"

Nick frowned, baffled, "Whose? Raina? She doesn't have any scars." At least none that could be seen, he thought.

"No, I mean Morgan's. The ones on her cheek."

Chapter 10

The distant sound of a hammer drew her from the bathroom and into the kitchen. Nick's big black Dodge was parked at the end of her driveway. Surprised by a brief jolt of pure joy she hurried back into her bathroom to check her appearance, wincing at the face staring back at her. Pale and red-eyed from working late nights on her paintings she looked like a living ad for zombies. Since she'd had no plans to go out today she hadn't bothered with any makeup, but now she grabbed up her Dermablend corrective foundation and carefully applied a light layer, paying special attention to the five silvery scars on her cheek. Jagged and ugly she had hoped that after four years they would have faded more, but unless she was wearing the special makeup they were one of the first things people noticed.

Morgan opened the jar of sealing powder that had to worn with the makeup to make it stay on and dusted a light layer across her cheek. Satisfied she squinted at herself in the mirror, carefully examining her work. Her cheek looked almost flawless, reminding her of how it used to be before Richard and how he had laughed when she had mentioned plastic surgery. He'd said that there was no way she was going to erase his 'mark,' that he wanted her to remember who she belonged to and what happened when she got mouthy.

It had worked. Everything he had done to her had

been very effective. He would have been very proud.

The hammering stopped, drawing Morgan out of her bathroom and across her bedroom to the big picture window near the bed. From it she had a clear view of the barn and Nick working beside it. Dressed in his usual jeans and a T-shirt he was standing by the two wooden saw-horses Jake had put up the other day and was in the process of measuring a gap along the barn's foundation. The same gap she had struggled with the other day. As she watched, helplessly admiring, he raised the hem of his shirt, displaying a set of abs that could have been carved in stone. Her fingers clutched the curtain, eyes glued to his deeply tanned six-pack, devouring him, tracing the rippling of his muscles up the sides of his body as he stretched his arms over his head and, before her dumbfounded gaze, shrugged out of his shirt.

Oh.

My.

God.

Morgan's mouth went dry, her blood turning molten in her veins. A pool of creamy wetness centered itself between her thighs.

Naturally dark skin stretched tightly over wide heavy shoulders and a broad, ridged chest. Muscles rippled and flexed in his arms as he lowered the shirt to his side. His body was smooth except for a light furring of dark hair that covered his naval and disappeared into the waistband of his jeans.

Morgan's brain ceased to function. If possible, the man looked even bigger half-naked and had a body that would make a Greek God bow down and cover himself in shame. Awesomely commanding to look at, he would make any woman in the world drool in an agony of lust and trembling need.

Morgan gripped the curtain in her fist, waiting for the habitual fear to surface, for Richard's legacy of terror to take hold of her. Eyes following his every move she waited, but the panic never came, leaving her confused and wholly aware of her physical response to Nick's body.

Seeming completely unaware that he was being watched, he rubbed the shirt across his abdomen and up to his chest and shoulders, wiping away the sweat as he went. Her eyes followed every move, every drip and swell of muscle…and she finally saw that the tattoos on his arms were thick chains. Shaded black and grey they wrapped each of his biceps several times from his elbows to the tops of his shoulders, where they curved around and trailed down either side of his spine, ending midway down his back. Morgan stared, riveted as the chains flexed with each muscle. Her hand hovered over the window, her fingertips barely touching the cool smooth glass while unconsciously she caressed each link.

In another display of purely unconscious masculine power, he walked over to one of the piles of timber Jake had left and effortlessly hoisted at least ten of the long boards onto one broad shoulder, carrying them back to his work area.

Oh…wow.

Morgan let the curtain flutter back into place and just stood there, feeling faint, unable to get his image out of her mind. A pulse had begun throbbing between her legs, making her loins feel empty, unfulfilled and she shifted, squeezing her thighs together to try and ease some of the ache.

My God, she thought, *I've never been this turned on in my whole life. And if the man could do that with just an innocent little strip tease, what in the world could he do if he actually ever touched me?*

****

"I-I brought you something to drink."

Nick quickly wrote down the measurements he had just taken and straightened from bending over the sawhorses. He had sensed her approach long before she had appeared in front of him looking fresh and absurdly fragile in a yellow sundress. Today her hair was flowing long and loose around her shoulders with strands trailing down her back to hit the backs of her knees, drawing his eyes to slender, lightly sun-kissed legs and sandaled feet. Her toes were painted a shimmery, pale pink. He breathed in her scent, enjoying the sensation of the mysterious floral fragrance tickling his nostrils.

A tall ice-filled glass of water was held out in front of her as an offering.

Three seconds and already she was testing his resolve. He reached for the glass, letting his fingers brush against hers.

"Thanks." He took a long swallow, then set the glass on one of the boards he had already cut and relaxed against it, studying her. Less than five minutes in his presence and she was already nervous, her cheeks bright and rosy and her gaze bouncing around, trying to land anywhere but on him. Of course, by the quick sneak peeks she kept taking at his naked torso he figured that might have something to do with it.

"I-I didn't think you would be back." When he said

nothing she bit her lip and gestured to the freshly patched barn. "You, um…you really didn't have to do all of this."

"I wanted to."

"Oh. Well, then…" Her full mouth trembled a little, and she let the sentence hang, seemingly at a loss as to what to do now. Nick studied her face, searching for the scars Jake had seen. It was hard to tell because he was no makeup expert by any means, but he thought her right cheek looked more heavily made up than the other.

What else had been done to her? He glanced at her leg but couldn't see any scars, or anything outwardly wrong other than she limped, but she had said it was an old injury, one she was used to.

"I, um…I guess I'll leave you alone then…" She backed away, ready to make her escape.

"What perfume do you wear?"

"What?" She stopped, gold eyes wide with surprise.

"Your perfume," he replied slowly, "what is it?"

"Oh, ah," she fiddled with the fabric of her dress, then twirled a strand of her hair, making Nick wonder if she was this nervous around everyone, or just him.

Or was it men in general?

Chapter 11

He was staring at her cheek, those blue, beautiful eyes that haunted her dreams almost black in anger and…something else.

Then it hit her, making her stomach drop to her feet. Making her want to wretch.

It was 'the look'. The one that she absolutely hated and yet had seen from everyone, sometimes even Lisa. Pity, or maybe disgust, she thought, just like everyone else. Her eyes filled with tears and the unfairness of it was like a physical blow to her chest. Fighting for breath she yanked herself out of his reach. For just a few days she had felt almost like a normal woman— one who had caught the attention of a startlingly gorgeous man. That illusion now shattered into a million sharp-edged pieces, each one slicing into her as they fell. Cutting her raw. Ashamed, she turned away from him, "I don't need your pity," she hissed, wrapping her arms tight around her middle and backing away so he wouldn't see how much she was trembling, how much she hurt," so why don't you just leave now and not come back."

She covered her cheek with her palm, still feeling the ghostly imprint of his touch. "Go!" she cried.

He stiffened, his thick black brows drawing low over his narrowed eyes. He cursed under his breath, low, foul and ugly and took a quick step towards her, reaching for her again.

Hastily she backed away, holding out both hands to ward him off. "S-Stay away from me!" She put a shaking hand to her forehead, confused by her conflicting desires. Part of her wanted him hold her again, but the other part was afraid of being made a fool.

He ignored her protests, advancing on her. "Pity? Morgan, for Gods sake! It's not what you—"

"No! You're just like everyone else!" she sobbed, glaring at him and stumbling away, "I bet you don't think I'm so beautiful now, do you?"

"Yes," he said quietly, his voice rumbling from the depths of his chest. "I do. If you only knew how much. But I also see plenty of evidence that you've been treated like shit. And I guessed right about your husband putting his hands on you, didn't I?"

The brusque statement hit like a blow, penetrating her mind and the hurt. Using her hand she dashed the tears away and looked at him. He was so blindingly handsome. The perfect male animal. No flaws to be found, so unlike scarred, gimpy her. Morgan laughed, but it came out as a sob; she had been so stupid to let herself be reeled in by a few scraps of hope. Maybe Richard had been right about her. He had always called her a weak-minded twit who was too stupid to know when to give up.

A man like Nick would have a new woman for each day of the week. Beautiful, perfect women. Ones who didn't limp and who had no scars and who didn't freak out when a man touched them. They'd enjoy sex and know how to please a man like him.

"You're lying. But that's okay; I'm used to it. And

yeah, you're right," her chin trembled and she clenched her jaw against the show of weakness, "my husband used to beat the crap out of me and then some. The pretty proof is right there on my face, every single day for the entire world to see." A sob caught in her throat and she gestured sharply at her face.

He cursed, reaching for her. "Sweetheart, just let me—."

"Stop!" She jerked backwards, dashing the wetness from her face. Crying had never done any good; she knew that for a fact. Making her voice low and hard, she said, "Please…just get away from me. I'm not one of your horses that needs saving."Nick went still, his heart slamming painfully against his ribs. Briefly he closed his eyes, imagining some of what she must have endured and wondering if he had pushed her too far. He knew full well how evil people could be and the knowledge that Morgan's husband had used his fists on her, tried to break her body and spirit, turned his blood to ice. The sick, sadistic bastard…

Nick drew in a deep breath, filling his lungs with crisp, clean air, calming himself and relaxing his tight fists while he contemplated how to handle the next step. God…if only he could take her in his arms, protect her from the world; absorb her pain into his body…

She was sobbing openly now, one hand covering her eyes while the other stayed clamped against her belly. She backed away from him towards the barn, her fragile shoulders jerking with each violent heave. He watched in helpless, enraged silence as she blindly bumped into the barn and slid down the wall to plop on her butt right there in the grass. Her hair tangled around her shoulders. Long strands, wet from tears, cut across her face and mouth as she continued to cry in great wrenching sobs.

He winced when her slight shoulders jerked with a particularly violent one. His emotions were in an uproar, his hands clenching and unclenching and he knew that if her husband had been alive and standing in front of him he would have ripped the son-of-a-bitches' throat out.

Shit…seeing her cry felt like somebody had sliced into his chest with a dull knife and was systematically carving off small pieces of his heart… very slowly and very painfully. He wanted to slam his fist through the wall—through the bloody bastard's face that had reduced her to this. Anything to take her pain away.

He wanted to—God.

Why did each of their encounters have to be so fucked up?

He shoved his hand through his hair, locking his fingers behind his head and pacing back and forth, shaken by the driving urge to comfort her but riddled with fear of not knowing how. If he came on too strong, too determined, she would run away from him as she had before, and possibly never let him near her again. She was already wary and hurt, thinking he had been playing with her…lying to her.

She was still huddled against the barn, head down and sobbing quietly into her arms. He started towards her, and was only a few feet from her when he stopped, cursing tightly under his breath. If she was one of his horses he would know instantly what to do—move slowly, take several days getting them used to him, and then begin— but this was Morgan, not a horse, and he was not a comforting man, had no experience with being tender outside of the bedroom, and even those instances were few and far between. And relationships? Those were pretty much zero. Women wanted to fuck him, not date him, and until now he had been okay with that. But now…now he felt utterly useless and the reality of that was harsh.

It was blazingly obvious that she came with some serious baggage. One misstep with Morgan and he could hurt her deeply, possibly even more deeply than she had been already.

And you're so skeleton-in-the-closet free?

Okay. Can't call the kettle black. Hell, if she knew his past it would most likely send her into an even bigger panic attack. Ex-con. Yeah, that's the type of man a woman who has been abused wants to get involved with. One who's been in prison, behind bars, judged too dangerous to for civilized society. Nick felt an odd pain in his throat, and a burning behind his eyelids. Ex-convict…dangerous…He looked down at Morgan, his eyes traveling over the exposed nape of her neck, so delicate and fragile and pictured her husband wrapping his hand around the slender column. He swallowed hard, dislodging the tightness in his throat and willed away the burning in his eyes. Not once since collapsing had she looked up at him.

Ex-con. Murderer…He had an ugly history and the why of it wouldn't matter.

Nick ground his jaw as a heavy weight settled between his shoulders and he realized that that was the truth of it. He was nobody's savior, especially not Morgan's, a woman who had already been through so much pain.

He had lived here for over ten years and whenever

he was in town some people still looked at the ground and hurried past as he walked down the street. Even Jake, who had never caused trouble a day in his life and usually had a smile for everyone had been treated to the same judgments, just because he happened to be the brother of an ex-con. It had been hard getting out of prison and trying to get on with his life. People, in general, did not like to give trust or second chances, especially not when faced with his black past. So for several months he had wandered, luckily getting an odd job on a ranch here and there before his past caught up with him and he was asked to leave. Again and Again. No matter what outside image he projected, once people found out he had been in 'the big house' doors were slammed shut...and locked. The stigma never went away.

And here he was, basically stalking a woman who had lived a life of pain and who was now struggling to make it on her own. He could unintentionally ruin that. Nick looked down at her still huddled against the barn, but was surprised to see that she had stopped crying and was now staring at him out of tearstained gold eyes, her expression bleak and resigned. Tired. She deserved so much more than being with a black-tempered ex-con whose past was always present, and who knew nothing except how to train horses and how to fuck.

She deserved someone like Jake.

Jake, the good brother, who had never been in trouble, and who was kind, patient, loyal, and a gentleman, especially when it came to women. Jake would know how to soothe her, how to help her move beyond the past. And sex...Jake would know exactly what she needed—would know exactly how to make love to her…Jake and Morgan. In a sick self-torture Nick's brain flashed with images of his brother covering her sweet body, of Jake parting those pale thighs…Oh… God…The pain of it was real, as if it had already happened and he had lost her, but the pain of knowing he could ruin her future, could only hurt her in the end, was just as strong. Leave…leave right now. You've already hurt her, she thinks you've made a joke out of her, so just turn around and move one foot in front of the other until you're in your truck and headed down the road.

No, goddamnit! Not like this.

Those huge eyes followed his every move, and she gasped slightly as he dropped to his knees in front of her. His hands were shaking as he cupped her face. The rough pad of his thumb traced the swollen softness of her bottom lip.

"Shhh, sweetheart, it's alright," he soothed when his fingers touched her scars and she tried to pull away. Raw emotion closed his throat, and the urge to kiss her, to lay her down in the overgrown yard and worship her with his mouth and hands and body until she understood how beautiful she was to him was nearly unbearable.

"Morgan?" Her name was a gruff whisper. He pressed his lips against her ear as she pushed her wet face into his shoulder, soaking his shirt with her tears, no longer fighting or lashing out. "Whatever it is baby, it'll be okay."

He rubbed her slender back, absorbing her shudders into his stronger body while she cried.

As he stroked her hair he memorized the smooth, silky feel of it between his fingers. Regret, hot and harsh, closed his throat and he had to glance away before he could speak. Coward. "Listen, sweetheart…" his throat tightened again, choking him. He swallowed once more and then forced out the words he didn't want to say. "I wish you understood…since the first time I saw you how much I—" he swiped a hand over his jaw, cursing.

No point in going there now, there was no way she would believe him.

"I'll, uh…I'll send Jake out here to help you get this place situated. He'll help with whatever you need. You won't have to see me." The words tasted bitter, regret poisoning each of them.

"No," she said, pulling away from him and rubbing her eyes. She didn't look at him; instead she stared at the distant line of trees that separated their properties. "I don't want to see either of you. Just like I don't need or want your pity."

Nick's mouth dropped open in shock while his brain tried to wrap around her statement. Pity? Holy shi— "Pity is the last thing I think about when I look at you, Morgan."

She gave a shaky little laugh, "Yeah…that was evident by the expression on your face. And to think that I—"

Nick knew by the way she clamped her mouth shut that something very important had been about to spill out.

"You what?" He asked softly.

Silence. Frustration mounting he swiped a hand over his head. "Damn it! You what, Morgan?"

That delicate jaw clamped even tighter. Throwing caution to the wind and ignoring her high-pitched squeak, Nick tunneled his hand through her hair until he cupped the back of her scalp. He tugged until her head tilted and she arched her neck, her gold eyes wide with alarm, black lashes spiky from her recent tears.

His first thought was to back off, comfort her, but he ignored it, sensing that right now comfort would only send her into a deeper zone where only she could go. He wanted her fired-up, pissed off, hell, anything she had to give him he'd take. Anything except this small, defeated shell sitting on the ground in front of a crumbling old barn.

He'd be damned if he was going to leave her thinking that pity had been his motive.

Staring straight into her eyes, keeping his voice fierce and low, he said, "You think its pity I feel for you? Well let me tell you sweetheart, it's not pity that makes me hard every damn night since I first saw you. And if you haven't figured it out, yes, I'm talking about my di—penis." Since he was still holding her head she couldn't move, but her eyes immediately dropped to his groin, then flew back up to his face. Bright spots of pink highlighted her cheeks and she reached up, grabbed his forearms and tugged. Gently resisting her he said, "No, don't try to get away; I'm not hurting you Morgan. I'm telling you this because you need to hear it and I'm damn well going to get it out before I leave."

His thumbs moved slowly over her cheekbones, back and forth, softly stroking. His eyes dipped to her lips, lingering as the tip of her tongue came out to wet her bottom lip. In any other woman he would take that as an invitation, but not Morgan. Even so he couldn't resist leaning nearer, so close now that he could see himself reflected in her eyes. She was tensing up again, but he remained close, willing her to believe him. "Look at me Morgan and tell me you still think I'm lying. Pity has nothing to do with the way my gut clenches, or the way my heart pounds each time you look at me with those huge golden doe eyes."

"N-Nick…" Her voice was a mere breath of sound and she tugged at his wrists again, fingers trembling and slipping on his skin with her efforts. "Stop…"

"Too late sweet, the ball's rolling now. Shhh…Relax, I'm not hurting you." He waited until she stopped pulling on him and sat quietly, her fingers loosening embracing his thick wrists. "And don't even get me started on what your hair does to me, drives me crazy is an understatement. But you really want to know what I think when I see you?" Tenderly he started massaging her scalp with his fingers, working his way along the back of her head to the nape of her neck. Her shoulders rose and fell on a slight sigh and her eyelids fluttered in enjoyment.

"I see a beautiful woman. Yes," he emphasized when she opened her mouth to protest, "I said beautiful because it's true. You're sweet and gorgeous Morgan. Life's given you some tough shit to deal with, but that's past now…you don't have to fight or be afraid anymore…you…" he swallowed, glancing away from her, needing a moment to get the words out, "you deserve to be happy." And that's why I'm going to let you go.

A lump formed in his throat and then his vision went blurry, shit. He hadn't cried since he was seventeen and his mom had died. Focusing on the woman in front of him he stroked his fingers softly over her cheek, over her scars, feeling the long rough edges that marred her otherwise baby-fine skin. Fresh tears rolled down her face, wetting his hand.

He swallowed hard, then gruffly whispered, "Every warrior has battle scars, sweetheart."

Chapter 12

Morgan sat at her kitchen table, staring sightlessly at the mess of paints and brushes on her kitchen floor, a glass of forgotten tea in front of her. A packet of sweetener sat unopened beside it. It was eight o'clock in the morning, the sun was shining outside and the kitchen walls were waiting on a last coat of paint, but she just couldn't find the will to get started. The brilliant yellow that had made her feel so cheerful just weeks ago had failed yet again today.

It had been two weeks since she had seen Nick and she didn't understand how she could miss someone she barely knew.

'I see a beautiful woman. Yes, I said beautiful because it's true.' The words replayed incessantly in her mind, especially when she looked at herself in the mirror. She kept the words with her, close to her heart.

A little bit of hope tucked away like a beloved treasure.

She thought about him constantly, wondered what he was doing at certain times of the day and night...pictured him riding a horse, or lying in his bed with the sheet pulled up just to his waist, heavy arms crossed behind his head on the pillow. She had even wondered what type of sheets he slept on or if he wore a robe around his house like her husband had. No, that didn't fit. A man like him doubtlessly preferred only briefs or boxers. An image of him leaning against a kitchen counter in only a pair of boxers, his big, dark hands wrapped around a steaming mug of coffee, filtered into her brain.

She would love to see that in person. But that would mean you'd have to wake up…with him. In bed. After a night of—she stopped herself.

If fantasies like that weren't ridiculous then she didn't know what was. Hadn't she learned by now?

His brother, Jake, had shown up once to collect the tools Nick had left and to offer his help if she needed it, but she had politely refused. He had hesitated, apparently wanting to say something, but then had just looked at her for a long moment before getting into his truck and driving away, leaving her feeling as if the door to something special had not only been slammed shut, but bolted.

In fact, she felt much the same as she had when Robert had first introduced her to his fist.

Shell-shocked.

Her head hurt, her lip burned, and the metallic tang of blood hit her tongue, soaking between it and the indentation behind her bottom teeth. Gagging and coughing she struggled to her knees. Blindly she fumbled and her hand hit the side of the bed. She gripped the thick comforter tightly, using it to pull herself halfway off the floor.

'Oh no you don't. You still have a lot to learn about being my wife.' Richard's voice came at her from above; right before his fist connected with her temple.

Morgan stared blindly into her tea glass, remembering that night and waking up in the cabins bed much, much later with several white towels between her bleeding head and the pillow. That had been during their Honeymoon cruise to Alaska. Richard had been very thorough in his lessons.

Stepford wife in public, slut in private. Every mans fantasy woman.

She'd had to stay in bed, barely able to move, until the end of their trip almost a week later.

Morgan shuddered; she had been so excited to see the Alaskan scenery, so excited to be Richard's wife… but had ended up with memories of the cabins white ceiling through blackened, swollen eyes.

And from then on the six years of marriage had been a private warzone, with no one to help, or to believe her except Lisa, and Richard had made sure her cousin had stayed away. Her only joy had been visiting her mother, but each visit, each time her mother hugged her and asked how Richard was doing, only reminded her of the awful life she was keeping a secret. Of how much she was hiding behind the makeup and expensive clothes. But battling cancer had been enough for her mother to deal with and she had died never knowing the truth.

Stop it Morgan.

Dropping her head into her hands Morgan let the tears she had held back all morning flow free. Considering the amount she had cried in the last two weeks she was surprised there were any left.

****

The first flowers showed up eighteen days later, wrapped in cellophane and sticking out of her mailbox. Pale pink rose buds that had yet to open. Attached was a handwritten note that said only, 'Sorry.'

Morgan bit her lip, torn for a moment and then

stuffed the fragile buds into her unused paperbox. The second bunch, this time multicolored daisies, she found lying on her front steps a couple days later. Another note read, 'Really sorry.' She stuffed them in the box with the rose buds, ignoring the creeping regret when she saw the wilted pink flowers still struggling to survive.

Two days later her doorbell rang. Her postman was on the other side, mail in one hand, a bouquet of daffodils, along with the two bunches from her paperbox in the other.

"Mrs. Fletcher, these," he handed her the daffodils and mail, "were stuck in the mailbox and I couldn't get any mail in. And these," he held up the two bunches of drooping, lifeless roses and daisies, "were in the paperbox. They need some help…fast." He smiled at her, "Looks like you have an admirer. I hope you can save them."

Morgan thanked him and shut the door, feeling petty and mean for leaving the innocent flowers out there to die for no reason. Setting her mail on the hall table for later viewing, she carried the flowers into the kitchen and ran water in three vases, dropping an aspirin into each and hoping it wasn't too late.

Two days later a dozen blood-red roses in full bloom were waiting on her.

****

Nick pounded the last nail into the wooden slat and straightened, glaring at the horse that watched him with complete and false innocence. Three days in his new stall near the feed room and already two boards had been knocked loose. Nick knew it was because he had yet to move Raina.

"The next time you kick this panel out I'm going to nail your hide, instead of the board." He threatened, moving closer to stroke the old Arabian's silky chestnut neck. It was an empty threat and both he and Sultan knew it. Nick had owned the horse since being released from prison and could not count how many stall boards or pasture railings he had replaced over the years, but installing a layer of heavy-duty rubber padding on the lower portion of the stall walls had helped some and lessened any chance of injury for the horse.

"Eat your hay, cranky. She'll be up here as soon as I get that stall ready."

Thunder, heavy and low, rumbled in the distance. Giving the horse one final, affectionate pat he latched the door behind him, went to check on the two Appaloosa fillies that had arrived a few days before, and then left the barn, breaking into a jog as fat raindrops began to fall from the darkening sky, soaking him before he reached the protection of his screened back porch. He shrugged out of his shirt, using it to wipe the rain and sweat off of his head and upper body and then collapsed onto the bench by the back door, watching as lighting lit the sky over the mountains and rain ran in rivulets through the stableyard, the flowing streams reminding him of Morgan's tears.

You left her crying her guts out and didn't do a damn thing but walk away. He slammed his eyes shut, refusing to acknowledge that little fact of truth. Instead, he searched his brain, calling forth an image of her with no tears. That morning, before he had fucked things up so royally. She had brought him a drink, shyly offering it to him and her eyes had been clear then, anxious yes, but not bloodshot from crying.

Weariness seeped into his bones; he had been running himself ragged for days, weeks, trying to get her out of his mind. Not that it had done any good. Trying to do the best thing was really not working out for him.

'No good deed goes unpunished'. If that wasn't the fucking truth then he didn't know what was.

Trying to do the 'right' thing was threatening to drive him mad. The days since had been hell. He had ridden through the woods by the stream almost every day hoping to see her, a fact that had had his brother laughing his ass off. She had never shown and he had since stopped.

He knew why, understood it completely. She was ashamed of her scars and what had happened to her. No matter what he said she thought he was just taking pity on her, playing with her. She clearly did not know how beautiful she was, even with the scars, and he wasn't certain, but he suspected she blamed herself for those scars.

And probably blamed herself for the abuse, each and every time her husband hurt her. He knew it was common among abuse victims, especially with domestic abuse. God knows he had heard his mother defending his father often enough.

Shit. Nick looked down at his broad, clenched fists with their huge knuckles. One blow from him would definitely break her jawbone, and she was so petite that he wouldn't even have to put much force behind it.

The thought sickened him.

He couldn't comprehend being violent with her on any level. The thought of hurting her in any way was physically repellent.

But he had hurt her. He had gotten personal too soon, and, like the arrogant, opportunistic bastard that he could be, he had pushed and it had backfired. Hell, he had even gone as low as to tell her about his fully functioning penis. Great job, Nick. Just great. Exactly what she needed to think about while she's on the ground crying—you and your hard-on.

So what, you won't be seeing her again. The voice of reason spoke inside his head. Plus you've done this before, gotten involved where you really shouldn't have and all it did was land your ass in prison. Go get laid and get her out of your mind.

Sound advice, too bad he wasn't really listening. The only woman he cared about getting laid with lived on the other side of his pasture, which, since he couldn't have her, might as well be on the other side of the continent. Sure, his hands worked and his mind ran rampant with fantasies about her, but they were a piss poor substitute for the real thing and offered little satisfaction. He knew her body, had held it against his and that little bit had only fanned the flame. He wanted more, so much more. He wanted her soft and yielding in his arms, skin to skin, her body flushed, wet with desire, not tense and panicky.

And definitely no goddamned tears.

"Nick," he muttered to himself, "You're too old for this adolescent shit."

Getting up he headed inside to the shower. Maybe a night out would do him some good. God knows it had been a long time. Some female companionship might be exactly what he needed to get him back on track.

The more he thought about it the more appealing the prospect became.

A few hours later he was in his truck and headed for the outskirts of town.

Chapter 13

The alarm clock blared at quarter to five the next morning; 'Here Without You' by Three Doors Down came on, piercing Nick's right eardrum. He groaned and slapped a hand over the radio, shutting off both the high-pitched beeping and the song, not needing to be reminded about lonely minds and dreaming about someone who wasn't there.

A quick, cold shower woke him up, but did nothing to relieve his mental exhaustion. He glared at himself in the mirror; bloodshot blue eyes stared back at him. Not a good combination. Looking and feeling like shit just confirmed the fact that last night's excursion hadn't helped. A fact that he layed firmly on Morgan Fletcher's slender shoulders.

The storm had passed during the night, leaving the morning misty and calm. Cool air clung to his face as he made his way from the house to the barn a little after six. Mud, thick and heavy, stuck to his boots, forcing a pit-stop by the wash-rack to hose them off before heading inside. Jake was already there, haltering the horses that would go out to pasture for the day according to the chalkboard schedule on the wall.

"Late start today?" Jake checked his watch, "I'm showing six-thirty-six. I was here at a prompt six-fifteen."

Nick grunted irritably, not in the mood after

catching only about an hours' worth of sleep. "Put Raina and Sultan together in the dry lot with some grass hay. I'm going to switch her stall today and put her beside Sultan. We also need to worm everyone later. Don't let me forget."

"Sure thing, sunshine." Jake muttered while slipping a halter over the lowered head of the sweet-faced Quarter Horse mare. "Thata girl Sarah." In her heyday she had been a pretty good barrel racer, but a fractured coffin bone had ended her career early, so the owners, unable to afford proper medical treatment for the mare, had donated her to the farm instead of putting her down. Now her only job was to baby-sit the rambunctious yearlings that Nick sometimes got in.

"Hey. Nick…" Jake's voice was extremely gentle, "you okay?"

Nick rolled his eyes and raised an eyebrow, "What's on your mind Jake?"

"I saw your truck leave late last night."

Nick waited, "And?"

"And you didn't come back for several hours. Not to mention your oh so slightly bloodshot eyes. Did you and Morgan—."

"No," he growled, "and I told you why."

It was Jakes turn to roll his eyes, "Yeah, I know, you're an ex-con. Not worthy of her. Give me a break."

Nick sighed, walked into the tack room and jerked a pail out of the pile in the corner. The sweet scent of oats mixing with the tanginess of well-used leather swept into Nick's nostrils. The smell always soothed him, bringing him back from his mood swings to what was important. The farm, the horses.

He felt Jakes presence near the door behind him

and busied himself with digging a handful of oats out of the container and dumping them in the bucket.

"I still say your reason is bullshit, Nick." Jake said in a disgusted voice. "You're screwing yourself out of something that could be really good if you gave it a half a chance. And it might even make you more pleasant to be around."

"Look Jake, shut up." Aware of his brother's close scrutiny Nick rubbed his eyes, then rolled his head on his shoulders, working out the kinks caused by a lousy night's sleep. "You want to know what I did? I'll tell you. I went to the bar outside of town hoping to find a woman who was short and had long dark hair so I could get a room, fuck her brains out until early morning and then send her on her way in hopes that maybe, just fucking maybe, it would get me back to normal."

He turned just in time to see shock flit through Jakes' deep green eyes. Even though he was six years older than Jake, those eyes always had the power to make him squirm. The same way their mothers had when he was little and would get caught doing something he wasn't supposed to.

Jakes mouth opened and closed. Opened. Before his brother could gather his wits together Nick continued, "But once I got there the idea seemed a little shitty, you know? Wrong somehow. So I sat back, thought of her, nursed two beers, politely refused the come-ons from women who were too drunk to know what they were doing or who they were doing, and then came home to sleep for about, oh, an hour. Now, I'm going to get that stall ready for Raina, and after that I'll be in the back working with Nightshade."

Leaving Jake to brood over that little disclosure he

walked down the aisle past numerous stalls and through the short hallway that connected the main barn to the indoor arena. Off to the side was a smaller pen, now the temporary home of the gelding. Progress with the horse had been exceedingly slow, but nothing less than he had expected.

The horse was watching him, huge brown eyes alert with suspicion, reminding him of Morgan.

Christ, would it never cease? Pushing the distraction away he entered the pen. Instantly the horse began rearing at the rails, trying to break through, but Nick noticed the efforts were more half-hearted than the last time. Progress, no matter how small, was progress.

Finally, after about ten minutes of Nick not moving any closer the horse stopped and turned towards him, white chest heaving with each deep breath.

"Easy now. That's right…" Nick murmured, "You know I'm not going to hurt you."

He moved closer, slowly, keeping his eyes off to the side of the nervous horse so as not to threaten him. Trust would be hard-earned with this guy, but worth every struggling moment.

Nick set the small pail of oats down in the center of the pen and crouched beside them. Immediately the geldings' ears pricked forward. He moved a step closer, stopping when he saw that Nick was not moving away. Nick knew he was waiting on him to leave the pen before coming to find out what kind of treat was in the bucket. He kept his eyes cast off to the side, his body loose, shoulders relaxed and unthreatening.

"Sorry boy, I know you don't like it but I'm staying for awhile." The horse's ears swiveled anxiously back and forth, monitoring the sound of his voice. "But I promise, no whips, sticks, or whatever the hell else the bastard used on you."

****

Heart pounding and palms sweating on the steering wheel Morgan maneuvered her car carefully onto the tree-lined dirt and gravel driveway. Nick's place was nothing like what she expected, although she didn't really know what she had expected. A huge sign labeled 'Evanoff Farm' hung above the drive, assuring her that she had the correct place. As she cautiously maneuvered around a sharp curve Morgan caught sight of horses grazing in the pastures on either side of her. She slowed her car to almost a stop and rolled her window down for a better look. A cool breeze ruffled her hair, lifting several flyaway strands and she angled her head up to catch it more fully in the face. Several of the horses raised their heads towards her, ears flicking back and forth in curiosity. They were all so beautiful, their sleek gleaming hides showcased against the backdrop of darkly wooded mountains. Absolutely perfect for her Majestic Montana series. The artist in her surfaced, eager for fresh material. Morgan put the car in park and reached over to the dash compartment, searching for her camera. Crap! The compartment door shut with a sharp click and a quick glance at the backseat told her the camera wasn't there either. If only…But memory would have to do and besides, a photo op had been the farthest thing from her mind when she had gotten in her car less than half an hour ago.

Which brought her back to her original reason for being here.

Biting her lip she put the car back into drive and

slowly pressed the accelerator, barely reaching ten miles an hour as she followed the fenced drive around. A rectangular two-story beige brick house with burgundy shutters finally came into view and behind it an enormous white with green trim barn. The large double-doors were open and Nick's huge black Dodge truck was parked off to the side, looming large and ominous in her line of sight.

"Oh God," she muttered, "What am I doing here?" Her foot faltered on the accelerator and her heart hammered, beating loud in her ears.

Giving herself time to gather some much-needed courage she looked around and spotted another house, this one smaller and made of red-brick, a little ways behind the barn. Beside it was a tin-roofed shed housing a black and tan four-horse trailer and two smaller ones. She could also see the tail-end of some type of motorcycle sitting inside. Probably a Harley. Of course a man like Nick would go for a Harley. And don't forget the half-naked biker babes that would go with it.

No…she didn't want to think about that. She looked around again, examining everything in an effort to dismiss the absurd feeling of jealously.

Apparently having heard her car approach, a Black Lab came racing full speed around the corner of the barn, barking and nipping her car's tires, announcing her arrival. Figuring her time to escape was now gone Morgan pressed the gas and maneuvered carefully, half afraid she'd run over the animal, and parked near a fence.

A rider on the far side of the ring beside the barn drew her attention and for a moment her stomach flip-flopped, but then she recognized Jake's lighter hair under the baseball cap he was wearing. He was mounted on a muscular Paint horse and as they got closer she realized he was riding bareback with only a halter. Easy and relaxed he and the horse moved together as one, hypnotizing in their graceful beauty.

Morgan cursed her hormones, wondering why they couldn't have picked this brother, the safe, charming one, to go all googly over.

Just when she was again contemplating putting her car in reverse and getting out of there he saw her, threw his hand up and loped the horse over to the gate. She watched, amazed, while in one smooth motion he leaned down, unlatched the gate, maneuvered the big horse through it and latched it back. She got out of the car, keeping one eye open for signs of Nick, and waited for him to ride over.

"Hi." She said shyly when he was within a few feet of her. "I was, um," she tapped her nails on the car door and swallowed, hard, "…looking for, ah, Nick."

Jake swung a leg over the Paints neck, paused, grimacing as if in pain, and slid off the animals back. The expression on his face did nothing to bolster her failing courage.

"Are you okay?" She asked, frowning at him. "You look like you're in pain."

He nodded, "Still a little sore."

She raised an eyebrow in question and he replied, "I fractured a rib several weeks ago, got stuck between a pony and a hard place."

When she opened her mouth he interrupted her, saying, "I think Nick's in the barn working with one of the horses." He fiddled with the reins, flicking them back and forth with his thumbs, and then reached up to stroke the Paints black and white neck. "Uh, today might not be a good time, Morgan. He's really…uh…busy. Maybe I can—"

"No. I'm not."

They both turned. Nick, looking gorgeous but tired in jeans and a dark blue T-shirt, was standing framed in the barn doorway, hands planted on his hips, a bridle dangling from one wrist.

Jakes' 'oh shit' and her 'Oh God' were muttered in unison.

"I have to go," Jake mumbled beside her, "stuff to do and all that."

He practically dragged the horse away and Morgan wondered at his sudden nervousness. She was the one being cut by piercing, heavy-lidded blue eyes and a not-too-welcoming expression. Nerves raw, she wet her lips, gathering her scattered wits while trying to catch her breath for the next step.

"I have to admit I never expected to see you here," Nick stated, gliding towards her, his brawny, tanned muscles bunching and flexing. The bridle jingled in his hand. Six-foot-plus of hulking male moved with pantherish grace towards her. Intimidated she shrank back before she could stop herself.

He stopped, raised an eyebrow and cocked his head to the side, assessing her. "You want me to stop here so you feel safer? Or back up a little?" He raised his hands, holding them out in front of himself as he moved several steps back away from her. The bridle swayed, suspended from his wrist. She blinked, uncertain how to respond. He seemed almost glad that she was here, yet…not.

"Nick, I don't…um. That is…I came to…"

As she stuttered to a stop, lost in confused silence about how to proceed, he heaved a loud sigh, muttered something under his breath, and walked right up to her, bracing his arms on either side of her and trapping her against the car. Morgan squeaked and her hands came up to push him away, only to land and rest on his chest. His heart pounded beneath her palms, its rapid rhythm mirroring her own. Suddenly he leaned down close, brushing her ear with his nose, then his mouth. Morgan's breath halted in her throat. Having him this close was wreaking havoc on her nerves and turning her blood flow into a sluggish pool centered low in her abdomen. Her skin felt too tight for her body...He nipped her ear, just barely, and she whimpered, jerking up against him.

"You came to me sweetheart," his mouth drifted down, oh so close to the fluttering pulse in her throat between her collarbones, "*you* came to *me*."

Morgan's head fell back. She forgot about the hard metal of the roof behind her and cringed just before the moment of impact. But the hard hit never came; Nick's hand was there, cradling her, shielding her from harm, his fingers tangling in her thick mane of hair.

"Nick..." she whispered, "please..." She didn't know what she was asking for exactly, only that he was so close, not quite touching her with his body but still...so close, and it felt so...good...so different from what she was used to feeling.

"Uh-uh sweetheart." His voice was low and soft. His fingers shifted through her hair, then came around to cup her chin. His eyes were the bluest she'd ever seen them as they touched upon every part of her face, lingering on her cheek. His thumbs stroked over her bottom lip, the contact light, just the way he had several weeks ago, but her nerve endings fired, making her conscious of the scorching heat of her body. Arousal. Just like that.

"You're going to have to give me some kind of guideline as to how to proceed sweetheart, because I admit…handling you can be damned confusing, tricky even, and from now on I'm not taking any risks."

Chapter 14

"So why did you come, Morgan?"

It took her a few seconds but then she looked up at him, blinking those lovely eyes in dazed confusion, as if she had just realized he had stopped nuzzling her and had spoken. If she didn't respond soon he was definitely going back to nuzzling. Never give away a good opportunity his grandfather had always said.

She cleared her throat and he noticed a fine layer of goose bumps had risen on her skin. One corner of his mouth kicked up, it damned sure wasn't cold.

"I-I wanted to tell you thank you...for the uh-flowers, but they aren't necessary. Really. There's nothing for you to be sorry about. So please...stop." The last word came out husky, slightly above a whisper and he got the feeling she didn't really want to say.

He frowned, "What flowers?"

"The flowers and notes...the ones in my mailbox and..." she nibbled her bottom lip and a frown creased her forehead, "porch."

He slowly shook his head and stepped back slightly, giving her, and him, some breathing room. "Sorry, sweetheart, but I don't know what you're talking about."

"Oh God...you didn't..." she trailed off, going pale. "I'm so sorry, I just thought....I-I need to go." She spun around, lunging for her car door and yanking on the handle.

"Morgan. Morgan stop." Damn it! Not again. This time was not going to end in a fucked-up mess.

His hand landed hard on her shoulder, harder than he meant and she shrieked, but then immediately went still with one hand on the door handle and the other hand clamped over her mouth. The sudden utter stillness in her body was almost eerie, especially when just one second ago she had been in a flurry of activity to escape him. Using as little force as he could manage, he turned her stiff body around until she faced him again.

"Nuh-uh Morgan. Don't go there, baby." She gave a slight flinch when he raised his hand, but when all he did was caress her jaw the tenseness begin to ebb from her body.

"Wh-where?"

"Wherever your mind went just then. It doesn't belong there. Not with us."

Her chest expanded on a deep breath. "I'm sorry…but someti—"

"Hush." He pressed a finger to her lips, shushing her. "First of all," he said, "I'm sick and tired of you running away from me. It makes it really hard to get to know you. Second," his voice changed, turning cold; "Second, I'd like to murder the fucker who hurt you."

Somewhere far away in her past life Morgan would have been offended by his blunt, crude language, but instead his low, savage voice mesmerized, pulling her out of that dark mental zone that was so familiar. He was angry for her, and it was thrilling. His words resonated through her head, making her body crave something she had never known.

"His name was Richard," she whispered, "and he's already dead."

"No," he caressed her throat, her collarbones. Each touch a featherlight exploration that had her quivering against him. "Every time you flinch from me you bring him back to life."

She ducked her head, letting her hair fall forward to hide her hot blush.

"Nick..."

"There's something between us, you know," he said softly. He pushed her hair back and his warm breath stroked her temple, fluttering the baby-fine hairs near her ear, "whether you or I want it or not. I've been fighting for weeks to get you out of my mind and nothing works. And the nights...you're with me there too, sweetheart. I tried to leave you alone for your sake, but here you are...messing with me again."

He eased his big body closer to hers, making her even more aware of the loose cage of his arms, of the hard metal at her back. Of how much she wanted him. He exuded raw masculine power but instead of being afraid of it, of him, she felt comforted...and she wanted more. For once in her life Richard wasn't winning, and if this shivery, heated flushed sensation running over her was anything to go by, then her body certainly didn't feel threatened either.

Nick's voice, low and husky, right above her brought her back from her inward examination.

"Trust me..." his head dipped and his lips smoothed over her forehead, then her temple, slowly to her cheekbone and down...She closed her eyes on a soft sigh when he reached the corner of her mouth. "I'm not going to hurt you, Morgan. All men aren't monsters. There are some decent guys in the world and you're going to have to trust one someday. It might as well be me." Then he kissed her, not hard or demanding, but soft and slow, barely touching her lips with his. Teasing her before backing off.

Her heart ached; her body sizzled. How she wanted to believe, wanted to allow herself to just feel, for once what it was like to be held tenderly. She wanted more of this, of what he was showing her right now.

He was watching her; she could feel the heated weight of his stare while his thumb stroked the sensitive spot just below her ear. Her body felt different, her stomach coiled tight, waiting…wanting. She was almost panting. Alarmed she pushed at him, her palms meeting the smooth material of his t-shirt and hard muscles of his chest beneath. He let her go and stepped back, giving them both some space, but the brief contact had shocked her, and her feelings, her…desire, she realized, didn't fade.

He blew out a deep breath. "Would it help if I admitted to doing the flower thing?"

She almost smiled, would have if her body wasn't in such turmoil. "Of course not, you'd be lying."

He grinned slightly, "Yeah, well, call me opportunistic."

She exhaled slowly, forcing her body back from the chaos he had unleashed inside her, and struggling with the impulse to let go and leap into the unknown. "I…have issues, Nick…big issues. You already know that. You've seen how I react sometimes. I don't do it on purpose…and I hate it." Her voice quivered along with her chin. "I have scars and I limp. I can't see what you—"

"Hush, it's not your fault."

She tucked her chin to her chest, letting her hair fall forward. Her shield against her shame.

"No, you don't." Using his fingertips he bullied her chin up. "Look at me," he demanded, "straight in the eyes." She blushed, meeting his warm indigo gaze. "None of that is your fault, Morgan."

She opened her mouth to negate him, but then the loud rumble of a diesel engine drew both their gazes to the driveway. A huge white horse van, the kind pulled by a semi, was slowly making its way towards them. Nick cursed, clearly upset by the interruption and then motioned the driver to park near the barn. He turned back to her, grasping her chin in his hand. "Did you hear what I said? None of what happened to you is your fault, Morgan."

She nodded as much as she could since he was still holding her chin, but something in her eyes must have upset him because he cursed again.

"Look, come back in a few days," he urged, "I'd say tomorrow but this," he jerked his head in the direction of the semi, "should be delivering six horses and I want to give them a few days of adjustment. This is Sunday, by Wednesday I should be clear. Come back and I'll show you around, tell you about some of the horses. No pressure, Morgan. I promise."

She hesitated for a long moment, balanced on the edge of an abyss, dizzy with the direction her life had suddenly taken and overwhelmed by the big man in front of her. You may never have this chance again, Morgan. Don't let Richard rule you again.

"Okay." She nodded, wondering if she had lost her mind. "Wednesday then."

****

Thirty minutes later, after dealing with the paperwork concerning the new arrivals, he found Jake cleaning out one of the empty stalls, readying it for one of the new horses, and planted himself in the doorway. "Happen to know anything about flowers and notes, little brother?"

Jake shrugged, not even bothering to look not-guilty, "That would depend on if they worked or not."

Nick snorted a laugh, "Well, lucky for you in a roundabout way they did, but next time mind your own business or I'll shove my boot up your ass." He turned in the doorway, and then paused, "Dare I ask what the notes said?"

Jake grinned in amusement, "Don't worry, I kept it very simple. She doesn't think you're Lord Byron or anything like that. But you do owe me about a hundred bucks."

Chapter 15

Hesitantly, Morgan stepped inside the spacious barn, becoming the immediate focus of at least forty curious horses. Instantly assaulted by the sweet smells of hay, sawdust, leather and the animals she walked over to the first stall and, standing on tiptoe, looked in. A chestnut Arabian glanced at her, flicked his ears, and then went back to munching his hay, dismissing her completely. Not put off she wiggled her fingers while making little clucking noises in her throat. All it produced was a chestnut ear turned her way.

"Oh well," she smiled, remembering the freedom that could be found on the back of a horse, "your loss."

"That's Sultan. He can be a snob unless you have an apple or carrot."

Morgan whipped around and looked up at Nick as he began descending the loft ladder. "You scared me," she gasped, one hand plastered against her pounding chest.

"Sorry. That does seem to be a habit."

"Jake said you were in here," she said, feeling the need to explain her presence. Morgan watched his muscles ripple as he maneuvered down the steep ladder. She hated to admit it but his forearms and biceps were mouth-watering, daring a woman to press her lips to each yummy bulge.

What would it be like to be held by him… made

love to by him? And why the heck are you even thinking about this Morgan Fletcher? Don't you remember how it was with Richard? What about the things he did to you while you were tied up or otherwise helpless? All men like to dominate a woman in some way. Nick may have treated you nicely so far but once he gets you alone he's probably no different, and he's big enough to force you, bigger than Richard, and Richard did whatever he wanted to you. Briefly an image flashed in her mind, of her in front of a mirror, bent over the skinny, hard-edged back of a chair, barely able to breathe because of the crushing pain in her stomach while Richard used her unprepared body in the most degrading way.

Unconsciously her arm went across her stomach. She closed her eyes and cleared her throat, hoping the brief, evil direction her mind had taken didn't show on her face. "Jake said just to wander around until I found you."

"Yeah, I was just on my way to give this alfalfa to the gelding." Nick gestured down to the far end of the barn, then seized the handles of the wheelbarrow sitting in the aisle. "Come on, he's a little afraid of everyone right now, but he might not mind meeting a beautiful woman like you."

She flushed under the compliment and flashed him a brief, bashful smile. She knew she wasn't beautiful, but it was nice of him to keep saying it. Each thoughtful action or word made the distance between him and Richard loom larger.

"All right." She trailed after him past countless stalls filled with horses of all kinds. "He's a rescue horse?"

"Yeah. I got him a couple of months ago, a few days before our first 'meeting'." He grinned and winked at her. "Out of all the horses I've dealt with he's been the toughest one yet. But it's understandable with what he went through."

"How many horses do you have?" The lines of stalls seemed endless.

"Fifty-one total. Thirty-seven are mine—well, Jake claims a couple too—the rest are here for training. "Do you like horses?" He asked casually.

She nodded without glancing up, "Oh yes. I love them."

"Do you ride?"

"I used to, I was taking lessons, but then—"

He looked down at her when she fell silent. "But then what?"

She glanced at him but didn't quite meet his eyes, then cast her gaze down at the ground again, never breaking stride. "But then I hurt my leg."

Nick said nothing, but when she looked back up there was a muscle ticking in his jaw that hadn't been there before.

They entered a short connecting hallway and he pushed the hay through a set of open double doors. Eyes widening in amazement at the huge open space in front of her Morgan stopped dead and just looked around. She realized that they had entered an indoor riding ring, complete with mirrored walls on one side, just like in Dressage barns, and a long sectioned off exercise pool at the far end. Morgan had only seen those used on a TV veterinary show. But apparently Nick spared no expense when it came to the horses.

Awed she turned around several times, taking in

the sheer size of the place. Tall oversized sections of wood made up the walls, with big screened-in windows every third section. Covering the whole ring was a tin roof. Eight large sun panels were fixed into the roof allowing natural light to brighten the arena and a humongous industrial sized fan swirled lazily at the far end near the roof line. A smaller metal ring sat off to the right side. Even the professional barn she had taken a few lessons at couldn't compete with this one.

Out of the corner of her eye she caught a movement in the smaller ring and glanced at it again. A large white horse was standing at the far end with his nose to the ground, gently pushing the dirt around. She followed Nick closer, trailing slightly behind him as they neared the pen.

"He's getting better," Nick said, "improving daily, it's just going to take time and patience."

"You must have a lot of that. Patience I mean."

He flashed her a grin and answered, "Tons. Although it's reserved for special people and animals."

She smiled back at him, blushing and feeling oddly dreamy. The moment was broken when the horse, agitated now by their approach, blew a sharp breath and kicked one of the metal railings with his back hoof. The whole ring shuddered. Nick picked up the flake of hay out of the wheelbarrow and went over to the gate. The harsh sound of scraping metal and clinking chains announced that he was unlatching the door. Morgan stood off to the side away from the ring in case the horse went crazy and tried to leap over it. Nick entered the ring and animal went stock still, then blew sharply through his nose and trotted off to the far side of the ring. Nick dropped the bundle of hay he had been holding and exited the pen.

"Usually I would stay in there with him for awhile, but not today. I think it would stress him too much having another person here."

Morgan let out the breath she had been holding and walked slowly to the panel rail. The horse was at the hay now, head down and munching quietly and for the first time she got a clear, close-up look at him. She stopped, gasping in horror. Her hand flew up to cover her mouth and she swallowed tightly, sensing Nick coming up behind her.

The horse was skin and bones, every rib could be counted, and its hips stuck out prominently beneath tightly stretched skin and his white coat. Morgan gripped the bar tightly for support as her breath hitched, stuck in her dry throat. Not only was he skinny, but he was covered in welts and old scars. Long and short, some deeper than others, they marred his face, his neck, his ears. Jesus God there was not a section of his body that was not marred. Her hand fluttered up towards her cheek. Most of the marks, like her own, would never fade. She wiped at her eyes and looked over her shoulder at Nick, not surprised to find his keen blue eyes focused on her.

"Who did that to him?" Her voice quivered. "Why?" Nick became a watery, out of focus blur, and his voice, when he spoke, was gruff.

"His previous owner." Nick's palms landed on her shoulders, then slid down along her arms until he covered both of her cold hands in his own. Gently he removed her fingers from the metal bars and criss-crossed their arms across her stomach. Morgan let herself be surrounded by the hard warmth of his body and timidly leaned back against him. He made an appreciative noise in his throat and she relaxed even more.

The horse raised its head, eyeing them briefly, then refocused on the hay, using his delicate pink muzzle to push bits here and there emitting soft, contented little snuffles while munching.

"Then his previous owner should be shot," she whispered. She wasn't sure, the contact had been too brief and could have been accidental, but she thought she felt Nick press a light kiss to the top of her head.

"Yeah…I was tempted to do some damage." Against her back she felt his chest expand on a deep breath. "But that wouldn't have solved anything, and would have only caused trouble for me and Jake." His voice lowered as if in afterthought, "Which I sure as hell don't need."

Morgan detected an odd note in there, but tamped down on her sudden curiosity, not about to pry into Nick's personal affairs. "Tell me about him." She gestured towards the horse.

"Well," he began in a deeply soft voice, "he's part Draft, part Quarter Horse and was used on his owner's farm to haul…well, whatever the guy had to haul, even though he had a tractor that could have done most of the work." He shifted against her, adjusting their positions so that his arms rested just below her breasts. Richard used to hold her this way, but unlike Nick's hold Richard's had been tight enough to almost crush her ribs. Morgan's breath stuttered in her chest and she shivered, clutching at Nick's forearm. This horse had been owned by a person exactly like Richard, and like her, had been marked forever by him. Goose bumps rose on her skin even though it was not cold in the arena.

"Relax Morgan." Nick's warm breath tickled her ear, the side of her neck. She closed her eyes on a low moan. "Just let me hold you, sweetheart." He waited until she gave a small nod and then continued. "Anyway, I never understood why he used the horse instead of it. But he was a cheap bastard and didn't feed the horse enough to keep up his strength and weight; so of course, even though he's part Draft he couldn't work like he used to."

The pictures played out clearly in her mind—the horse, emaciated and weak but bravely struggling, trying its best to please its master before giving out and collapsing, too broken down to care about whatever fate awaited him. Too tired to care. Whether it was death or something else at least it would be a departure from a hellish life.

Unconsciously her hand went to her cheek. "So he started to whip him." She whispered.

"Yeah," Nick's voice was soft, "he started whipping him."

One big rough hand slid up her arm over the material of her shirt and her skin tingled through the thin cotton. Those questing fingers reached her shoulder and then caressed along the line of her throat. A slight mewling sound escaped her. "Shhh…" He soothed. She flinched, but didn't pull away when his fingers moved up and skimmed the slightly raised marks on her cheek. He stroked her skin for moment, then turned her face to his, his indigo eyes touching on each scar line and as she watched the muscles in his darkly stubbled jawbone went rigid.

"Nick?" Morgan waited until his eyes flicked to hers. "It's alright."

"The hell it is." He growled. "That miserable bas—" He stopped, closed his eyes briefly and heaved a deep breath. "Christ Morgan, I'm sorry. I really didn't mean to go there…to bring him up again. Not today at least." Giving her a small, self-deprecating smile Nick pressed a kiss to the top of her head, then let his hand fall to his side and moved away from her. Immediately Morgan experienced a sense of loss, missing his warmth, the secure feeling of just being held close.

Nick walked over to the wheelbarrow and grabbed each handle, knuckles flexing as he adjusted his grip. Morgan followed him as he wheeled the cart out of the arena and into connecting walkway of the main barn. "I've been working each day with him, trying to gain his trust. Once that's done then I can have him examined again by the vet and see what he needs. When he first came here we had to tranquilize him and I really don't want to do that again if it can be helped."

He looked so sincere, his expression so at odds with his big, dark, severe appearance that there was no faking it. She felt his sincerity in every pulse-pounding cell of her body. "You really do care about these horses, don't you?"

The muscles in his jawbones started ticking again, and his voice deepened to almost a growl. "It kills me to see how people can treat them." He was silent a moment, then, "Just like it kills me to know you went through the same."

Morgan's mouth opened, but no response seemed a worthy comeback to that matter-of-fact statement, so she remained silent while inside her heart turned over and over and over.

They stopped at each stall, and each stall had a horse with a story; there was Goldie, the twenty-nine year old pony that had worked at fairs riding kids around in endless circles even after she had foundered twice. There was a black Thoroughbred racehorse named Sweet Sinjun that had broken down during her first race and, like so many others, been on her way to the slaughterhouse before Nick had intervened; Hiero, the ex-police horse that had been shot up in the line of duty and blinded in one eye and retired to Nick's farm instead of being put down. There were so many other sad, heartrending stories that Morgan's mind was whirling, struggling with the information overload and the myriad of emotions that each story heaped upon her. If not for Nick and Jake most of these beautiful animals would have been dead by now, one way or another, and some possibly even served up as the latest delicacy in some European restaurant.

Somehow she managed to keep her roiling emotions from showing and said, "Wow, Nick, I just don't see how you and Jake manage it all."

Nick grinned at her, "We have schedules and a rhythm, it's the way we like it," he explained. "Plus on weekends a couple of high school kids come out to help with cleaning stalls and grooming. The horses here that take most of our time are the ones in training, the rest are here permanently, so they don't require as much focus, just grooming and feeding."

There were so, so many horses, so many cases of mistreatment that it was hard for her to comprehend even though she had been through the same thing. The difference was that unlike her, the animals couldn't hide what had been done to them. It's crazy, she thought to herself …they're horses, not people…but I don't feel so alone anymore.

As Nick continued talking Morgan realized that she felt more at ease in this huge barn than she had living with her husband in their—no his home. Morgan looked at Nick, past the tattoos and the outwardly tough 'don't fuck with me' demeanor, to the sincere love he felt for these horses shining in his dark blue eyes. Her heart swelled with an emotion she didn't want acknowledge, but couldn't ignore. Don't be a fool again, Morgan. Don't you dare.

"Morgan?" Nick's voice penetrated her musing and she looked up questioningly. They had stopped at a stall marked Nearctic. Nick opened the latch and was now looking at her, concern plain in the lines of his dark face, blue eyes keen. "You okay? You went really quiet on me. And not just with your voice." He took a black halter off the hook by the door, his worried eyes never leaving her.

Oh God, it's too late. Richard's summarization of her as a 'weak-minded twit' was dead on. She was a complete fool…one that was already half-way in love with Nick.

Panic coursed through her, filling her mouth with a flat metallic twang, almost like the taste of blood. She remembered the taste of her own blood; she'd had firsthand multiple opportunities to learn its flavor. Oh, God…It would never end. She had to leave, had to get out of there and away from Nick's gentle draw before she did something supremely stupid and fell in love completely. He was a good man; she knew that truth to her bones and he didn't deserve to have the dark poison of Richard and her past contaminate his life. Morgan knew she would only disappoint him and seeing that disappointment growing in his eyes, day by day, would destroy her.

She couldn't take anymore heartache, and caring for someone…trusting them and letting them into her life meant she would have to take that chance, the chance of failing and of being hurt again. It was too much, too soon.

"I-I think I'd better go, Nick." Ignoring the bewilderment darkening of his eyes she backed away, her heels sliding over the sawdust covered aisleway. "No, I have to go. For both of us."

"What?" his voice roughened in disbelief, "Why? What the hell for?" In two seconds his expression changed from one of concern to brooding incredulity, reminding her of a darkening sky before a thunderstorm. He stalked towards her and grabbed her elbow before she could turn and run. Bravely she faced him, an oversized wall of unmovable male who was twice her size. But for the first time in six years she felt no fear. No mind-crippling apprehension.

Only a dull, aching sadness.

"Talk to me, Morgan." He demanded, "What the hell's wrong? Did I do something that scared you?"

She looked down, past his hand holding her elbow to the halter dangling forgotten from his wrist. It was still swaying from his sudden movements, bumping her in the thigh. If he had been Richard she would have already felt that concoction of metal and leather against her skin, and she would have been face-down at his feet, bleeding and eating sawdust.

If only she had met Nick first, before Richard had

ruined her.

"No Nick," she answered, "I scared myself." I'm scared because you make me want things, she added silently, and that's a risk I can't take. Then, knowing this was her last opportunity to touch him, she rose up to her tiptoes and using his shoulders as leverage she brushed a kiss over his darkly stubbled jaw. Her lips moved slowly, memorizing the texture of his beard shadow and the slightly salty taste of his skin. He jerked slightly, no doubt from shock, but before he could respond or react, she whispered, "Self-preservation, Nick. It's all I have left."

Chapter 16

He was staring at her cheek, those blue, beautiful eyes that haunted her dreams almost black in anger and…something else.

Then it hit her, making her stomach drop to her feet. Making her want to wretch.

It was 'the look'. The one that she absolutely hated and yet had seen from everyone, sometimes even Lisa. Pity, or maybe disgust, she thought, just like everyone else. Her eyes filled with tears and the unfairness of it was like a physical blow to her chest. Fighting for breath she yanked herself out of his reach. For just a few days she had felt almost like a normal woman—one who had caught the attention of a startlingly gorgeous man. That illusion now shattered into a million sharp-edged pieces, each one slicing into her as they fell. Cutting her raw. Ashamed, she turned away from him, "I don't need your pity," she hissed, wrapping her arms tight around her middle and backing away so he wouldn't see how much she was trembling, how much she hurt," so why don't you just leave now and not come back."

She covered her cheek with her palm, still feeling the ghostly imprint of his touch. "Go!" she cried.

He stiffened, his thick black brows drawing low over his narrowed eyes. He cursed under his breath, low, foul and ugly and took a quick step towards her, reaching for her again.

Hastily she backed away, holding out both hands to ward him off. "S-Stay away from me!" She put a shaking hand to her forehead, confused by her conflicting desires. Part of her wanted him hold her again, but the other part was afraid of being made a fool.

He ignored her protests, advancing on her. "Pity? Morgan, for God's sake! It's not what you—"

"No! You're just like everyone else!" she sobbed, glaring at him and stumbling away, "I bet you don't think I'm so beautiful now, do you?"

"Yes," he said quietly, his voice rumbling from the depths of his chest. "I do. If you only knew how much. But I also see plenty of evidence that you've been treated like shit. And I guessed right about your husband putting his hands on you, didn't I?"

The brusque statement hit like a blow, penetrating her mind and the hurt. Using her hand, she dashed the tears away and looked at him. He was so blindingly handsome. The perfect male animal. No flaws to be found, so unlike scarred, gimpy her. Morgan laughed, but it came out as a sob; she had been so stupid to let herself be reeled in by a few scraps of hope. Maybe Richard had been right about her. He had always called her a weak-minded twit who was too stupid to know when to give up.

A man like Nick would have a new woman for each day of the week. Beautiful, perfect women. Ones who didn't limp and who had no scars and who didn't freak out when a man touched them. They'd enjoy sex and know how to please a man like him.

"You're lying. But that's okay; I'm used to it. And

yeah, you're right," her chin trembled and she clenched her jaw against the show of weakness, "my husband used to beat the crap out of me and then some. The pretty proof is right there on my face, every single day for the entire world to see." A sob caught in her throat and she gestured sharply at her face.

He cursed, reaching for her. "Sweetheart, just let me—."

"Stop!" She jerked backwards, dashing the wetness from her face. Crying had never done any good; she knew that for a fact. Making her voice low and hard, she said, "Please…just get away from me. I'm not one of your horses that needs saving."

Nick went still, his heart slamming painfully against his ribs. Briefly he closed his eyes, imagining some of what she must have endured and wondering if he had pushed her too far. He knew full well how evil people could be and the knowledge that Morgan's husband had used his fists on her, tried to break her body and spirit, turned his blood to ice. The sick, sadistic bastard…

Nick drew in a deep breath, filling his lungs with crisp, clean air, calming himself and relaxing his tight fists while he contemplated how to handle the next step. God…if only he could take her in his arms, protect her from the world; absorb her pain into his body…

She was sobbing openly now, one hand covering her eyes while the other stayed clamped against her belly. She backed away from him towards the barn, her fragile shoulders jerking with each violent heave. He watched in helpless, enraged silence as she blindly bumped into the barn and slid down the wall to plop on her butt right there in the grass. Her hair tangled around her shoulders. Long strands, wet from tears, cut across her face and mouth as she continued to cry in great wrenching sobs.

He winced when her slight shoulders jerked with a particularly violent one. His emotions were in an uproar, his hands clenching and unclenching and he knew that if her husband had been alive and standing in front of him he would have ripped the son-of-a-bitches' throat out.

Shit…seeing her cry felt like somebody had sliced into his chest with a dull knife and was systematically carving off small pieces of his heart… very slowly and very painfully. He wanted to slam his fist through the wall—through the bloody bastard's face that had reduced her to this. Anything to take her pain away.

He wanted to—God.

Why did each of their encounters have to be so fucked up?

He shoved his hand through his hair, locking his fingers behind his head and pacing back and forth, shaken by the driving urge to comfort her but riddled with fear of not knowing how. If he came on too strong, too determined, she would run away from him as she had before, and possibly never let him near her again. She was already wary and hurt, thinking he had been playing with her…lying to her.

She was still huddled against the barn, head down and sobbing quietly into her arms. He started towards her, and was only a few feet from her when he stopped, cursing tightly under his breath. If she was one of his horses he would know instantly what to do—move slowly, take several days getting them used to him, and then begin— but this was Morgan, not a horse, and he was not a comforting man, had no experience with being tender outside of the bedroom, and even those instances were few and far between. And relationships? Those were pretty much zero. Women wanted to fuck him, not date him, and until now he had been okay with that. But now...now he felt utterly useless and the reality of that was harsh.

It was blazingly obvious that she came with some serious baggage. One misstep with Morgan and he could hurt her deeply, possibly even more deeply than she had been already.

And you're so skeleton-in-the-closet free?

Okay. Can't call the kettle black. Hell, if she knew his past it would most likely send her into an even bigger panic attack. Ex-con. Yeah, that's the type of man a woman who has been abused wants to get involved with. One who's been in prison, behind bars, judged too dangerous to for civilized society. Nick felt an odd pain in his throat, and a burning behind his eyelids. Ex-convict...dangerous...He looked down at Morgan, his eyes traveling over the exposed nape of her neck, so delicate and fragile and pictured her husband wrapping his hand around the slender column. He swallowed hard, dislodging the tightness in his throat and willed away the burning in his eyes. Not once since collapsing had she looked up at him.

Ex-con. Murderer...He had an ugly history and the why of it wouldn't matter.

Nick ground his jaw as a heavy weight settled between his shoulders and he realized that that was the truth of it. He was nobody's savior, especially not Morgan's, a woman who had already been through so much pain.

He had lived here for over ten years and whenever he was in town some people still looked at the ground and hurried past as he walked down the street. Even Jake, who had never caused trouble a day in his life and usually had a smile for everyone had been treated to the same judgments, just because he happened to be the brother of an ex-con. It had been hard getting out of prison and trying to get on with his life. People, in general, did not like to give trust or second chances, especially not when faced with his black past. So for several months he had wandered, luckily getting an odd job on a ranch here and there before his past caught up with him and he was asked to leave. Again and Again. No matter what outside image he projected, once people found out he had been in 'the big house' doors were slammed shut…and locked. The stigma never went away.

And here he was, basically stalking a woman who had lived a life of pain and who was now struggling to make it on her own. He could unintentionally ruin that. Nick looked down at her still huddled against the barn, but was surprised to see that she had stopped crying and was now staring at him out of tearstained gold eyes, her expression bleak and resigned. Tired. She deserved so much more than being with a black-tempered ex-con whose past was always present, and who knew nothing except how to train horses and how to fuck.

She deserved someone like Jake.

Jake, the good brother, who had never been in trouble, and who was kind, patient, loyal, and a gentleman, especially when it came to women. Jake would know how to soothe her, how to help her move beyond the past. And sex…Jake would know exactly what she needed—would know exactly how to make love to her...Jake and Morgan. In a sick self-torture Nick's brain flashed with images of his brother covering her sweet body, of Jake parting those pale thighs...Oh... God...The pain of it was real, as if it had already happened and he had lost her, but the pain of knowing he could ruin her future, could only hurt her in the end, was just as strong. Leave...leave right now. You've already hurt her, she thinks you've made a joke out of her, so just turn around and move one foot in front of the other until you're in your truck and headed down the road.

No, goddamnit! Not like this.

Those huge eyes followed his every move, and she gasped slightly as he dropped to his knees in front of her. His hands were shaking as he cupped her face. The rough pad of his thumb traced the swollen softness of her bottom lip.

"Shhh, sweetheart, it's alright," he soothed when his fingers touched her scars and she tried to pull away. Raw emotion closed his throat, and the urge to kiss her, to lay her down in the overgrown yard and worship her with his mouth and hands and body until she understood how beautiful she was to him was nearly unbearable.

"Morgan?" Her name was a gruff whisper. He pressed his lips against her ear as she pushed her wet face into his shoulder, soaking his shirt with her tears, no longer fighting or lashing out. "Whatever it is baby, it'll be okay."

He rubbed her slender back, absorbing her shudders into his stronger body while she cried.

As he stroked her hair he memorized the smooth,

silky feel of it between his fingers. Regret, hot and harsh, closed his throat and he had to glance away before he could speak. Coward. "Listen, sweetheart…" his throat tightened again, choking him. He swallowed once more and then forced out the words he didn't want to say. "I wish you understood…since the first time I saw you how much I—" he swiped a hand over his jaw, cursing.

No point in going there now, there was no way she would believe him.

"I'll, uh…I'll send Jake out here to help you get this place situated. He'll help with whatever you need. You won't have to see me." The words tasted bitter, regret poisoning each of them.

"No," she said, pulling away from him and rubbing her eyes. She didn't look at him; instead she stared at the distant line of trees that separated their properties. "I don't want to see either of you. Just like I don't need or want your pity."

Nick's mouth dropped open in shock while his brain tried to wrap around her statement. Pity? Holy shi— "Pity is the last thing I think about when I look at you, Morgan."

She gave a shaky little laugh, "Yeah…that was evident by the expression on your face. And to think that I—"

Nick knew by the way she clamped her mouth shut that something very important had been about to spill out.

"You what?" He asked softly.

Silence. Frustration mounting he swiped a hand over his head. "Damn it! You what, Morgan?"

That delicate jaw clamped even tighter. Throwing

caution to the wind and ignoring her high-pitched squeak, Nick tunneled his hand through her hair until he cupped the back of her scalp. He tugged until her head tilted and she arched her neck, her gold eyes wide with alarm, black lashes spiky from her recent tears.

His first thought was to back off, comfort her, but he ignored it, sensing that right now comfort would only send her into a deeper zone where only she could go. He wanted her fired-up, pissed off, hell, anything she had to give him he'd take. Anything except this small, defeated shell sitting on the ground in front of a crumbling old barn.

He'd be damned if he was going to leave her thinking that pity had been his motive.

Staring straight into her eyes, keeping his voice fierce and low, he said, "You think its pity I feel for you? Well let me tell you sweetheart, it's not pity that makes me hard every damn night since I first saw you. And if you haven't figured it out, yes, I'm talking about my di—penis." Since he was still holding her head she couldn't move, but her eyes immediately dropped to his groin, then flew back up to his face. Bright spots of pink highlighted her cheeks and she reached up, grabbed his forearms and tugged. Gently resisting her he said, "No, don't try to get away; I'm not hurting you Morgan. I'm telling you this because you need to hear it and I'm damn well going to get it out before I leave."

His thumbs moved slowly over her cheekbones, back and forth, softly stroking. His eyes dipped to her lips, lingering as the tip of her tongue came out to wet her bottom lip. In any other woman he would take that as an invitation, but not Morgan. Even so he couldn't resist leaning nearer, so close now that he could see himself reflected in her eyes. She was tensing up again, but he remained close, willing her to believe him. "Look at me Morgan and tell me you still think I'm lying. Pity has nothing to do with the way my gut clenches, or the way my heart pounds each time you look at me with those huge golden doe eyes."

"N-Nick…" Her voice was a mere breath of sound and she tugged at his wrists again, fingers trembling and slipping on his skin with her efforts. "Stop…"

"Too late sweet, the ball's rolling now. Shhh…Relax, I'm not hurting you." He waited until she stopped pulling on him and sat quietly, her fingers loosening embracing his thick wrists. "And don't even get me started on what your hair does to me, drives me crazy is an understatement. But you really want to know what I think when I see you?" Tenderly he started massaging her scalp with his fingers, working his way along the back of her head to the nape of her neck. Her shoulders rose and fell on a slight sigh and her eyelids fluttered in enjoyment.

"I see a beautiful woman. Yes," he emphasized when she opened her mouth to protest, "I said beautiful because it's true. You're sweet and gorgeous Morgan. Life's given you some tough shit to deal with, but that's past now…you don't have to fight or be afraid anymore…you…" he swallowed, glancing away from her, needing a moment to get the words out, "you deserve to be happy." And that's why I'm going to let you go.

A lump formed in his throat and then his vision went blurry, shit. He hadn't cried since he was seventeen and his mom had died. Focusing on the woman in front of him he stroked his fingers softly over her cheek, over her scars, feeling the long rough edges that marred her otherwise baby-fine skin. Fresh tears rolled down her face, wetting his hand.

He swallowed hard, then gruffly whispered, "Every warrior has battle scars, sweetheart."

Chapter 17

Morgan sat at her kitchen table, staring sightlessly at the mess of paints and brushes on her kitchen floor, a glass of forgotten tea in front of her. A packet of sweetener sat unopened beside it. It was eight o'clock in the morning, the sun was shining outside and the kitchen walls were waiting on a last coat of paint, but she just couldn't find the will to get started. The brilliant yellow that had made her feel so cheerful just weeks ago had failed yet again today.

It had been two weeks since she had seen Nick and she didn't understand how she could miss someone she barely knew.

'I see a beautiful woman. Yes, I said beautiful because it's true.' The words replayed incessantly in her mind, especially when she looked at herself in the mirror. She kept the words with her, close to her heart.

A little bit of hope tucked away like a beloved treasure.

She thought about him constantly, wondered what he was doing at certain times of the day and night...pictured him riding a horse, or lying in his bed with the sheet pulled up just to his waist, heavy arms crossed behind his head on the pillow. She had even wondered what type of sheets he slept on or if he wore a robe around his house like her husband had. No, that didn't fit. A man like him doubtlessly preferred only briefs or boxers. An image of him leaning against a kitchen counter in only a pair of boxers, his big, dark hands wrapped around a steaming mug of coffee, filtered into her brain.

She would love to see that in person. But that would mean you'd have to wake up…with him. In bed. After a night of—she stopped herself.

If fantasies like that weren't ridiculous then she didn't know what was. Hadn't she learned by now?

His brother, Jake, had shown up once to collect the tools Nick had left and to offer his help if she needed it, but she had politely refused. He had hesitated, apparently wanting to say something, but then had just looked at her for a long moment before getting into his truck and driving away, leaving her feeling as if the door to something special had not only been slammed shut, but bolted.

In fact, she felt much the same as she had when Robert had first introduced her to his fist.

Shell-shocked.

Her head hurt, her lip burned, and the metallic tang of blood hit her tongue, soaking between it and the indentation behind her bottom teeth. Gagging and coughing she struggled to her knees. Blindly she fumbled and her hand hit the side of the bed. She gripped the thick comforter tightly, using it to pull herself halfway off the floor.

'Oh no you don't. You still have a lot to learn about being my wife.' Richard's voice came at her from above; right before his fist connected with her temple.

Morgan stared blindly into her tea glass, remembering that night and waking up in the cabins bed much, much later with several white towels between her bleeding head and the pillow. That had been during their Honeymoon cruise to Alaska. Richard had been very thorough in his lessons.

Stepford wife in public, slut in private. Every man's fantasy woman.

She'd had to stay in bed, barely able to move, until the end of their trip almost a week later.

Morgan shuddered; she had been so excited to see the Alaskan scenery, so excited to be Robert's wife… but had ended up with memories of the cabins white ceiling through blackened, swollen eyes.

And from then on the six years of marriage had been a private warzone, with no one to help, or to believe her except Lisa, and Richard had made sure her cousin had stayed away. Her only joy had been visiting her mother, but each visit, each time her mother hugged her and asked how Richard was doing, only reminded her of the awful life she was keeping a secret. Of how much she was hiding behind the makeup and expensive clothes. But battling cancer had been enough for her mother to deal with and she had died never knowing the truth.

Stop it Morgan.

Dropping her head into her hands Morgan let the tears she had held back all morning flow free. Considering the amount she had cried in the last two weeks she was surprised there were any left.

****

The first flowers showed up eighteen days later, wrapped in cellophane and sticking out of her mailbox. Pale pink rose buds that had yet to open. Attached a handwritten note that said only, 'Sorry.'

Morgan bit her lip, torn for a moment and then

stuffed the fragile buds into her unused paperbox. The second bunch, this time multicolored daisies, she found lying on her front steps a couple days later. Another note read, 'Really sorry.' She stuffed them in the box with the rose buds, ignoring the creeping regret when she saw the wilted pink flowers still struggling to survive.

Two days later her doorbell rang. Her postman was on the other side, mail in one hand, a bouquet of daffodils, along with the two bunches from her paperbox in the other.

"Mrs. Fletcher, these," he handed her the daffodils and mail, "were stuck in the mailbox and I couldn't get any mail in. And these," he held up the two bunches of drooping, lifeless roses and daisies, "were in the paperbox. They need some help…fast." He smiled at her, "Looks like you have an admirer. I hope you can save them."

Morgan thanked him and shut the door, feeling petty and mean for leaving the innocent flowers out there to die for no reason. Setting her mail on the hall table for later viewing, she carried the flowers into the kitchen and ran water in three vases, dropping an aspirin into each and hoping it wasn't too late.

Two days later a dozen blood-red roses in full bloom were waiting on her.

****

Nick pounded the last nail into the wooden slat and straightened, glaring at the horse that watched him with complete and false innocence. Three days in his new stall near the feed room and already two boards had been knocked loose. Nick knew it was because he had yet to move Raina.

148

"The next time you kick this panel out I'm going to nail your hide, instead of the board." He threatened, moving closer to stroke the old Arabian's silky chestnut neck. It was an empty threat and both he and Sultan knew it. Nick had owned the horse since being released from prison and could not count how many stall boards or pasture railings he had replaced over the years, but installing a layer of heavy-duty rubber padding on the lower portion of the stall walls had helped some and lessened any chance of injury for the horse.

"Eat your hay, cranky. She'll be up here as soon as I get that stall ready."

Thunder, heavy and low, rumbled in the distance. Giving the horse one final, affectionate pat he latched the door behind him, went to check on the two Appaloosa fillies that had arrived a few days before, and then left the barn, breaking into a jog as fat raindrops began to fall from the darkening sky, soaking him before he reached the protection of his screened back porch. He shrugged out of his shirt, using it to wipe the rain and sweat off of his head and upper body and then collapsed onto the bench by the back door, watching as lighting lit the sky over the mountains and rain ran in rivulets through the stableyard, the flowing streams reminding him of Morgan's tears.

You left her crying her guts out and didn't do a damn thing but walk away. He slammed his eyes shut, refusing to acknowledge that little fact of truth. Instead he searched his brain, calling forth an image of her with no tears. That morning, before he had fucked things up so royally. She had brought him a drink, shyly offering it to him and her eyes had been clear then, anxious yes, but not bloodshot from crying.

Weariness seeped into his bones; he had been running himself ragged for days, weeks, trying to get her out of his mind. Not that it had done any good. Trying to do the best thing was really not working out for him.

'No good deed goes unpunished'. If that wasn't the fucking truth then he didn't know what was.

Trying to do the 'right' thing was threatening to drive him mad. The days since had been hell. He had ridden through the woods by the stream almost every day hoping to see her, a fact that had had his brother laughing his ass off. She had never shown and he had since stopped.

He knew why, understood it completely. She was ashamed of her scars and what had happened to her. No matter what he said she thought he was just taking pity on her, playing with her. She clearly did not know how beautiful she was, even with the scars, and he wasn't certain, but he suspected she blamed herself for those scars.

And probably blamed herself for the abuse, each and every time her husband hurt her. He knew it was common among abuse victims, especially with domestic abuse. God knows he had heard his mother defending his father often enough.

Shit. Nick looked down at his broad, clenched fists with their huge knuckles. One blow from him would definitely break her jawbone, and she was so petite that he wouldn't even have to put much force behind it.

The thought sickened him.

He couldn't comprehend being violent with her on any level. The thought of hurting her in any way was physically repellent.

But he had hurt her. He had gotten personal too soon, and, like the arrogant, opportunistic bastard that he could be, he had pushed and it had backfired. Hell, he had even gone as low as to tell her about his fully functioning penis. Great job, Nick. Just great. Exactly what she needed to think about while she's on the ground crying—you and your hard-on.

So what, you won't be seeing her again. The voice of reason spoke inside his head. Plus, you've done this before, gotten involved where you really shouldn't have and all it did was land your ass in prison. Go get laid and get her out of your mind.

Sound advice, too bad he wasn't really listening. The only woman he cared about getting laid with lived on the other side of his pasture, which, since he couldn't have her, might as well be on the other side of the continent. Sure, his hands worked and his mind ran rampant with fantasies about her, but they were a piss poor substitute for the real thing and offered little satisfaction. He knew her body, had held it against his and that little bit had only fanned the flame. He wanted more, so much more. He wanted her soft and yielding in his arms, skin to skin, her body flushed, wet with desire, not tense and panicky.

And definitely no goddamned tears.

"Nick," he muttered to himself, "You're too old for this adolescent shit."

Getting up he headed inside to the shower. Maybe a night out would do him some good. God knows it had been a long time. Some female companionship might be exactly what he needed to get him back on track.

The more he thought about it the more appealing the prospect became.

A few hours later he was in his truck and headed for the outskirts of town.

Chapter 18

The alarm clock blared at quarter to five the next morning; 'Here Without You' by Three Doors Down came on, piercing Nick's right eardrum. He groaned and slapped a hand over the radio, shutting off both the high-pitched beeping and the song, not needing to be reminded about lonely minds and dreaming about someone who wasn't there.

A quick, cold shower woke him up, but did nothing to relieve his mental exhaustion. He glared at himself in the mirror; bloodshot blue eyes stared back at him. Not a good combination. Looking and feeling like shit just confirmed the fact that last night's excursion hadn't helped. A fact that he layed firmly on Morgan Fletcher's slender shoulders.

The storm had passed during the night, leaving the morning misty and calm. Cool air clung to his face as he made his way from the house to the barn a little after six. Mud, thick and heavy, stuck to his boots, forcing a pit-stop by the wash-rack to hose them off before heading inside. Jake was already there, haltering the horses that would go out to pasture for the day according to the chalkboard schedule on the wall.

"Late start today?" Jake checked his watch, "I'm showing six-thirty six. I was here at a prompt six-fifteen."

Nick grunted irritably, not in the mood after

catching only about an hour's worth of sleep. "Put Raina and Sultan together in the dry lot with some grass hay. I'm going to switch her stall today and put her beside Sultan. We also need to worm everyone later. Don't let me forget."

"Sure thing, sunshine." Jake muttered while slipping a halter over the lowered head of the sweet-faced Quarter Horse mare. "Thata girl Sarah." In her heyday she had been a pretty good barrel racer, but a fractured coffin bone had ended her career early, so the owners, unable to afford proper medical treatment for the mare, had donated her to the farm instead of putting her down. Now her only job was to baby-sit the rambunctious yearlings that Nick sometimes got in.

"Hey. Nick…" Jake's voice was extremely gentle, "you okay?"

Nick rolled his eyes and raised an eyebrow, "What's on your mind Jake?"

"I saw your truck leave late last night."

Nick waited, "And?"

"And you didn't come back for several hours. Not to mention your oh so slightly bloodshot eyes. Did you and Morgan—."

"No," he growled, "and I told you why."

It was Jakes turn to roll his eyes, "Yeah, I know, you're an ex-con. Not worthy of her. Give me a break."

Nick sighed, walked into the tack room and jerked a pail out of the pile in the corner. The sweet scent of oats mixing with the tanginess of well-used leather swept into Nick's nostrils. The smell always soothed him, bringing him back from his mood swings to what was important. The farm, the horses.

He felt Jakes presence near the door behind him

and busied himself with digging a handful of oats out of the container and dumping them in the bucket.

"I still say your reason is bullshit, Nick." Jake said in a disgusted voice. "You're screwing yourself out of something that could be really good if you gave it a half a chance. And it might even make you more pleasant to be around."

"Look Jake, shut up." Aware of his brothers close scrutiny Nick rubbed his eyes, then rolled his head on his shoulders, working out the kinks caused by a lousy nights sleep. "You want to know what I did? I'll tell you. I went to the bar outside of town hoping to find a woman who was short and had long dark hair so I could get a room, fuck her brains out until early morning and then send her on her way in hopes that maybe, just fucking maybe, it would get me back to normal."

He turned just in time to see shock flit through Jakes' deep green eyes. Even though he was six years older than Jake, those eyes always had the power to make him squirm. The same way their mothers had when he was little and would get caught doing something he wasn't supposed to.

Jakes mouth opened and closed. Opened. Before his brother could gather his wits together Nick continued, "But once I got there the idea seemed a little shitty, you know? Wrong somehow. So I sat back, thought of *her*, nursed two beers, politely refused the come-ons from women who were too drunk to know what they were doing or who they were doing, and then came home to sleep for about, oh, an hour. Now, I'm going to get that stall ready for Raina, and after that I'll be in the back working with Nightshade."

Leaving Jake to brood over that little disclosure he

walked down the aisle past numerous stalls and through the short hallway that connected the main barn to the indoor arena. Off to the side was a smaller pen, now the temporary home of the gelding. Progress with the horse had been exceedingly slow, but nothing less than he had expected.

The horse was watching him, huge brown eyes alert with suspicion, reminding him of Morgan.

Christ, would it never cease? Pushing the distraction away he entered the pen. Instantly the horse began rearing at the rails, trying to break through, but Nick noticed the efforts were more half-hearted than the last time. Progress, no matter how small, was progress.

Finally, after about ten minutes of Nick not moving any closer the horse stopped and turned towards him, white chest heaving with each deep breath.

"Easy now. That's right…" Nick murmured, "You know I'm not going to hurt you."

He moved closer, slowly, keeping his eyes off to the side of the nervous horse so as not to threaten him. Trust would be hard-earned with this guy, but worth every struggling moment.

Nick set the small pail of oats down in the center of the pen and crouched beside them. Immediately the geldings' ears pricked forward. He moved a step closer, stopping when he saw that Nick was not moving away. Nick knew he was waiting on him to leave the pen before coming to find out what kind of treat was in the bucket. He kept his eyes cast off to the side, his body loose, shoulders relaxed and unthreatening.

"Sorry boy, I know you don't like it but I'm staying for awhile." The horse's ears swiveled anxiously back and forth, monitoring the sound of his voice. "But I promise, no whips, sticks, or whatever the hell else the bastard used on you."

****

Heart pounding and palms sweating on the steering wheel Morgan maneuvered her car carefully onto the tree-lined dirt and gravel driveway. Nick's place was nothing like what she expected, although she didn't really know what she had expected. A huge sign labeled 'Evanoff Farm' hung above the drive, assuring her that she had the correct place. As she cautiously maneuvered around a sharp curve Morgan caught sight of horses grazing in the pastures on either side of her. She slowed her car to almost a stop and rolled her window down for a better look. A cool breeze ruffled her hair, lifting several flyaway strands and she angled her head up to catch it more fully in the face. Several of the horses raised their heads towards her, ears flicking back and forth in curiosity. They were all so beautiful, their sleek gleaming hides showcased against the backdrop of darkly wooded mountains. Absolutely perfect for her Majestic Montana series. The artist in her surfaced, eager for fresh material. Morgan put the car in park and reached over to the dash compartment, searching for her camera. Crap! The compartment door shut with a sharp click and a quick glance at the backseat told her the camera wasn't there either. If only…But memory would have to do and besides, a photo op had been the farthest thing from her mind when she had gotten in her car less than half an hour ago.

Which brought her back to her original reason for being here.

Biting her lip, she put the car back into drive and

slowly pressed the accelerator, barely reaching ten miles an hour as she followed the fenced drive around. A rectangular two-story beige brick house with burgundy shutters finally came into view and behind it an enormous white with green trim barn. The large double-doors were open and Nick's huge black Dodge truck was parked off to the side, looming large and ominous in her line of sight.

"Oh God," she muttered, "What am I doing here?" Her foot faltered on the accelerator and her heart hammered, beating loud in her ears.

Giving herself time to gather some much needed courage she looked around and spotted another house, this one smaller and made of red-brick, a little ways behind the barn. Beside it was a tin-roofed shed housing a black and tan four-horse trailer and two smaller ones. She could also see the tail-end of some type of motorcycle sitting inside. Probably a Harley. Of course, a man like Nick would go for a Harley. And don't forget the half-naked biker babes that would go with it.

No…she didn't want to think about that. She looked around again, examining everything in an effort to dismiss the absurd feeling of jealously.

Apparently having heard her car approach, a Black Lab came racing full speed around the corner of the barn, barking and nipping her car's tires, announcing her arrival. Figuring her time to escape was now gone Morgan pressed the gas and maneuvered carefully, half afraid she'd run over the animal, and parked near a fence.

A rider on the far side of the ring beside the barn drew her attention and for a moment her stomach flip-flopped, but then she recognized Jake's lighter hair under the baseball cap he was wearing. He was mounted on a muscular Paint horse and as they got closer she realized he was riding bareback with only a halter. Easy and relaxed he and the horse moved together as one, hypnotizing in their graceful beauty.

Morgan cursed her hormones, wondering why they couldn't have picked this brother, the safe, charming one, to go all googly over.

Just when she was again contemplating putting her car in reverse and getting out of there he saw her, threw his hand up and loped the horse over to the gate. She watched, amazed, while in one smooth motion he leaned down, unlatched the gate, maneuvered the big horse through it and latched it back. She got out of the car, keeping one eye open for signs of Nick, and waited for him to ride over.

"Hi." She said shyly when he was within a few feet of her. "I was, um," she tapped her nails on the car door and swallowed, hard, "…looking for, ah, Nick."

Jake swung a leg over the Paints neck, paused, grimacing as if in pain, and slid off the animals back. The expression on his face did nothing to bolster her failing courage.

"Are you okay?" She asked, frowning at him. "You look like you're in pain."

He nodded, "Still a little sore."

She raised an eyebrow in question and he replied, "I fractured a rib several weeks ago, got stuck between a pony and a hard place."

When she opened her mouth he interrupted her, saying, "I think Nick's in the barn working with one of the horses." He fiddled with the reins, flicking them back and forth with his thumbs, and then reached up to stroke the Paints black and white neck. "Uh, today might not be a good time, Morgan. He's really…uh…busy. Maybe I can—"

"No. I'm not."

They both turned. Nick, looking gorgeous but tired in jeans and a dark blue T-shirt, was standing framed in the barn doorway, hands planted on his hips, a bridle dangling from one wrist.

Jakes' 'oh shit' and her 'Oh God' were muttered in unison.

"I have to go," Jake mumbled beside her, "stuff to do and all that."

He practically dragged the horse away and Morgan wondered at his sudden nervousness. She was the one being cut by piercing, heavy-lidded blue eyes and a not-too-welcoming expression. Nerves raw, she wet her lips, gathering her scattered wits while trying to catch her breath for the next step.

"I have to admit I never expected to see you here," Nick stated, gliding towards her, his brawny, tanned muscles bunching and flexing. The bridle jingled in his hand. Six-foot-plus of hulking male moved with pantherish grace towards her. Intimidated she shrank back before she could stop herself.

He stopped, raised an eyebrow and cocked his head to the side, assessing her. "You want me to stop here so you feel safer? Or back up a little?" He raised his hands, holding them out in front of himself as he moved several steps back away from her. The bridle swayed, suspended from his wrist. She blinked, uncertain how to respond. He seemed almost glad that she was there, yet…not.

"Nick, I don't…um. That is…I came to…"

As she stuttered to a stop, lost in confused silence about how to proceed, he heaved a loud sigh, muttered something under his breath, and walked right up to her, bracing his arms on either side of her and trapping her against the car. Morgan squeaked and her hands came up to push him away, only to land and rest on his chest. His heart pounded beneath her palms, its rapid rhythm mirroring her own. Suddenly he leaned down close, brushing her ear with his nose, then his mouth. Morgan's breath halted in her throat. Having him this close was wreaking havoc on her nerves and turning her blood flow into a sluggish pool centered low in her abdomen. Her skin felt too tight for her body…He nipped her ear, just barely, and she whimpered, jerking up against him.

"You came to me sweetheart," his mouth drifted down, oh so close to the fluttering pulse in her throat between her collarbones, "*you* came to *me.*"

Morgan's head fell back. She forgot about the hard metal of the roof behind her and cringed just before the moment of impact. But the hard hit never came; Nick's hand was there, cradling her, shielding her from harm, his fingers tangling in her thick mane of hair.

"Nick…" she whispered, "please…" She didn't know what she was asking for exactly, only that he was so close, not quite touching her with his body but still…so close, and it felt so…good…so different from what she was used to feeling.

"Uh-uh sweetheart." His voice was low and soft. His fingers shifted through her hair, then came around to cup her chin. His eyes were the bluest she'd ever seen them as they touched upon every part of her face, lingering on her cheek. His thumbs stroked over her bottom lip, the contact light, just the way he had several weeks ago, but her nerve endings fired, making her conscious of the scorching heat of her body. Arousal. Just like that.

"You're going to have to give me some kind of guideline as to how to proceed sweetheart, because I admit...handling you can be damned confusing, tricky even, and from now on I'm not taking any risks."

Chapter 19

"So why did you come, Morgan?"

It took her a few seconds but then she looked up at him, blinking those lovely eyes in dazed confusion, as if she had just realized he had stopped nuzzling her and had spoken. If she didn't respond soon he was definitely going back to nuzzling. Never give away a good opportunity his grandfather had always said.

She cleared her throat and he noticed a fine layer of goose bumps had risen on her skin. One corner of his mouth kicked up, it damned sure wasn't cold.

"I-I wanted to tell you thank you…for the uh-flowers, but they aren't necessary. Really. There's nothing for you to be sorry about. So please…stop." The last word came out husky, slightly above a whisper and he got the feeling she didn't really want to say.

He frowned, "What flowers?"

"The flowers and notes…the ones in my mailbox and…" she nibbled her bottom lip and a frown creased her forehead, "porch."

He slowly shook his head and stepped back slightly, giving her, and him, some breathing room. "Sorry, sweetheart, but I don't know what you're talking about."

"Oh God…you didn't…" she trailed off, going pale. "I'm so sorry, I just thought….I-I need to go." She spun around, lunging for her car door and yanking on the handle.

"Morgan. Morgan stop." Damn it! Not again. This time was not going to end in a fucked-up mess.

His hand landed hard on her shoulder, harder than he meant and she shrieked, but then immediately went still with one hand on the door handle and the other hand clamped over her mouth. The sudden utter stillness in her body was almost eerie, especially when just one second ago she had been in a flurry of activity to escape him. Using as little force as he could manage he turned her stiff body around until she faced him again.

"Nuh-uh Morgan. Don't go there, baby." She gave a slight flinch when he raised his hand, but when all he did was caress her jaw the tenseness begin to ebb from her body.

"Wh-where?"

"Wherever your mind went just then. It doesn't belong there. Not with us."

Her chest expanded on a deep breath. "I'm sorry...but someti—"

"Hush." He pressed a finger to her lips, shushing her. "First of all," he said, "I'm sick and tired of you running away from me. It makes it really hard to get to know you. Second," his voice changed, turning cold; "Second, I'd like to murder the fucker who hurt you."

Somewhere far away in her past life Morgan would have been offended by his blunt, crude language, but instead his low, savage voice mesmerized, pulling her out of that dark mental zone that was so familiar. He was angry for her, and it was thrilling. His words resonated through her head, making her body crave something she had never known.

"His name was Richard," she whispered, "and he's already dead."

"No," he caressed her throat, her collarbones. Each touch a featherlight exploration that had her quivering against him. "Every time you flinch from me you bring him back to life."

She ducked her head, letting her hair fall forward to hide her hot blush.

"Nick…"

"There's something between us, you know," he said softly. He pushed her hair back and his warm breath stroked her temple, fluttering the baby-fine hairs near her ear, "whether you or I want it or not. I've been fighting for weeks to get you out of my mind and nothing works. And the nights…you're with me there too, sweetheart. I tried to leave you alone for your sake, but here you are…messing with me again."

He eased his big body closer to hers, making her even more aware of the loose cage of his arms, of the hard metal at her back. Of how much she wanted him. He exuded raw masculine power but instead of being afraid of it, of him, she felt comforted…and she wanted more. For once in her life Richard wasn't winning, and if this shivery, heated flushed sensation running over her was anything to go by, then her body certainly didn't feel threatened either.

Nick's voice, low and husky, right above her brought her back from her inward examination.

"Trust me…" his head dipped and his lips smoothed over her forehead, then her temple, slowly to her cheekbone and down…She closed her eyes on a soft sigh when he reached the corner of her mouth. "I'm not going to hurt you, Morgan. All men aren't monsters. There are some decent guys in the world and you're going to have to trust one someday. It might as well be me." Then he kissed her, not hard or demanding, but soft and slow, barely touching her lips with his. Teasing her before backing off.

Her heart ached; her body sizzled. How she wanted to believe, wanted to allow herself to just feel, for once what it was like to be held tenderly. She wanted more of this, of what he was showing her right now.

He was watching her; she could feel the heated weight of his stare while his thumb stroked the sensitive spot just below her ear. Her body felt different, her stomach coiled tight, waiting…wanting. She was almost panting. Alarmed she pushed at him, her palms meeting the smooth material of his t-shirt and hard muscles of his chest beneath. He let her go and stepped back, giving them both some space, but the brief contact had shocked her, and her feelings, her…desire, she realized, didn't fade.

He blew out a deep breath. "Would it help if I admitted to doing the flower thing?"

She almost smiled, would have if her body wasn't in such turmoil. "Of course not, you'd be lying."

He grinned slightly, "Yeah, well, call me opportunistic."

She exhaled slowly, forcing her body back from the chaos he had unleashed inside her, and struggling with the impulse to let go and leap into the unknown. "I…have issues, Nick…big issues. You already know that. You've seen how I react sometimes. I don't do it on purpose…and I hate it." Her voice quivered along with her chin. "I have scars and I limp. I can't see what you—"

"Hush, it's not your fault."

She tucked her chin to her chest, letting her hair fall forward. Her shield against her shame.

"No you don't." Using his fingertips he bullied her chin up. "Look at me," he demanded, "straight in the eyes." She blushed, meeting his warm indigo gaze. "None of that is your fault, Morgan."

She opened her mouth to negate him, but then the loud rumble of a diesel engine drew both their gazes to the driveway. A huge white horse van, the kind pulled by a semi, was slowly making its way towards them. Nick cursed, clearly upset by the interruption and then motioned the driver to park near the barn. He turned back to her, grasping her chin in his hand. "Did you hear what I said? None of what happened to you is your fault, Morgan."

She nodded as much as she could since he was still holding her chin, but something in her eyes must have upset him because he cursed again.

"Look, come back in a few days," he urged, "I'd say tomorrow but this," he jerked his head in the direction of the semi, "should be delivering six horses and I want to give them a few days of adjustment. This is Sunday, by Wednesday I should be clear. Come back and I'll show you around, tell you about some of the horses. No pressure, Morgan. I promise."

She hesitated for a long moment, balanced on the edge of an abyss, dizzy with the direction her life had suddenly taken and overwhelmed by the big man in front of her. You may never have this chance again, Morgan. Don't let Richard rule you again.

"Okay." She nodded, wondering if she had lost her mind. "Wednesday then."

****

Thirty minutes later, after dealing with the paperwork concerning the new arrivals, he found Jake cleaning out one of the empty stalls, readying it for one of the new horses, and planted himself in the doorway. "Happen to know anything about flowers and notes, little brother?"

Jake shrugged, not even bothering to look not-guilty, "That would depend on if they worked or not."

Nick snorted a laugh, "Well, lucky for you in a roundabout way they did, but next time mind your own business or I'll shove my boot up your ass." He turned in the doorway, and then paused, "Dare I ask what the notes said?"

Jake grinned in amusement, "Don't worry, I kept it very simple. She doesn't think you're Lord Byron or anything like that. But you do owe me about a hundred bucks."

Chapter 20

Hesitantly, Morgan stepped inside the spacious barn, becoming the immediate focus of at least forty curious horses. Instantly assaulted by the sweet smells of hay, sawdust, leather and the animals she walked over to the first stall and, standing on tiptoe, looked in. A chestnut Arabian glanced at her, flicked his ears, and then went back to munching his hay, dismissing her completely. Not put off she wiggled her fingers while making little clucking noises in her throat. All it produced was a chestnut ear turned her way.

"Oh well," she smiled, remembering the freedom that could be found on the back of a horse, "your loss."

"That's Sultan. He can be a snob unless you have an apple or carrot."

Morgan whipped around and looked up at Nick as he began descending the loft ladder. "You scared me," she gasped, one hand plastered against her pounding chest.

"Sorry. That does seem to be a habit."

"Jake said you were in here," she said, feeling the need to explain her presence. Morgan watched his muscles ripple as he maneuvered down the steep ladder. She hated to admit it but his forearms and biceps were mouth-watering, daring a woman to press her lips to each yummy bulge.

What would it be like to be held by him… made

love to by him? And why the heck are you even thinking about this Morgan Fletcher? Don't you remember how it was with Richard? What about the things he did to you while you were tied up or otherwise helpless? All men like to dominate a woman in some way. Nick may have treated you nicely so far but once he gets you alone, he's probably no different, and he's big enough to force you, bigger than Richard, and Richard did whatever he wanted to you. Briefly an image flashed in her mind, of her in front of a mirror, bent over the skinny, hard-edged back of a chair, barely able to breathe because of the crushing pain in her stomach while Richard used her unprepared body in the most degrading way.

Unconsciously her arm went across her stomach. She closed her eyes and cleared her throat, hoping the brief, evil direction her mind had taken didn't show on her face. "Jake said just to wander around until I found you."

"Yeah, I was just on my way to give this alfalfa to the gelding." Nick gestured down to the far end of the barn, then seized the handles of the wheelbarrow sitting in the aisle. "Come on, he's a little afraid of everyone right now, but he might not mind meeting a beautiful woman like you."

She flushed under the compliment and flashed him a brief, bashful smile. She knew she wasn't beautiful, but it was nice of him to keep saying it. Each thoughtful action or word made the distance between him and Richard loom larger.

"All right." She trailed after him past countless stalls filled with horses of all kinds. "He's a rescue horse?"

"Yeah. I got him a couple of months ago, a few days before our first 'meeting'." He grinned and winked at her. "Out of all the horses I've dealt with he's been the toughest one yet. But it's understandable with what he went through."

"How many horses do you have?" The lines of stalls seemed endless.

"Fifty-one total. Thirty-seven are mine—well, Jake claims a couple too—the rest are here for training. "Do you like horses?" He asked casually.

She nodded without glancing up, "Oh yes. I love them."

"Do you ride?"

"I used to, I was taking lessons, but then—"

He looked down at her when she fell silent. "But then what?"

She glanced at him but didn't quite meet his eyes, then cast her gaze down at the ground again, never breaking stride. "But then I hurt my leg."

Nick said nothing, but when she looked back up there was a muscle ticking in his jaw that hadn't been there before.

They entered a short connecting hallway and he pushed the hay through a set of open double doors. Eyes widening in amazement at the huge open space in front of her Morgan stopped dead and just looked around. She realized that they had entered an indoor riding ring, complete with mirrored walls on one side, just like in Dressage barns, and a long sectioned off exercise pool at the far end. Morgan had only seen those used on a TV veterinary show. But apparently Nick spared no expense when it came to the horses.

Awed she turned around several times, taking in

the sheer size of the place. Tall oversized sections of wood made up the walls, with big screened-in windows every third section. Covering the whole ring was a tin roof. Eight large sun panels were fixed into the roof allowing natural light to brighten the arena and a humongous industrial sized fan swirled lazily at the far end near the roof line. A smaller metal ring sat off to the right side. Even the professional barn she had taken a few lessons at couldn't compete with this one.

Out of the corner of her eye she caught a movement in the smaller ring and glanced at it again. A large white horse was standing at the far end with his nose to the ground, gently pushing the dirt around. She followed Nick closer, trailing slightly behind him as they neared the pen.

"He's getting better," Nick said, "improving daily, it's just going to take time and patience."

"You must have a lot of that. Patience I mean."

He flashed her a grin and answered, "Tons. Although it's reserved for special people and animals."

She smiled back at him, blushing and feeling oddly dreamy. The moment was broken when the horse, agitated now by their approach, blew a sharp breath and kicked one of the metal railings with his back hoof. The whole ring shuddered. Nick picked up the flake of hay out of the wheelbarrow and went over to the gate. The harsh sound of scraping metal and clinking chains announced that he was unlatching the door. Morgan stood off to the side away from the ring in case the horse went crazy and tried to leap over it. Nick entered the ring and animal went stock still, then blew sharply through his nose and trotted off to the far side of the ring. Nick dropped the bundle of hay he had been holding and exited the pen.

"Usually I would stay in there with him for awhile, but not today. I think it would stress him too much having another person here."

Morgan let out the breath she had been holding and walked slowly to the panel rail. The horse was at the hay now, head down and munching quietly and for the first time she got a clear, close-up look at him. She stopped, gasping in horror. Her hand flew up to cover her mouth and she swallowed tightly, sensing Nick coming up behind her.

The horse was skin and bones, every rib could be counted, and its hips stuck out prominently beneath tightly stretched skin and his white coat. Morgan gripped the bar tightly for support as her breath hitched, stuck in her dry throat. Not only was he skinny, but he was covered in welts and old scars. Long and short, some deeper than others, they marred his face, his neck, his ears. Jesus God there was not a section of his body that was not marred. Her hand fluttered up towards her cheek. Most of the marks, like her own, would never fade. She wiped at her eyes and looked over her shoulder at Nick, not surprised to find his keen blue eyes focused on her.

"Who did that to him?" Her voice quivered. "Why?" Nick became a watery, out of focus blur, and his voice, when he spoke, was gruff.

"His previous owner." Nick's palms landed on her shoulders, then slid down along her arms until he covered both of her cold hands in his own. Gently he removed her fingers from the metal bars and criss-crossed their arms across her stomach. Morgan let herself be surrounded by the hard warmth of his body and timidly leaned back against him. He made an appreciative noise in his throat and she relaxed even more.

The horse raised its head, eyeing them briefly, then refocused on the hay, using his delicate pink muzzle to push bits here and there emitting soft, contented little snuffles while munching.

"Then his previous owner should be shot," she whispered. She wasn't sure, the contact had been too brief and could have been accidental, but she thought she felt Nick press a light kiss to the top of her head.

"Yeah…I was tempted to do some damage." Against her back she felt his chest expand on a deep breath. "But that wouldn't have solved anything, and would have only caused trouble for me and Jake." His voice lowered as if in afterthought, "Which I sure as hell don't need."

Morgan detected an odd note in there, but tamped down on her sudden curiosity, not about to pry into Nick's personal affairs. "Tell me about him." She gestured towards the horse.

"Well," he began in a deeply soft voice, "he's part Draft, part Quarter Horse and was used on his owner's farm to haul…well, whatever the guy had to haul, even though he had a tractor that could have done most of the work." He shifted against her, adjusting their positions so that his arms rested just below her breasts. Richard used to hold her this way, but unlike Nick's hold Richard's had been tight enough to almost crush her ribs. Morgan's breath stuttered in her chest and she shivered, clutching at Nick's forearm. This horse had been owned by a person exactly like Richard, and like her, had been marked forever by him. Goose bumps rose on her skin even though it was not cold in the arena.

"Relax Morgan." Nick's warm breath tickled her ear, the side of her neck. She closed her eyes on a low moan. "Just let me hold you, sweetheart." He waited until she gave a small nod and then continued. "Anyway, I never understood why he used the horse instead of it. But he was a cheap bastard and didn't feed the horse enough to keep up his strength and weight; so of course, even though he's part Draft he couldn't work like he used to."

The pictures played out clearly in her mind—the horse, emaciated and weak but bravely struggling, trying its best to please its master before giving out and collapsing, too broken down to care about whatever fate awaited him. Too tired to care. Whether it was death or something else at least it would be a departure from a hellish life.

Unconsciously her hand went to her cheek. "So he started to whip him." She whispered.

"Yeah," Nick's voice was soft, "he started whipping him."

One big rough hand slid up her arm over the material of her shirt and her skin tingled through the thin cotton. Those questing fingers reached her shoulder and then caressed along the line of her throat. A slight mewling sound escaped her. "Shhh…" He soothed. She flinched, but didn't pull away when his fingers moved up and skimmed the slightly raised marks on her cheek. He stroked her skin for moment, then turned her face to his, his indigo eyes touching on each scar line and as she watched the muscles in his darkly stubbled jawbone went rigid.

"Nick?" Morgan waited until his eyes flicked to hers. "It's alright."

"The hell it is." He growled. "That miserable bas—" He stopped, closed his eyes briefly and heaved a deep breath. "Christ Morgan, I'm sorry. I really didn't mean to go there…to bring him up again. Not today at least." Giving her a small, self-deprecating smile Nick pressed a kiss to the top of her head, then let his hand fall to his side and moved away from her. Immediately Morgan experienced a sense of loss, missing his warmth, the secure feeling of just being held close.

Nick walked over to the wheelbarrow and grabbed each handle, knuckles flexing as he adjusted his grip. Morgan followed him as he wheeled the cart out of the arena and into connecting walkway of the main barn. "I've been working each day with him, trying to gain his trust. Once that's done then I can have him examined again by the vet and see what he needs. When he first came here we had to tranquilize him and I really don't want to do that again if it can be helped."

He looked so sincere, his expression so at odds with his big, dark, severe appearance that there was no faking it. She felt his sincerity in every pulse-pounding cell of her body. "You really do care about these horses, don't you?"

The muscles in his jawbones started ticking again, and his voice deepened to almost a growl. "It kills me to see how people can treat them." He was silent a moment, then, "Just like it kills me to know you went through the same."

Morgan's mouth opened, but no response seemed a worthy comeback to that matter-of-fact statement, so she remained silent while inside her heart turned over and over and over.

They stopped at each stall, and each stall had a horse with a story; there was Goldie, the twenty-nine-year-old pony that had worked at fairs riding kids around in endless circles even after she had foundered twice. There was a black Thoroughbred racehorse named Sweet Sinjun that had broken down during her first race and, like so many others, been on her way to the slaughterhouse before Nick had intervened; Hiero, the ex-police horse that had been shot up in the line of duty and blinded in one eye and retired to Nick's farm instead of being put down. There were so many other sad, heartrending stories that Morgan's mind was whirling, struggling with the information overload and the myriad of emotions that each story heaped upon her. If not for Nick and Jake most of these beautiful animals would have been dead by now, one way or another, and some possibly even served up as the latest delicacy in some European restaurant.

Somehow she managed to keep her roiling emotions from showing and said, "Wow, Nick, I just don't see how you and Jake manage it all."

Nick grinned at her, "We have schedules and a rhythm, it's the way we like it," he explained. "Plus on weekends a couple of high school kids come out to help with cleaning stalls and grooming. The horses here that take most of our time are the ones in training, the rest are here permanently, so they don't require as much focus, just grooming and feeding."

There were so, so many horses, so many cases of mistreatment that it was hard for her to comprehend even though she had been through the same thing. The difference was that unlike her, the animals couldn't hide what had been done to them. It's crazy, she thought to herself …they're horses, not people…but I don't feel so alone anymore.

As Nick continued talking Morgan realized that she felt more at ease in this huge barn than she had living with her husband in their—no his home. Morgan looked at Nick, past the tattoos and the outwardly tough 'don't fuck with me' demeanor, to the sincere love he felt for these horses shining in his dark blue eyes. Her heart swelled with an emotion she didn't want acknowledge, but couldn't ignore. Don't be a fool again, Morgan. Don't you dare.

"Morgan?" Nick's voice penetrated her musing and she looked up questioningly. They had stopped at a stall marked Nearctic. Nick opened the latch and was now looking at her, concern plain in the lines of his dark face, blue eyes keen. "You okay? You went really quiet on me. And not just with your voice." He took a black halter off the hook by the door, his worried eyes never leaving her.

Oh God, it's too late. Richard's summarization of her as a 'weak-minded twit' was dead on. She was a complete fool…one that was already half-way in love with Nick.

Panic coursed through her, filling her mouth with a flat metallic twang, almost like the taste of blood. She remembered the taste of her own blood; she'd had firsthand multiple opportunities to learn its flavor. Oh, God…It would never end. She had to leave, had to get out of there and away from Nick's gentle draw before she did something supremely stupid and fell in love completely. He was a good man, she knew that truth to her bones and he didn't deserve to have the dark poison of Richard and her past contaminate his life. Morgan knew she would only disappoint him and seeing that disappointment growing in his eyes, day by day, would destroy her.

She couldn't take anymore heartache, and caring for someone…trusting them and letting them into her life meant she would have to take that chance, the chance of failing and of being hurt again. It was too much, too soon.

"I-I think I'd better go, Nick." Ignoring the bewilderment darkening of his eyes she backed away, her heels sliding over the sawdust covered aisleway. "No, I have to go. For both of us."

"What?" his voice roughened in disbelief, "Why? What the hell for?" In two seconds his expression changed from one of concern to brooding incredulity, reminding her of a darkening sky before a thunderstorm. He stalked towards her and grabbed her elbow before she could turn and run. Bravely she faced him, an oversized wall of unmovable male who was twice her size. But for the first time in six years she felt no fear. No mind-crippling apprehension.

Only a dull, aching sadness.

"Talk to me, Morgan." He demanded, "What the hell's wrong? Did I do something that scared you?"

She looked down, past his hand holding her elbow to the halter dangling forgotten from his wrist. It was still swaying from his sudden movements, bumping her in the thigh. If he had been Richard she would have already felt that concoction of metal and leather against her skin, and she would have been face-down at his feet, bleeding and eating sawdust.

If only she had met Nick first, before Richard had

ruined her.

"No Nick," she answered, "I scared myself." I'm scared because you make me want things, she added silently, and that's a risk I can't take. Then, knowing this was her last opportunity to touch him, she rose up to her tiptoes and using his shoulders as leverage she brushed a kiss over his darkly stubbled jaw. Her lips moved slowly, memorizing the texture of his beard shadow and the slightly salty taste of his skin. He jerked slightly, no doubt from shock, but before he could respond or react she whispered, "Self-preservation, Nick. It's all I have left."

Chapter 21

Some dim part of Morgan's brain thought surely this was a stranger talking; surely she couldn't be boldly asking this man to kiss her. But the brief taste of him at his barn had not been nearly enough, and no matter how hard she tried to put him out of her mind he was always there, drawing her in despite her fear, using kind words, sweet gestures, or frustrating touches—touches that left her body aching for him.

His horses, those beautiful abused animals, trusted him. Why shouldn't she?

"Morgan—"

"Make love to me, Nick."

Holy hell. His body snapped taut, disbelief and arousal invading every pore. He could not have heard her right. That whisper, those low, seductive words, had to be his mind playing a trick on him, trying to make him screw up more than he already had.

His gaze lowered to her face. Her eyes were wide, both fear and desire evident in the beautiful hazel depths. She held his stare. A blush began to creep over her cheeks ending at her nose and turning the tip red. Her chin trembled and she swallowed hard, the small convulsive movement in her throat showing him just how hard she was pushing herself.

"What did you say?" He had to hear it again, just to be sure. Kiss me, Make love to me, Nick…

The soft pink tinge that had colored her cheekbones just a moment before now flooded her whole face. His mouth quirked, even her sweet little ears were red. She pressed her forehead into his chest, hiding. The way she was plastered against him she had to be feeling the obvious hard-on in his pants.

She cleared her throat and he felt the vibrations all the way through his T-shirt and into his skin. "I asked you to, um, m-make love to me."

Holy hell.

She had just spoken the words that he had dreamed about, fantasized about, for over two months—

And he had no clue what to do now. Any other woman and he would have had her naked and under him in two seconds flat, but this was Morgan. His sweet, precious, innocent-no-matter-what-she-had-been-through, fantasy woman. She deserved so much more than to just be taken to the ground and fucked in some mindless animal act. Her bastard husband had given her plenty of that and more. He'd be damned if he'd treat her with the same callous disregard. The trust she was handing him was too precious and in return he wanted to love her, cherish her…destroy her demons for her.

"Um, Nick?" her voice quivered like she was about to cry. "Please say something. If you don't want to…"

Oh fuck no; this wasn't going to go that way. Quickly he hugged her to him, easing up only when she grunted in protest. "Believe me baby, I more than want to. But…"

Deep grooves creased her forehead and he felt her fingers clench on his shirt. Her bottom lip disappeared between her teeth and she ducked her head, but not before he caught a glimpse of what could be shame on her face. Oh no…no way.

"Baby…look at me." At his urging she raised her head, but avoided meeting his gaze. He so did not want to do this, especially not now. But she had been hurt enough and sleeping with her without telling her about his past would be a big betrayal. "Before we go any further there's something you need to know."

Gently, being careful of her leg, he pushed her towards the table and sat her down. Then, so he wouldn't be crowding her if she decided to hightail it out of there after hearing what he was about to say, he went back to stand with his back against the wall. Missing the feel of her against him, and knowing that this could be the last time he held her, he crossed his arms over his chest wanting to feel the imprint of her body heat as long as possible.

"I need to tell you…" Shit. A sick, burning sensation almost like nausea twisted his gut. He ran a hand over his head and to the back of his neck, rubbing the skin until it burned like fire. He welcomed the pain, hoping it might give him the balls to do this. The words hung heavy and savage in his mind…Killer. Murderer.

Nick looked across the small room to where Morgan sat at the table looking at the floor. Her back was straight and stiff, her face lined with tension. He sighed and glanced out of the kitchen window, but found no help in the bright light of day. When he turned back to her those beautiful antique gold eyes were watching him, dark with concern. It was time to end the suspense, quick and clean, and reveal his fucked-up past. Nick heaved a sigh, feeling relationship death riding towards him on a fast horse.

He felt a line of sweat bead on his forehead and raked another hand through his hair, aware of how his heart was pounding. Meeting her eyes he forced himself to speak. "Something happened when I was younger, Morgan...much, much younger. I...I-uh...made a serious mistake and...shit."

Morgan held her breath, her stomach coiled in knots, waiting while he hesitated, but then he squeezed his eyes shut and his dark head thumped back against her wall, looking a far cry from the confidant man she had become used to.

"Morgan...I'm sorry. I-I can't do this right now." Deep grooves embedded themselves around his mouth, giving his face a haunted expression. His jaw was locked; he stuck his hands in his jeans pockets and pushed away from the wall. He looked at her, started to say something but then closed his mouth and Morgan sensed that whatever inner demon he was fighting had just won.

No. Unlike herself Nick was big and so strong, physically more capable than most to handle whatever life threw his way. But like her there was something in his past that still affected him and, judging by his defeated stance right now, that something was still capable of making him feel less than he was. Who or what could have done that? Drawn to him despite her clear-thinking brain yelling 'no' Morgan decided that whatever he'd had to say made no difference. She knew what it felt like to be judged—during her marriage Richard had known exactly how to lay on the charm and elicit sympathy from friends and family, so much so that whenever he alluded to marital issues she was automatically blamed. By everyone except Lisa.

Good or bad she and Nick both had their pasts…so maybe there had been enough secrets told today.

Feeling stronger and more sure of herself Morgan got up and went over to him, putting her palms against his torso to stop him from leaving. He didn't move, in fact he barely breathed, as if afraid any movement or sound at all would send her away. The tension in his big body was palpable and for a moment she did nothing but stare up into his deep blue eyes, now bleak and shadowed with secrets and a hint of shame…Morgan's heart squeezed in on itself, feeling heavy and tight behind her ribcage. She knew shame, saw it mirrored in her own eyes everyday, although recently less and less, thanks to Nick.

Slowly, with hands trembling, she ran them up his chest and to his shoulders. Her fingertips grazed the pulse between his collarbones, and then moved along his dark skin to find the fine line of hair at the back of his neck. His nostrils flared, reminding her of a wild stallion scenting the breeze and her resolve slipped for a moment. But then she looked back up into his eyes, eyes that were guarded but tender.

Richard's eyes had never held a moment's tenderness and the memory of that made Morgan realize how much she had missed, and how much she wanted it now.

"It doesn't matter Nick." She needed something good to come from the bad. "Please, don't go."

"The problem is it does matter." His voice was deep, rough and husky with what she recognized as desire. His eyes, darkened now to the color of midnight, lowered to her mouth and his thumb brushed her chin, then her bottom lip, stroking lightly over the fullness, making her nerve endings sizzle. His groan as she licked the tip of his thumb made her feel powerful, more aware than ever that women do indeed have strength over men.

"It doesn't matter,' she repeated, realizing it was true, "and I don't care, Nick." Her terror and humiliation at the hands of her husband would not follow her forever. He would not win. "I—I," she hesitated, nerves scattered, "I want to know what…what being a woman is like, Nick. Please," her voice shook, "all I ask is that you don't…don't hurt me." The last was whispered and she cringed at the note of begging in it.

He made a harsh sound deep in his throat and a tremor shook his body. He lowered his mouth to her ear and whispered, "Never." A breath shuddered out of her and he tightened his arms around her protectively. "I would never hurt you, Morgan. You need to understand and trust that with your whole being. If I do something you don't like, no matter what it is, you tell me. Hell—slap me, punch me, bite me— whatever it takes to get my attention. Okay?"

She nodded shortly and then whispered "Okay."

Nick grinned at her and pressed a quick kiss to her mouth, then picked her up, cuddling her close against his chest. She squeaked, digging her nails into his shoulders as turned towards the hallway. Her hair hung loose and long, flowing over both of them like a silken cape. His boot heels sounded abnormally loud in the small quiet house, seeming to mimic pounding of her heart. He held her high and tight against his chest, so securely wrapped in his arms that she really didn't need to hang on. But she did and even as her bedroom door loomed closer and closer Morgan knew she could still say no. As if reading her mind he paused and glanced down at her, one black brow raised in silent question. In answer she snuggled her head into the side of his neck, breathing in his dark masculine scent, as once again his boot heels clicked rhythmically on her hardwood floor.

With no help from her he zeroed in on her bedroom door and strode inside, kicking it shut with his heel.

"How did you—?"

"I used to do odd repairs for Eliza. Let me know if your tub starts leaking again."

The bed loomed before them, and for the first time Morgan felt a niggling of unease. Soon she would be spread out beneath him on her yellow butterfly sheets with his weight and strength pinning her down while he pounded into her. A brief memory flashed through her mind—hard hands holding her down, hurting her, leaving bruises all over her body… She stared at the bed and a small sound escaped her. She wouldn't be able to move, and Nick was so much bigger and stronger than she was…how would he know if he was hurting her? The room spun crazily and she swallowed, shoving the vein of fear back into its box.

He must have either heard her whimper or felt the slight change in her body because he stopped and his eyes flicked down to her. "We don't have to do this right now. We don't have to do this at all if you aren't ready. I don't want there to be any regrets for you Morgan."

'We don't have to do this at all…' The words were so different from what she was used to, so unlike Richard's angry commands and hard, hurting hands. 'You're my wife, and you'll fuck me whenever and however I want, whether you want it or not!' Morgan shuddered as cold washed over her, freezing the blood in her veins. Memories of Richard still controlled her—still dictated her reactions. But now there were other memories as well, ones of Nick and the kindness he'd shown her numerous times, of the way her pulse quickened and her breath left her whenever he was near, of how her body responded even when her mind had not wanted to.

She needed this. She needed him.

She shook her head, twining her arms around his neck and cupping the back of his head of his head for balance.

Have some guts, Morgan. Women do this all the time and according to the romance books they love it. Her fingers tunneled into the short hairs at the back of his neck. The feel of it against her palm was amazing, coarse and soft at the same time; the short black bristles tickled her hand, sending goosebumps running up and down her arms. Even her breasts responded, becoming fuller, heavier, her nipples stiff and tight. Ready for him.

Desire and anxiety battled for supremacy inside her. Nick was still holding her high against him, waiting and watching her with a softness in his eyes she hadn't seen before and she knew that if she even hinted at stopping he would. Like a soft summer breeze her anxiety drifted away and desire cloaked her body.

"I need this Nick," she said softly, "I need to feel something different than what I've been feeling for six years. And I need it with you."

Urging his head down she kissed him.

****

Nick hugged her to him, barely able to control his trembling as he returned her shy kiss, softly at first. But then, when he felt her shivery response and heard her soft moan, he took her mouth harder, deeper, thrusting his tongue between her parted lips to explore the velvety softness inside, sipping at the sweet, peachy nectar that was all her.

This was what he had dreamed of and he was damned well going to make it good for her.

Keeping contact with her mouth he located the bed. Situated across the room it was a feminine, frilly-looking thing completely decked out with virginal white lace and yellow butterflies. Like Morgan, it was the picture of sweetness. Innocently sexy and twice the turn-on as anything he had experienced in his life.

His cock hardened, feeling about the size of a baseball bat.

He hated having to leave her mouth but if he didn't, he'd have her shoved up against the wall with her legs wrapped around his waist before either of them realized what had happened. A fine prospect for later, but not for her first time with him. He broke the kiss; she sighed, snuggling her face into the side of his neck again. Her tongue, warm and wet, slowly licked up the side of his throat, teasing the thick vein there. He winced, assaulted by a small but sharp pain, then grinned. She had nipped him. His cock, already iron hard, jerked in pleased response.

That was good, he thought, that was damn good. If he could keep her relaxed enough maybe she'd bite him again.

Her mouth moved tenderly against his skin, right over the spot she had just abused, "Sorry…" she whispered, "But your skin smells so good…I've never…I just had to see what you tasted like."

He adjusted her, brought his mouth down to hers for a sweet kiss, torn between fury at what she had been through before him, and tenderness because of how innocent she, was even with her past.

Holding her full weight with one arm he ripped back the delicate white lace comforter with more force than necessary. "Don't ever apologize for wanting to touch me. In fact I'll expect it; often and as much as you want." he said, laying her down sideways across the yellow butterfly print sheets and bracing himself above her with a fist on either side of her head, "Besides sweetheart…" he grinned and winked at her, "in less than five minutes I plan to be eating you alive."

Her eyes got huge, her mouth opening on a silent gasp and he knew she hadn't even considered that possibility. Fast as lightening he wrenched his shirt off and then took immediate advantage, swooping down and claiming her lips, first sucking on the fuller bottom one and then pushing his tongue in, moving rhythmically in her mouth the way his body wanted to move within her slick heat. He groaned, lost in her mind-druggingly sweet taste.

Grasping her hands in his Nick slid her arms up until they were pinned above her head, and then slowly lowered his torso to hers. Their bodies connected and she stiffened in uncertainty, beginning to pull against his hold. Shushing her he used his thumbs to rub soothing circles in the middle of her palm and over her wrists while raining kisses over her cheeks, along her jaw and finally capturing her mouth. She writhed against him, whimpering into his mouth, but he kept his exploration leisurely and soft, not forceful or hurried. Sliding his tongue inside he sparred with hers, patiently teaching her the intricate art of French kissing. He released her wrists and tangled his hands in her hair, cupping and massaging the back of her head. Tenderness flooded him when he pulled back and she impatiently raised her head, trying to catch his lips again.

"Slow down sweetheart." he teased, "there's no rush." He licked her bottom lip while his blood belied his words, pumping harshly through his veins in a primitive surge that threatened to make him forget about going slow, urging him to spread her legs and pump himself to oblivion.

He felt her small hands run up his sides to tightly grip the back of his biceps and he reined his urgings in. This was Morgan, not some bar-whore, and he reminded himself that she had been wounded both physically and mentally but was now lying beneath him, trusting him with her body.

She clutched at his shoulders and obligingly he lowered himself to kiss her again, more forcefully this time while still keeping tight control, not wanting to ruin this experience for her by moving too fast. Moments like this and unexpected innocence like hers were special and to be savored, not conquered. Hell, he'd lay here and just kiss her all night if that's what she wanted.

Her needs were first and foremost.

His cock screamed in protest, wanting to be inside her now.

Nick ignored it, easing back and raising his head. She was panting, her eyes closed tightly, mouth swollen from his rough kisses; the fragile column of her throat was arched, submissively bared for him. He kissed it, felt her swallow.

Yeah, he had to make this all about her. She deserved nothing less.

"Look at me." He punctuated the command with a tender kiss and angled his hips, nudging his arousal into her soft stomach for the first time. She gasped, eyes flying open to stare directly into his.

God, he could drown in those liquid gold depths and die a happy man. "I want you to know exactly who you're with, not who your mind is remembering."

"I'm not remem—" He nudged her again, lower this time and used a circular motion that made her moan. "Nick…" His name came out as a breathy exhalation. Her fingers flexed on his biceps, slipped, and then gripped again.

Damn these clothes… "That's right." He flexed his hips again, "Say it again."

No way were her demons going to insinuate themselves between them this time.

"Nick."

He hummed his approval against her skin, kissing his way down the smooth column of her throat to the neck of her t-shirt. He frowned at the barricade of grey fabric, irritated that his progress had been halted but cornered the urge to shred it down the middle. Instead he shifted his weight and, using his free hand, smoothed his palm down her side to the bottom of the shirt and snaked his hand inside. She let out a small, choked sound and the silky, warm skin of her belly quivered beneath his touch, making him wonder if her bastard husband had ever taken the time to touch her other than to hit her.

"Shhh…remember it's just me, no one who wants to hurt you."

Chapter 22

He kissed her lips, tenderly, worshipfully, absorbing her nervous little pants into his mouth while caressing his way up her ribcage. His fingers met the soft underside of her thin, lacy bra and he covered one breast with his palm. Instantly her nipple stiffened and he brushed his thumb back and forth over it, alternating between lazy circles and sharp, flicking contact. She whimpered into his mouth and he paused, waiting until the sudden tension eased from her body before applying firm pressure to the eager tip.

Oh…Sweet Jesus…She was so soft, the feel of her breasts an ample treat for his greedy fingers…He wanted his mouth on her, right now.

Nick ground his teeth together. Control. If ever he needed it it was now.

He put his mouth against her ear, fingers still tormenting the tender bud. "Your skin is so damned soft…Tell me what you want, sweetheart. What you like."

She bit her lip, made a small helpless sound and hid her face against his chest. "I don't-I don't know." It ended as a frustrated cry, her hands clenching and unclenching against the muscles in his shoulders. He leaned down and kissed the flushed curve of her cheek soothingly. Of course she didn't know what she liked.

She'd always been taken, never served.

That made her as close to a virgin as Nick had ever gotten. His cock hardened even more, a rigid length of steel threatening to bust through the denim of his jeans if he didn't do something about it soon.

"It's all right." He pressed his lips to the shallow indentation between her collarbones where her pulse kicked madly. Nibbling his way up her throat to her ear he distracted her long enough to slide his hand from under her shirt to the waistband of her shorts where he flicked open the button that held them closed.

The zipper followed suit, sliding down smoothly and easily. He caught a glimpse of baby-fine skin and creamy lace panties and swallowed hard, reminding himself of his earlier oath to go slow.

In a voice so deep he barely recognized it he said, "I'll take care of you. You don't have to do anything." Giving her a brief hard kiss he slid down her body, going to his knees beside the bed.

"Wait! What are you…?"

"Shush…let me…" He broke off, distracted by the smooth skin of her bare calves. Christ…Even her ankles were beautiful. Kissing and stroking his way up her legs he waited until she was once again relaxed and gasping for breath, then grasped the hem of her shorts and pulled them down her legs. Her arms shot out, small hands frantically grabbing at the material.

He stopped pulling and gazed at her. "Are we stopping?"

She bit her lip and her hands clenched on the fabric. "Um…you—"

He cut her off. "This isn't about me. Not this time." He slid his hands up and covered her fists where they bunched on the material of her shorts. Softly he asked again, "Are we stopping?" She quivered and their eyes locked. The tip of her tongue came out to caress her bottom lip. Gazing at her, at the flushed well-loved woman look on her face Nick knew he could stop if she said so, but the knowledge that he might actually have to felt like a fate worse than death.

Her "no" was no more than a breath of sound, yet the word rang loud and clear in Nick's ears. He flashed her a grin, then kissed her thigh before slowly tugging her shorts down her legs. As each smooth inch of her upper thighs was finally bared to him Nick felt his mouth going dry. One final tug and the shorts came off. He tossed them over his shoulder, not caring where they landed, completely focused on the near nude woman laid out like a sacrifice before him. Starting at her ankles Nick ran his hands up the insides of her legs, using firm pressure to part them as he went. Her thighs spread wide and Morgan let out a small, embarrassed cry, immediately trying shield herself from his view.

"Oh no, sweet," he said, taking a wrist in each hand and gently pressing her hands into the bed at her sides. "I can't allow that."

He wedged his chest between her knees, spreading her thighs wide, then leaned down and pressed his open mouth to her soft belly.

"The view from here is too beautiful."

****

Morgan let her head fall back onto the mattress with a moan, unable to think of anything except the extraordinary feel of his warm, wet mouth moving lazily across her stomach. She should be afraid, wary at least with her hands still trapped at her sides by a half-naked man who was twice her size, but…oh…um…Her brain froze while his tongue swirled around her belly button. His breath, warm and moist, tickled her skin. The light rasping of his tongue stirred already over-sensitized nerves, making her skin tingle and her loins tighten excruciatingly. Morgan's stomach quivered and she drew in a deep breath as her hips jerked, reacting to each sweeping lick of his tongue. She groaned, squirming against him, wanting…no needing him to move lower…

Ohh…that felt so good.

She must have said it out loud because she felt him smile against her skin and then he said, "I'm going to let go of your hands, but unless I scare you I want them out of my way. Okay?"

He rubbed his bristly jaw along her side and over the sensitive skin covering her ribs, then nuzzled the underside of one breast through her bra. Her nipples, already tight, hardened even more, almost to the point of pain. Nick's rough jaw brushed lightly over one peak, sending sparks throughout her swollen breast and shattering her thought process.

"Morgan?"

Unable to form a coherent reply she drew in a great breath of air and nodded.

Nick leaned over her, brushed a featherlight kiss along her jaw and then let her go. Morgan fisted her hands in the sheets, uncertain as to what to do with them while he pushed her shirt out of the way and nuzzled her skin, whispering reassurances against her flesh as he eased the cups of her bra down, baring her nipples. Growling 'easy' low in his throat he sucked one engorged nipple into his mouth. Morgan felt the sharp edge of his teeth grip her, then the soft flicking of his tongue on the tip. Even as heat seared through her veins she froze, barely breathing as memories of another mouth on her breast, this one cruel and hurtful, rushed to the forefront of her mind: Richard, biting her hard enough to make her bleed and then laughing as she screamed.

No. She made a noise low in her throat and reached up to push Nick's head away.

"Just me Morgan." Nick's thumb caressed her cheek, "No one else."

Yes…This was Nick, and his mouth was tasting her so slowly, his lips suckling, pulling at her tingling nipples until they were red and throbbing. He let her nipple pop out of his mouth and she breathed a sigh of relief as the sensual torment was removed, only to have him grin and suck the exquisitely sensitized tip back into the warmth of his mouth. His tongue played, circling around her areola. She felt the edge of his teeth rim her nipple, then a sharp pain as he briefly bit her. She whimpered slightly and her hands clenched on his skin. He shushed her and then the soothing softness of his tongue and lips was easing the sting away. Morgan moaned, bowing her back off the bed and urging his head closer to her breast. He obliged, licking long and slowly, sometimes taking almost her whole breast in his mouth and tasting her as if she were a rare dessert to be savored.

To ensure herself that it really was Nick and not her mind playing a cruel trick she ran her hands up his sides, feeling the heavy bands of muscle and mile wide shoulders. His purr of approval vibrated through her skin and, gasping, she lifted her head, watching as his dark head moved to her other breast, lavishing it with the same thorough attention.

Now his large hands were squeezing her breasts together, plumping the firm mounds, nipping at the soft undersides with his teeth. She tensed, expecting the sharp needlelike pricks of pain she was used to, but instead of pain sharp jolts of pleasure raced up her spine, bowing her back off the bed and lifting her breasts towards Nick. She moaned, lost in the blind need of her blood pumping, impatient to have her body against his, his hands and mouth on her—everywhere.

"Shit," his voice was muffled against her flesh, "You drive me so fucking crazy."

His voice, harsh and layered with sensual craving, only added to her torment. Then he was rubbing his face against her, using the bristly surface of his jaw against her sensitive nipples and laving away the slight burn with his tongue, alternating between gentleness and roughness, setting her on fire from top to bottom. Her clit throbbed painfully, and she could feel wetness gathering between her thighs, dampening the bed underneath her butt. Her vaginal muscles clenched, opening and closing like a fist, milking air, making her cry out as heavy need spiked inside her. She tossed her head back and forth on the bed, aching with the need that Nick was fueling within her body.

"Nick!" She twisted under him, scissoring her legs apart. "I-I need...I want..." Trembling she clutched him to her, trying to use her body to communicate her desire.

"You need to cum." He stated, using his wicked mouth on her again. "And I want to make you cum." His lips brushed her swollen nipple as he spoke, driving her higher and higher with each deliberate word. "I want you wide open, my mouth on your cunt, my tongue inside you where I can lick and feel every sweet part of you until you're dripping honey down my throat."

"Oh…God." The unexpected image of Nick with his head down there was so erotic that her breath caught in her throat and she arched against him, pleading, her body needing…what? "Nick."

"Hang on sweetheart, I'm about to make you feel very good." With barely a reprieve he started nibbling his way down her stomach, across to each hipbone and then lower, his rough jaw grazing the line of her pubic hair. Morgan felt him nuzzle her with his nose and sucked in a deep breath.

Surely, he couldn't really mean to…

Out of breath and embarrassed she dug her nails into his back, trying to drag him back up. Before she could draw breath to protest he had shoved her legs up and draped them over his shoulders. Nick's hot wet breath wafted over her and the smooth, firm tip of his tongue briefly touched her exposed nub in a firm caress. Shockwaves of tight, focused pleasure bolted through her vagina and she shrieked, heaving under him, but he only gripped her thighs tighter and pushed his face closer, sliding his tongue deep inside of her, burning her sensitive inner tissues with each gentle thrust. Her breathing froze, centered on the strange feel of his tongue moving inside her, licking and rubbing against her inner walls. Her core pulsed and she felt herself tightening around him. Against her will she began to rotate her hips, arching her aching center against mouth.

"Nick!" she wailed, "No…I-I can't…" Oh God! His tongue lapped, twisting and tickling around her clit, building stroke upon stroke of need.

With his mouth wide open around her, his rough beard bristles teasing her soft folds, he mumbled, "Oh yes…you can."

Morgan's mind went blank, her whole focus centered on the searing, burning waves of heat caused by Nick's tongue.

Richard had never, ever done this, had never even attempted…

Shaking, moaning Morgan levered herself up enough to see her legs splayed over Nick's wide shoulders and his dark bristly head against her core. She saw his head move, felt his tongue, hot, soft and wet, as it slipped inside her, almost burning…she whimpered and he glanced up, caught her watching him and his blue eyes blazed to almost black. Slowly, deliberately holding her gaze he pulled his tongue out and placed his lips over her clit, sucking strongly. Wild, sharp shards of pleasure struck her. Bright light flashed behind her closed eyelids, pulsing in time with each strong pull of his mouth on her throbbing flesh. Sharp little cries tore from her throat and with a wrenching sob Morgan fell back on the bed, shaking, body and mind splintering to bits as a violent orgasm pulsed through her, burning her nerve endings, stealing the breath from her body, yet still leaving her aching and empty.

And still Nick's mouth worked, torturing her oversensitive flesh. Reflexively she clutched at his ears, trying to pull him away from her but it was like trying to remove a starving dog from his meal. He growled, long and low in his throat, and then licked up the middle of her vagina to her throbbing clitoris.

There was no stopping him. Holding her hips in

both hands he ate at her ravenously, his tongue swirling around and around her clit, giving her mind and body no quarter. No leeway for her inexperience. Each hot rasp of his tongue sent bolts of painful pleasure through her body, sensation piling on top of sensation as he licked and sucked her wet flesh. She struggled to draw breath, frightened by the intensity of the coiling pressure within her vagina, pressure that rose from her core and spread to her abdomen and thighs. Small inner muscles, delicate and helpless against Nick's tormenting mouth, began to clench rhythmically and she could feel herself growing wetter and wetter. Surely Nick could feel it…taste it as well. Slightly embarrassed she tried to pull away only to have his hands tighten on her hips, restraining her.

"Cum, Morgan," his smooth voice whispered, "You know you want to. Your body needs to. Relax and let go for me."

He slid a finger inside of her and she moaned, her muscles clenching tightly around it. He hissed as though burned, and then began moving it slowly back and forth, "Fuck…You feel so good…so wet and hot. So perfect…. Feel me stroking you."

She whimpered, feeling his thick finger piercing her, moving inside of her. Mindlessly she writhed against him while shards of pleasure speared her inside and out. Helplessly, shamelessly she moaned his name, arching herself against him and opening her thighs wider, "Please…"

He increased the pace of his finger, slid another in beside it, stretching her with their combined width and put his mouth back between her legs, sucking hard.

The coils tightened on themselves, growing bigger

and bolder with every firm sweep of his tongue against her tender clit. Then suddenly, unexpectedly, the coils released, exploding inside of her, sending stabbing shafts of bright light streaking behind her closed eyelids. Crying out she arched her body, sobbing and twisting wildly as her ravished sex pulsed and clamped hard onto his fingers, tugging them inside with greedy pulls. Her body jerked, lunging against Nick, forcing his fingers deeper. He muttered something and then the heavy weight of his arm came across her stomach, holding her in place while she rode out the orgasm.

When the aftershocks had finished and she was aware once more she felt Nick gently pull his fingers out of her slick passage, and in an unexpectedly considerate move, adjust her panties so that she was covered. But his hand lingered on top of the material, stroking and petting her drenched flesh tenderly.

"First one?" he whispered.

Gasping, her body still twitching from aftershocks she nodded, beyond embarrassment. Feeling tears prick behind her eyelids she said, "Richard n-never…he didn't see any reason to…"

"Good thing the bastards dead." He muttered against her skin.

Giving him a shaky smile, she clasped her arms behind Nick's neck and pulled him up her body, feeling the hard, heavy prod of his erection brush against her as he moved. She mentally braced herself for the invasion that would come next, hoping that she would be able to get through it. But instead of opening his jeans and freeing himself, Nick carefully wiped her tears away, straightened her sweat-soaked hair so it wouldn't get caught under either of them and rolled onto his back so that she rested with her head on his chest. Her arm fell limp across his chest.

She waited, catching her breath and wondering what would come next.

Chapter 23

Long moments went by while she lay there, listening to his thumping heart and the steady sound of his breathing. She frowned, wondering if something was wrong. She chanced a glance up at his face, but his eyes were closed and his face relaxed, telling her nothing. Maybe he had fallen asleep…she moved her arm and her eyes latched onto his wide chest; all that smooth, dark skin packed with firm muscle…

Biting her lip she cautiously ran the tip of her finger from his sternum down to the ladder of his abdomen, carefully tracing each dip and swell. His skin was hot, rougher and thicker than hers. The line of hair on his stomach was soft, much softer than that on his head and she tangled her fingers in it, fascinated as a strand curled around her finger.

Beneath his jeans his erection was still obvious, and before her wide eyes it twitched, lengthening even more. Nick blew out a long breath, reached down and shifted it to a more comfortable position.

Morgan blushed and vaguely noticed that the room was darker, and that she could hear the chirping of insects outside her window. While she had been having the first orgasm of her entire life the earth had continued its trek around the sun and day had switched to night.

Her hand rose on Nick's stomach as he took

another deep breath and she knew that he had opened his eyes and was watching her.

"Nick?" her throat was scratchy, as if she needed a drink of water. She cleared it before continuing, "Aren't you going to…?" She faltered and gestured towards his erection.

He sighed, kissed the top of her head and pressed her closer to him, crushing her so close it felt like he wanted her to crawl right into his skin and be part of him forever, just like his tattoo.

"This was for you, Morgan." His voice was deep. The gravelly sound reminding her exactly of where his mouth had been. On her. Inside her. "Besides, I don't have anything here to protect you with and it's getting late."

Condoms. He was talking about condoms.

Against her will she imagined Nick's seed flooding her womb and she smoothed a hand over her flat belly, picturing it swollen and heavy. Oh, wow. This was so dangerous. He was dangerous.

"You, um…you don't have to worry about that. I mean…I take birth control pills." She drew in a shaky breath, "Never missed a day, even after—" She stopped, about to say 'even after Richard died'.

There was a long, thick silence while he absorbed that news. Then she felt him stroking her hair, letting the long dark strands run through his fingers until he caught the ends in a soothing and repetitive movement.

"You're so goddamned beautiful Morgan, and so damned tempting." He stroked her shoulder with the tip-end of her hair, using it like a feather to tickle her skin. "But I'm on edge right now, starving for you, and that's why I'm leaving here without going any further. I can't make love right now, not gently like you deserve. Especially not now that that I know I'd be able to feel you, dripping wet and tight, on every inch of my cock. It would only be fucking—hard—all night long, and then in the morning, when we're both tired and achy, when you've cum so many times you can't remember your own name…Then maybe I could slow down and make love to you. But not now."

****

"I've already fed for the night." Jake said as Nick walked into the lighted barn an hour later. "And I gave Lucky some Alfalfa."

Nick raised an eyebrow, "Lucky?"

"The gelding. I figured we had to call him something. I almost went with Scarface, but that didn't seem very nice."

"You aren't even going to ask where I've been?"

Jake grinned, "When Nearctic came home alone I went looking for you. The next time you're…involved with Morgan you might want to make sure the windows are shut. You could end up embarrassing some innocent bystander."

Nick muttered a curse and swiped a hand over his head, then couldn't help the little grin that kicked up the corner of his mouth. "Don't mention that to her."

"Are you kidding?" Jake exclaimed, placing a hand over his heart. "I'm not an idiot. A gentleman never tells." He hit the light switch, plunging the barn into darkness as they walked outside into the moonlit night. "So I take it that things are okay between the two of you now?"

"I took advantage of her."

Jake stopped dead, his shock a heavy weight

between them. "Come again?"

Nick walked on towards his house, knowing it wouldn't take Jake long to find his composure and hound him. "You heard me. And the hell of it is is that I'll keep doing it too."

"Yeah, I heard you, but I don't believe you. You care too much about her to use her or hurt her like that. I know you do, it's been obvious for weeks."

"Jake, I rode over there like some conquering nutcase and basically coerced her to let me in. I didn't take no for an answer."

"Nick…what are you saying? You didn't—"

"What? No! For fucks sake Jake you know I would never do that."

He could feel Jake's eyes boring into his back he stomped up the back steps and into the cool interior of his kitchen. Nick threw his brother an irritated scowl. "It's nine o'clock. You have your own home you know and this is really is none of your business."

Jake sauntered over to the kitchen table and sprawled into one of the chairs, propping his booted feet on another. "I know. But I haven't eaten yet and I know you have some leftover pizza in the refrigerator. So grab some plates and get to talking."

"Oh for fuck's sake!" Nick snapped. 'Fuck' and 'sake' were fast becoming his two favorite words, especially around Jake. "Why the hell couldn't dad have become impotent after I was born?"

Jake's green gaze flashed amusement, then back to concern. "Pizza and then talk, big brother."

Nick grabbed a plate out of the cabinet and the pizza out of the refrigerator and slapped two cold pieces onto his brother's plate. Then he took a handful of napkins and plopped everything on the table in front of Jake. Jake raised an eyebrow before calmly biting into one of the slices. Nick folded his arms and leaned back against his counter, calling back the urge to pick his brother up and toss him out the door. "She told me that she had been married for six years to the asshole and was tired of having him as her only experience. Obviously she was feeling vulnerable and I gave in to her without a struggle. End of story."

"Okay." Jake grabbed a napkin and wiped his mouth, then tapped his fingers on the table and nodded thoughtfully, "I see. So you had sex with her because she wanted you to. Um…how is that using her? Sounds to me like she was the one using you."

Feeling a huge headache coming on Nick shook an aspirin out of the bottle in the cabinet and stalked to the refrigerator, jerking open the door and grabbing a coke. Keeping his back to Jake he popped the top on the soda can and swallowed, grimacing as the cold liquid fizzed down his throat. Then admitted, "We didn't have sex."

"But I heard—oh…crap; thanks, now I have to get that visual out of my head."

Nick turned around. His brothers' face was red. "You wanted to know."

Jake cleared his throat, trying hard to hide his embarrassment. "Sorry, Nick. But I'm still not seeing the problem."

Nick sighed deeply. Everything in his life led back to this. "She doesn't know about me. She doesn't know she let an ex-con get…close to her."

He ran a hand across his face and mouth, remembering how her silky thighs had clenched on his head and how good, how sweetly hot she had tasted.

How her cries of pleasure— pleasure only he had ever given her—had been the most beautiful sounds he had ever heard. Leaving her alone in that bed knowing she was rosy and wet from her first orgasm, her body completely ready to take him inside, had been the hardest thing he had ever done. Even now he wanted to race right back over there and plunge his tongue into her again and again.

And then he would fuck her, exactly like he had told her, all night long, consequences be damned.

Jake pointedly clearing his throat brought him back to the present, and made him aware of the erection straining his jeans.

"Jesus, Nick. Go take a cold shower." Jake stood up, apparently figuring that this was his time to leave. "And after that you need to tell her the truth, before you go any further with her. I personally think you're making too big a deal out of nothing, but you know it's the right thing to do or, from what I heard this afternoon, you wouldn't be standing here pointing at me from below the waist."

Chapter 24

She had seduced a man, Morgan thought as she came awake the next morning. Of course, after the initial 'make love to me, Nick' he had taken over all control, but still she was the one who had gotten the ball rolling.

Smiling she pressed her face into the sheets, inhaling Nicks' lingering scent, then stretched her arms above her head and rolled over, facing the ceiling, picturing his ruthlessly stunning face and indigo eyes above her. A fierce, powerful delight swelled inside of her. She had had an orgasm. And to think that all of these years you thought those romance books were lying.

She had finally experienced that mysterious sexual grail and for the first time in six years she felt complete. Richard may have used her body, many times in ways that had made her feel lower than an animal. But Nick…Nick had given her that illusive, missing piece of the puzzle and had made her truly feel like a woman. Tentatively Morgan lowered her hand to the juncture between her thighs. Lightly she stroked the same spot his mouth had worshipped. Her breath caught, remembering the soft, damp heat of his tongue on her.

He had been merciless in his efforts to give her pleasure and now she wanted more of it. More of Nick…She moaned, stroking more firmly, losing herself in the building sensations as moisture gathered and spread.

The phone rang. Morgan screeched and jerked her hand from between her legs, glancing in horror at her bedside table as if the person on the other end could see exactly what she had been doing. Heart pounding, she leaned over the other side of the bed reaching for it, thinking it might be Nick. The moment her shaking fingers touched the receiver she hesitated, remembering that he didn't have her number. Besides, he was probably busy with the horses right now and with all that he had to do she would be the last thing on his mind.

Morgan picked up the receiver and sat up on the bed, wincing as her abused leg protested. She grinned even though the pain was sharp. Her muscles just weren't used to being spread over a man's wide shoulders like that.

"Hello?"

"Hey, hon. How are things over there in big sky country?" Lisa's bright, crisp voice came over the line.

Hey Lisa, guess what? I got naked with my hot, total package goliath neighbor and he made me come like there was no tomorrow.

Morgan winced, mentally shoving the little red devil off her shoulder. "Fine…things are…fine."

"You sure? You sound kind of breathless."

Before responding Morgan pulled in a deep, silent breath. Relax. Focus. "I've just been really busy getting a painting ready to ship to you; it'll be finished in a few days. It's the first for the 'Majestic Montana' series."

"Already? Wow. That's wonderful, Morgan."

Just then Morgan remembered the messy paint

splatter on her workroom floor and groaned. No doubt it was going to take loads of paint thinner and elbow grease to get it up. Hopefully it hadn't stained the wood floor permanently.

"Shoot Lisa, I hate to cut this short but I spilled paint all over my floor last night and completely forgot about cleaning it up. I'll have to let you go."

"Oh Morgan, how in the world did you forget to clean it up?"

Because my neighbors head was between my legs. Morgan bit back an embarrassed snort. Darn that little red devil!

"I just got busy with something else and it totally slipped my mind." While he slipped you the tongue—

Stop it!

"I'll talk to you soon, Lisa. I'll call you and let you know when to expect the painting."

"Okay sweetie. Bye."

Morgan hung up the phone feeling a rush of relief. Those little reminiscent scenes about last night had gotten her wet again; she could feel her panties dampening. Sure as the sun rose she had become addicted. A Nickoholic.

Wearing a goofy little smile she headed towards the bathroom to run water in the tub.

****

At seven-thirty that evening Morgan's doorbell rang. Nick was a looming presence on her porch looking wonderfully surly in his customary black T and faded jeans.

A delicious shivery sensation shook and her nipples peeked, pushing against the thin cups of her bra. Her breath quickened as memories roared through her brain. Hard and sensual his mouth had closed firmly around one tight nub, pulling and licking at the tight crest, manipulating her flesh until she was writhing beneath him, arching and begging him with her body.

Morgan groaned, closing her eyes as waves of embarrassment pinkened her skin. Surely he would take one look at her and know exactly where her mind had been.

Steeling herself she turned the doorknob.

"Do you like cats?" he asked as soon as she opened the door. Cats? Her brain slowed, back-peddling from embarrassment, sex, and maybe a 'hello' kiss to…cats. Morgan blinked several times, uncertain if she had heard him right. Okaay…so maybe you're the only one still stuck on last night.

"Um…Cats? As in the animal or the musical?"

Those black eyebrows lowered for an instant. "Animal."

"Well, uh…yes." Uncertain as to where this was leading she nodded, frowning slightly, "Yes I do."

Those dark eyes studied her for moment and then his lips tilted up in a slow, satisfied smile. In a move so quick she had no time to react he shackled her upper arm with his fingers and pulled her tight against his chest. In the next instant his large hands had slid smoothly down her back to firmly cup her butt. He squeezed, the movement lifting her against him, surprising a small shriek out of her.

"Nick!"

He made a soothing sound and cupped her closer; her belly pressed against him, leaving no doubt that he was fully aroused.

"I missed you." He nuzzled her ear with his nose,

nibbled his way down her throat. "You smell so damn good, Morgan."

"I-I just got out of the tub."

His breath hissed between his teeth, "Damn sweetheart, don't tell me that. I've been walking around with a hard-on all day because I couldn't stop thinking about you." He nipped her neck, right in the curve of her shoulder, making her gasp. On their own her hips arched, pressing against him. "I kept picturing the way you looked last night, spread out before me like a feast on the bed. Your legs wide open. That sexy hair framing your body like a living piece of art…" his voice lowered, growing strained and hoarse as his hot, wet mouth traveled up her throat. Morgan's head fell to the side, granting his free access. "And the way you tasted, so creamy …like the sweetest syrup…" a deep rumbling growl came from the depths of his chest, "fuck…I could eat you all day long and never get tired." She moaned as his lips traveled along her skin, giggling when he hit a tickle spot near the back of her neck and lingered there to abuse it.

"Mmm," she sighed breathily, "that feels sooo good Nick…"

His hands slid up her back to cup the back of her head. He planted a hard, quick kiss on her mouth, then threw a grin at her, "Made it damned difficult to ride a horse. Not to mention it embarrassed the hell out of Jake."

Morgan felt her whole face begin to redden. "He knows?"

Nick grinned again and using his body began to back her into the house. "He's a man, Morgan. It didn't take long for him to figure it out."

"Oh God," she cringed, "please tell me I'll never have to face him again."

Nick chuckled and his breath huffed across the top of her head. "Sorry honey, but if I have my way you'll be seeing a lot of each other."

"W-Wait!" She twisted in his hold as he maneuvered her into the front hallway. "Why did you want to know if I liked cats?"

"Because you can tell a lot about a person by if they like cats or not."

After all they had done last night that's how he judged her? Whether or not she liked cats? "Oh really?" She raised an eyebrow at him. "That's kind of a lame answer Nick."

"Um hmm. But that's the one you're getting." His tongue licked along her collarbone and then he nibbled his way back up her throat to her earlobe, biting it, making her melt. "Go for a drive with me."

His breath caressed her ear, warm and soft. His hands slid low on her back, over her buttocks and around. Large palms settled high on her outer thighs, his fingers resting under the curve of her cheeks. Thick and strong the tips of his thumbs caressed the front juncture where her thighs met her groin.

"Where—where to?" His tongue followed the fragile outer rim of her ear. She trembled and goosebumps rose along her forearms. Oh… God… the man was so good… His mouth and hands were setting her body ablaze, each touch lighting a firecracker of need that sizzled and popped in her lower body. Her legs trembled as the area between them became an aching throb, growing tight and moist at the same time. If she let him she knew he would move his thumbs just a little higher and stroke her, making her come right here her hallway. With her front door wide open. "Nick…please. Stop, it's too much."

Instantly he released her, raising his palms and backing off, though his eyes remained almost black. Hungry. "I'm sorry; I didn't mean to come on so strong." Worry flashed through his eyes, dimming some of that raw need. "I didn't scare you did I? Because—"

"Hush, Nick. It's alright. I know you won't hurt me." Morgan reached up and cupped his jaw, stroking his sandpapery chin with her fingertips, showing him she wasn't afraid. Cautiously and while watching her face closely he lowered his hands to rest on her hips again. "You might be big and intimidating sometimes, but I know you're not like him at all. I knew that that day at the barn. And probably, deep down, even before then." His blue gaze bored into hers and she blushed, dropping her eyes. "But the fact is I've only…I've never…only my husband has…"

Nick cut in, "Are you trying to tell me that you've only been with your husband? That you were a virgin when you got married?"

Morgan nodded, "Yes…and, I'm sure you've already figured it out but my experiences with him weren't….good. I mean I know I shouldn't feel this way after l-last night—," boy did her cheeks feel like they were going to spontaneously combust— "but it's all so new to me. So…intense." He opened his mouth but she put her hand up, covering his lips. He pressed a kiss into the center of her palm, making her smile. "I love the way you make me feel, Nick. It's just so new and-and I want you so much it's a little scary."

His hands settled on her waist, then stroked up her

back and down again in a soothing motion. She settled against him, then raised her face for his kiss. It was slow, soft, and infinitely tender.

"Come with me, there's a place I want to show you. Then we'll take it as slow and as sweet as you want."

Chapter 25

Morgan relaxed in Nick's arms and exhaled a contented sigh, watching as the sheets of water poured down to pound the lake's surface below. "Oh Nick…It's so beautiful…so peaceful. I can see why you brought me."

They were sitting on a small outcropping of rock about halfway up between the lake and the falls and he had her sideways on his lap, petting her hair and alternating between kissing and cuddling her. His mouth pressed briefly against her temple. "Somehow I knew you would like it."

She flashed him a grin and shivered slightly as a light mist drifted up, coating their skin. "I've never seen a waterfall at night, much less highlighted by a full moon. It's absolutely breathtaking."

"The water in the river above flows from Glacier National Park." Nick told her. "I used to come here a lot and just sit, thinking. Then I got the barn and the horses and I didn't need to come out here anymore. They were therapeutic enough."

She smiled at him, breathing in the crisp, cool air. "The air is so fresh…so clean. It was never like this in Chicago. I just wish I had my camera, the falls would be great for my Montana series."

"I can bring you back anytime, just say the word. Is your leg okay?" She nodded but he still looked concerned and shifted her against him so that her bad leg was supported completely on his thigh. His hand lingered, stroking her calf. She shivered, but this one had nothing to do with the coolness of the air. "Mind if I ask how long you lived in Chicago?"

"All of my life."

"Do you still have family there?"

She smiled wistfully, "Yes. I have a cousin, Lisa. She owns the gallery where I show and sell my paintings. She's the only thing I miss about Chicago, but she's also the one who gave me the 'push' to move out here."

Nick flashed a grin, "Remind me to send her some Thank You flowers."

Morgan huffed a laugh. "She'd be shocked senseless, and then she'd be on the first plane down here to make sure I hadn't lost my mind. By getting involved again, I mean." The air was getting chillier and she snuggled deeper against Nick's brawn for warmth, sighing in pleasure. "It feels so wonderful to be able to paint again, it's been years."

"Years?" One black brow shot up almost to his hairline. "If you're good and it's how you make money why did you sto—never mind. I don't need to ask. I already know." He hugged her against him, holding her completely and securely. "Are you too cold? Do you want to go back to the truck?" A wash of warmth flooded her. He was always so concerned about the littlest things; like her comfort, how she felt, if her leg was bothering her…it was so strange, so alien too her. And yet it felt so right.

"No, let's stay for just a little longer. You can tell me how you got into rescuing abused horses."

He shrugged as if it was no big deal but when he spoke his voice was husky and she heard him swallow several times. "I had a horse when I was a kid, a big old Appaloosa named Buckshot. I could do anything with that horse, even sit under his belly and read a book. My grandfather gave him to me, but then when my grandfather died my father didn't see a reason for me having a horse and he sold him. Years later I learned that my father hadn't sold him but had given him to a friend of his in order to pay off a gambling debt. The friend gave Buckshot to his kids who didn't know how to take care of him. They left him out in a dirt field one winter with no food and no shelter and he died." He was looking away from her, focused on the waterfall but his voice had gone flat and Morgan felt the tension in his body. "I hated my father then. Really, truly hated him. We had had our differences in the past but that was the final blow."

Morgan could clearly picture Nick as a little boy, completely in love with an old horse and then having that love shattered. She stroked the back of his neck soothingly, petting him while her chest tightened with unshed tears. She wished she could take away the pain and knowledge of what had happened to his horse. But the past can never be changed, no matter how much wishing one did.

"I'm sorry Nick."

His heavy shoulders lifted in a shrug and he snuggled her closer, resting his chin on the top of her head. "Yeah, well, it was a long time ago." She heard him swallow, then he sighed heavily. "Anyway…anger is what brought me into rescuing horses. I used the money that my grandfather left me to buy land and eventually I built the barn. My first rescue horse was Sultan and I've been doing it ever since. I guess I wanted to make up for what happened to Buckshot by making sure other horses didn't have the same fate."

"It wasn't anger, Nick. It was love." She spoke softly and squeezed the arm he had wrapped around her. "If you didn't love those horses, you wouldn't do it."

He was quiet for a long moment. She could almost see him replaying the events in his mind. "I guess it was a mixture of both, although anger helped a whole hell of a lot."

The differences between him and Richard were amazing. Impulsively she leaned forward and nuzzled her nose against his bristly jaw, receiving a surprised, yet pleased, grin in return. He made no move to take advantage of her sudden playfulness, just sat and let her test her new-found confidence, making Morgan even more aware of the reasons she had quickly and easily fallen for him. Richard's likeable smooth-talking businessman exterior had hidden a heartless, black-souled abuser while Nick's big, rough, tattooed don't-mess-with-me appearance probably fooled everyone into thinking he was dangerous.

But Morgan was in on the secret—he had a heart of gold. Instinctively she knew a woman could put her whole trust into Nick Evanoff and he would never use it against her or abuse it. Like tonight, she had spent most of the night sitting in his lap, snuggled against him and he had shown her she was important in so many little ways, probably most of them just instinctual for him…so unlike Richard who had never been remotely considerate of her feelings or things that mattered to her, much less take her anywhere special like a moonlit waterfall.

A good time for her had been any time she wasn't lying in bed with a new bruise or fractured bone.

"What's wrong, sweetheart?" She looked up, realizing she must have tensed up because his head was tilted down towards her and the intensity with which he was studying her was very disconcerting.

"Nothing," she hedged, "just thinking."

"Want to tell me about it?" When she remained silent he blew out a long breath, his chest flexing against her side. "Do you trust me, Morgan? Have we gotten that far yet?"

"I-oh Nick…" She sighed, sitting up and resting her elbows on her knees. Dropping her head forward she covered her face with her hands, at a loss as how to explain the feelings that bombarded her since meeting him. "If you understood how much of a big deal just being here with you is—and last night… you would never ask that question again." She put her hands down and looked at him helplessly, pleadingly. "My husband, Richard, did awful things to me. Physically and…sexually. When he died I was…God forgive me, but I was elated. Ecstatic…overjoyed. The police showing up at my door and giving me the news was honestly one of the best moments in my life, and I swore off all men for the rest of my life thinking that it was the safest route." A short little laugh escaped her. "But then I moved out here to be away from people and I met you and you make me feel so much…I'm afraid that it's going to turn wrong, bad somehow."

"All it takes are a few words sweetheart, everything out in the open so I know what demons I'm dealing with."

Demons. She had never thought of her nightmares and memories as in such a way. Even demons could be exorcised. Maybe confessing to Nick the darkness that had been her life would finally free her.

She struggled to find an opening. "I don't know really how to tell this...or how to begin...but if he hadn't been killed in a car accident over a year ago I would most likely still be married to him right now." Morgan paused as a sudden chill pulsed through her blood, and then whispered. "Or dead."

"Christ Morgan." He took her chin between his thumb and forefinger, "Are you telling me you think he would have—?"

"I have very few doubts." She stared at him, letting his eyes search hers until he found whatever answer he was looking for, then he released her jaw. "For several months before his wreck I had been getting the feeling that he was, uh, tired of me." She bit her lip and stared off into space until Nick's gentle nudge brought her back to earth. "It might sound funny, but I suspected it because the beatings were getting less often, but much more aggressive. You have to understand that he enjoyed hurting me; it was his pastime like other men play football or golf. There were also other women; he started to purposefully leave evidence lying around so that I would find out. In the beginning of our marriage he did his best to hide his affairs...but I always knew. Now it was like he was broadcasting them."

She pressed her face to his chest, letting his warmth and strength seep into her bones while he stroked her hair.

"He-uh..." She fiddled with a lock of her hair,

twisting the strand through her fingers, "Richard…he-he came home one day and accused me of seeing another man. Yeah right, like I would want a man after what he had taught me. I hardly ever left the house. But he went into a screaming rage and pushed me down the basement stairs. That's when I broke my hip. It shattered when I hit the concrete floor. Richard stood at the top of the stairs, a dark silhouette framed in the doorway, and he just stared at me for the longest time. I-I really think he was hoping that I would break my neck and die right then."

Nick dropped his head to rest against the top of hers. She felt his jaw clench against her hair and beneath her his muscles had gone rigid. After what seemed an eternity he finally spoke, his voice low and harsh in her ear. "God I wish I had met that bastard, I'd have killed him long before and ran away with you."

Morgan turned towards him and laid her palm against his cheek. "But then you'd be in prison and not here with me."

Morgan felt his whole body stiffen against her and something dark and undecipherable flashed behind his eyes. He looked almost…guilty. But then, before she could ask what was wrong he stood up and started ushering her towards the truck. "Let's go, you're cold. I can feel the chill-bumps on your skin."

Chapter 26

He was a selfish, selfish bastard. There it had been the perfect opening for the truth that she so rightly deserved, and his backbone had turned to mush.

But God, he loved her so much that the thought of—

He stopped dead in his tracks, so suddenly that she stumbled against him and he had to grab her to keep her from falling.

Love? Were his feelings for her really that deep? He spun the word around in his mind, tasting it and examining it from all angles. Love. He had never loved a woman before, except his mother, but, yes, he could see himself loving Morgan. She was so sweet and special, so small in stature yet possessed of an inner courage that outsized most people he knew. Hell, from the first moment he had seen her he had wanted to mark her, make it so every other male in the world knew she was his.

"Nick? Is something wrong?" Her soft voice pulled him from his thoughts.

Love. He loved her. "No, why do you ask?"

"You were frowning at me. Scowling very fiercely, actually."

He tucked her in close to his side, "I guess I was still thinking about what you went through, wishing I could take it all away." He opened the door and helped her into the truck, but her hand on his arm stopped him from closing it and the pure yearning in her voice sent shafts of lust straight to his so-far-tonight-well-behaved-cock. So much for that record.

"Nick?" her voice was low, tremulous. Her gold eyes bashful with the hint of sexual awakening. Her skirt had ridden up on her thighs, drawing his eyes like a magnet to the long bare length of her legs.

"What sweetheart?" Man, his voice was raspy.

Her gaze slid shyly away, her fingers rubbed nervously up and down his arm, driving him crazy. "You can try," she murmured. "Tonight. You did promise me slow and sweet, remember?"

No man could resist that temptation. Nick ground his jaw, wanting to lunge right into the cab and pull her on top of him and start licking and sucking on whatever part of her he touched first. But the gentleman in him reared his ugly head. Even though the cab of the truck was large it was no place to make love, especially not with her. He might get carried away and inadvertently hurt her leg or, or worse, scare her. Plus the area was dark and remote, surrounded by thick woods and wild animals. Not the best ambiance for slow and sweet.

She was sitting there in the truck watching him, waiting for his answer, her face angelic in the blue glow of the moonlight, her hair a long dark veil around her, looking much like the first time he had seen her. The effect was otherworldly, as if God or fate had seen fit to dump this ethereal, wounded woman in his life and give him the chance not to screw up.

At a loss for words he tunneled his hands into the heavy fall of hair on either side of her head and pulled her forward for a kiss. Her mouth opened, slowly and shyly at first, then becoming more confidant as he deepened the kiss and slid his tongue in to touch hers. Her hands slid around his waist to rest low on the middle of his back and briefly he broke contact with her mouth.

"That's a tempting offer, sweetheart. You sure you want to make it?"

****

Morgan's' nerves were stretched tight with anticipation as he rounded the front of the truck and opened the drivers' side door. She could have called a halt to this whole thing at any time and she knew he would have driven her back home, maybe not cheerfully, but he would have done it nonetheless. But she didn't want to; tonight was about experiencing that ultimate act of trust with a man she really, truly desired.

She had offered this moment to him and couldn't back out now. Wouldn't back out now. He had already shown her how much unbelievable pleasure he could give her and this was just naturally the next step.

So when he climbed into the cab and gruffly stated that they were going back to his place she did not argue.

Nick cleared his throat, drawing her attention as he carefully maneuvered the truck down the steep, shadowy mountain road. "I know you're going to be nervous, Morgan, and that's okay. What I don't want is for you to be scared. Fear and what we're going to be doing have no place together." He tapped a finger on the steering wheel, his expression serious. "But I do need to know if there's anything…specific…about it that scares you."

Morgan's stomach clenched. Cold and harsh the memories came flooding back of the times she had lain beneath Richard, biting her lip to hold in the cries of pain he so loved. And then there were the times when she had had to pleasure him orally. A wave of nausea hit as she remembered him coming in her mouth, gagging her with his hot semen. She pressed a hand to her stomach. Deep breaths…

"Morgan?"

Deep breaths…

"I--," she sucked in a deep breath and swallowed against the bile, "Everything. I-I hated everything about it." Morgan squeezed her eyes shut and curled her hands in her lap. "It always hurt; he always wanted it to hurt because that's what gave him pleasure." She heard Nick stir in his seat, heard his harsh indrawn breath and forced her eyes open, focusing on the darkness beyond the windshield. "And he would…he would make me…use my mouth…on him. It was disgusting. I always felt so dirty afterwards, I could never scrub myself clean enough." Her voice dropped to a whisper, "I still feel dirty, tainted. Please…I need you to take away the dirt Nick. I don't want to live with it anymore."

Silence reined throughout the roomy cab and Morgan slid a glance at the man beside her. Nick's jaw was locked, a muscle jumped visibly under his dark skin and there was an unnatural stillness in his big body. His fingers on the steering wheel flexed and unflexed as if he were holding himself back from strangling something. Morgan's lip slipped between her teeth and she swallowed uneasily, wondering if she had made a mistake by telling him her story. But then he must have become aware of her gaze because his body shifted and relaxed and in the next instant her chin was cupped in his palm and she was staring into glittering indigo eyes. He moved and she flinched, unable to help the instinctive reaction, but all she felt were his lips touching hers, lingering for a moment and then sliding across her cheekbone to her temple.

"I'll erase every stain or mark that bastard ever put on you, Morgan." His whisper stroked her ear, "And I swear you'll never feel dirty again."

****

Morgan listened to the gravel crunching under the tires as they followed the curves around until the barn and Nick's house came into view. Security lights came on as they passed the barn and pulled up in front of the brick ranch house. Everything was dark and quiet, as if the whole world had gone to sleep, leaving just the two of them. The silence closed in on her, rubbing against her nerves, making her even more aware of Nick and exactly what she intended to do with him.

Make love. Here. Tonight.

"Um…Nick?"

"Yeah, sweetheart?" He put the truck in Park and cut the engine.

"What—" her throat closed up as unbidden an image of Nick, muscular and naked and over her prone body, flashed in her brain. He planned to erase every stain and mark from Richard…Morgan swallowed tightly and forced the rest of the words out, "What about Jake? Won't he, uh…be here?" She looked at the house in front of her, only the porch light was lit and each window was black, evidencing no signs of activity inside.

Nick shook his head, "No. He and I like space to ourselves so Jake has his own house behind the barn.

230

Don't worry, we'll have total privacy."

Total privacy. Perspiration slickened Morgan's palms, making her grip on the door handle clumsy. Hands shaking she wiped them against her clothing and tried again. This time she managed to get the door open and carefully stepped down out of the high truck, putting most of her weight on her good leg, not wanting to freak her other one out before things even got started. The slamming of Nick's drivers' side door made her jump. Morgan wrapped her arms around herself and watched him come around the front of the truck towards her. He stopped in front of her, used one hand to push her door closed and then pulled her trembling body into the warm circle of his arms, snuggling her up against his chest.

"You're all nerves right now, aren't you?" He rested his chin on the top of her head and just held her. Wondering at his intuitiveness she nodded against his chest. His heart thudded slow and steady in her ear. Long moments passed while he held her and gradually her raw nerves began to relax, lulled into submission by the feel of his hard warm body against hers, especially since he seemed quite content to just stand there all night and hold her.

But it couldn't last…she knew that. He might have more patience—a lot more patience than any man in her experience, but he was still just a man. And she had offered him tonight.

Morgan drew in a shaky breath and pushed her face into his chest, squashing her nose into his shirt, breathing deeply, letting his earthy, fresh scent comfort her nerves. He began playing in her hair, shifting his fingers through the long strands much like he had just last night. The unhurried motion meant to soothe and distract. It worked, calming the chaos inside her.

"Morgan…I," he hesitated, "I care about you." One rough fingertip touched her cheek and stroked softly over her cheekbone like her skin was fragile silk. "I care about you more than any other woman I've known." His deep, rumbling voice stirred the delicate hairs at her temple while his stroking finger left trails of fire across her mouth, her jaw, her neck. "I don't want you to feel embarrassed or ashamed by anything we do."

His arousal was a thick obvious ridge straining against the front of his jeans, and pushing into her belly. Soon it would be pushing into her.

A searing bolt of sensation shot through her— anxiety or anticipation, she didn't know which— but right on its heels was definite arousal. Her breasts tingled, nipples hard and aching. Her skin grew warmer, and the place between her thighs clenched, becoming a stinging source of need, straight to her womb. Her body was readying itself, becoming wet in preparation of welcoming this man. She could feel the evidence pooling between her thighs. Dampening her panties. She pictured herself in his bed, accepting him as she had done so many times with Richard…

But this time she wanted it…her body wanted it. Her cautious mind might continue to say, 'wait just a minute, are you crazy?' But her body couldn't lie. And she was just a little bit tired of heeding all the red-flags waving in her brain.

Hope bloomed in the pit of her stomach, suppressing the acid of six years of horrific memories. Nick was not going to humiliate her and he would not abuse her, she knew that deep down to her gut. The knowledge freed her last little bit of restraint. She reached up and cradled his jaw, tugging his head down, loving how the bristly texture of his stubble scraped her palms.

Pressing her open mouth against his, she whispered, "Its cold out here, Nick. Take me inside and make me warm."

He took her hand, his burning gaze swallowing her whole. A gentle tug and without any extra urging she followed him across the driveway and into the darkened house.

Nick didn't release her hand once inside but held her close to him as he led her through a small front hallway and into a large living area. He flipped a switch on the wall and a low light courtesy a table lamp brightened the room. A large comfortable looking leather sofa sat sideways beside the fireplace, situated so one could sit and enjoy the fire while watching the outside world through the huge picture window in front of it. Morgan saw two heavy-looking western saddles sitting on the floor below it and various other items of horse tack hanging on the walls or laying on the floor.

Nick's arms came around her from behind and he snuggled her against him. Morgan's heart leapt into her throat.

"You're trembling." His nose nuzzled her ear; his teeth nipped her earlobe. She gasped, arching her head against him and his lips slid down her exposed throat.

"Oh…" The blood in her veins thickened and coherent thought left her for a few seconds while her body focused solely on the man behind her. She felt him smile against her skin and then his grip loosened.

"Why don't I make a fire?" He rubbed his hands up and down her arms. Morgan wondered if he knew the goosebumps had nothing to do with the temperature of the room. "It's chilly enough and watching the flames might help you relax. I know it does me." He said as he moved away from her, going over to a pile of logs beside the fireplace. She wondered how often he sat in front of the fire, brooding and staring into the flames.

She watched the muscles in his broad back bunch and shift under his shirt as he loaded several logs into the fireplaces' darkened mouth. Some crumpled paper, the flair of a match and soon bright yellow flames began to appear around and between the logs. The dry wood cracked and whistled, casting dancing shadows throughout the low-lit room. Nick stood up and turned to face her, crossing his arms and leaning a shoulder against the mantle. He looked so big and dangerous, his body painted light and dark by the flames, that Morgan swallowed nervously and took a step backwards. One black eyebrow cocked up and he straightened, unfolding his arms.

"I'm sorry…" she said, "it's not you—"

"I know," he interrupted, "and I understand. That's why we're here."

A huge picture window dominated one wall. Beyond the partly closed curtains she saw the security lights come on at the barn. Clasping her hands together in front of her she went and stood before the window, thinking how wonderful it must be to stand here during winter and watch the snow fall outside, painting everything with its gentle white kiss. As she stared the small form of a cat appeared at the corner of the barn.

"That's Boo. She hunts about this time each night."

She jumped slightly when Nick's arms came around her from behind. For such a big man he moved very quietly and she thought it must come from working with frightened horses. He pulled her back against him, molding her back to his front. "Except of course when it rains. Then she's snuggled up in the loft."

Morgan smiled at him over her shoulder before turning her attention back to Boo. The moist tip of his tongue stroked the sensitive area where her neck and shoulder met. She shuddered, breathing hard while a mix of hot and cold chills rose on her skin. She watched, his image reflected in the glass, as one of his hands slid up from her stomach to rest just below her breast, almost cupping its weight, and she let her head fall back against his chest in surrender. She felt strange inside, burning and almost breathless, as if he were stealing her oxygen, absorbing it into himself and the only way to get it back was through his touch.

"Come by the fire," he commanded softly, brushing her cheek with his lips and nipping the tender corner of her mouth, "you're still shivering."

She let him lead her to the sofa. Her skin, warmed by the blazing fire, lost its chill as she settled into the plush well-used leather. A tremor ran through her as Nick knelt down in front of her legs and cupped her knees in his hands. Inch by inch he coaxed her legs apart until he was settled directly between them with her thighs bracketing his ribs. He was so close that she could see the black pinpoints of his iris's and herself, looking pale and uncertain, mirrored in them. He smiled, a brief flashing of even white teeth and then he leaned forward, pressing her back against the cushions with his hands on her waist. Morgan's heart stuttered in her chest and she felt her shirt raised, inching up her body, baring her stomach. Like two lovers cool air caressed her skin on the left while warm air licked on the right.

Nick's mouth landed on her quivering stomach where he began to trace small designs on her skin with his lips and tongue. Back and forth, swirls, feather-light licks, long slow lapping strokes…all bombarding and confusing to her senses. She heard herself moan and whimper and couldn't stop from arching against him, pleading with her body for more. She sighed; gripping his head to hold him to her while his tongue rimmed her belly button.

After what had to be an eternity of torture, he lifted his mouth and caught her wrists, intertwining their fingers. Eyes darkened to black midnight burned into hers. "I promise you Morgan," he said solemnly, "nothing but heaven tonight."

He sounded sure of that, positive in fact, but still her stomach muscles tightened. Determined not to give fear leverage again she met his eyes and squeezed his fingers with hers. "I don't know what heaven is, Nick," she whispered to him, "I've never found it before."

He stared down at her, his deep blue eyes narrowed and shadowed by thick black lashes. Something, some emotion she couldn't catch flashed through those beautiful eyes and then a smile tilted the corner of his mouth. His hands came up to cup her face, thumbs stroking her skin. "You've found it now, sweetheart."

Chapter 27

Nick released her long enough to pull his shirt off and toss it on the back of the sofa. Immediately her wide eyes went to his naked chest and the tip of her pink tongue came out to wet her bottom lip. It was purely an unconscious gesture, but it made his blood several degrees hotter. It might have been a long time since he had been in any type of relationship with a woman, but he recognized plain desire when he saw it.

Her eyes crept up from his chest to meet his. He smiled and pressed a kiss to the tip of her nose. "Trust me, Morgan." He shifted to his back on the floor and pulled her, kneeling, to straddle his abdomen. Her hair slid forward in thick silken waves to cover them both. Her skirt rode up above her thighs, allowing him a glimpse of silky pale pink panties. Immediately she tried to shift off of him but he flashed a quick grin and put his hands on her waist. Gently but firmly he held her still on top of him. "No, don't be afraid. Sit on me— fully. Get used to it. You won't hurt me."

He traced her ribcage and sternum with his thumbs, feeling her heart pounding under heated skin. He watched her as she wiggled on her knees, jerking a groan out of him as her butt shifted and then settled on the length of his rigid cock still trapped inside his jeans. Something like a hiss came out of her and then her warm hands were drifting over his abs in a light caress, his muscles tightened in response and he saw the wonder on her face as she touched him. Nick closed his eyes, hands clenched on her waist, ready to rip open his jeans and shove himself inside her as he had fantasized about so many times.

Instead he gritted his teeth, reined his urges in and said softly, "You're beautiful, Morgan…" he stroked up her stomach, his fingers flitting over the cups of her bra and then back down. Gentling her. "So soft and silky. I love putting my mouth on you, tasting you." Watching her expression he raised her shirt, higher and higher until her lacy bra was bare. "No," he said when she tried to tug it back down, "don't try to hide."

Her knuckles were white on her shirt. Hazel eyes, wary yet wanting, stared at him. He tugged at the fabric, feeling her grip give a little.

"You trust me, don't you Morgan?" He persuaded. "You must trust me because you're sitting on me…and my cock, while I'm half-naked."

She bit her lip, shifted against him, eyes widening when she felt his cock jerk in his jeans.

"You trusted me enough to let me in your house the other day, lay you across your bed and put my tongue on the most delicate part of you until you came against my mouth." She turned such a bright red that if a blush could burn Nick knew his skin would be seared off his bones. He grinned at her dazed expression and quickly whipped her shirt off over her head, tugging until it was free of the length of her hair.

"You have the most amazing hair." He slid his hands through the heavy mahogany locks, dragging several thick pieces of it over her shoulders and arranging them so that they framed her breasts and trailed down over her stomach. "I've dreamed of seeing you like this, with your hair surrounding you like a dark cloud, for a long time." If only she were naked, then his dream would be fully realized.

Later. Too much too fast won't get you anywhere except back at square one, having to win her trust all over again.

He folded his hands behind his head, giving her complete freedom to do what she wanted. "Surely you've wondered what it would be like to explore a man's body, Morgan…so do it. Learn that I won't hurt you—no, I can't hurt you, even though my body is bigger and stronger than yours."

"Anywhere?" Her voice was a husky whisper.

He grinned at her, "Everywhere. Make me yours."

For an instant she hesitated, avoiding his gaze and nibbling her bottom lip. Then color bloomed into her cheeks and her eyes, lit by the fire, turned to molten glittering gold. She leaned down to touch her tongue to his Adams apple and her hair, a mass of tangled waves, cascaded around them. Nick swept it back over her shoulders, clutching it in one fist while using his free hand to stroke her spine. She moaned against his neck, arching slightly into his touch while the tip of her tongue traced the line of his beard stubble. He groaned, shut his eyes and tilted his head back to give her better access.

Her warm, slender hands slid from his abdomen, up along his sides and to his underarms, briefly skimming the tufts of hair that grew there, and then up to his shoulders. He shuddered, breath sawing heavily in and out as he forced himself not to move, not to do anything that might scare her into backing off.

"That feels so good, sweetheart." He encouraged, sliding his hands over her hips and down her thighs to the hem of her bunched-up skirt. Slowly, aware of her muscles tensing, he slid his hands up bare skin until his palms cupped her buttocks. "Remember how good it felt when I touched you here?" He flicked the tip of one finger against the damp crotch of her panties.

She gasped sharply, sitting up and jerking against his hand. "Yes."

"So touch all you want," he encouraged, groaning at the feeling of her wetness against his stomach through the thin fabric, "and so will I." He watched her, seeing for himself each expression that crossed her lovely face: wonder, anticipation, awe…pleasure, and even happiness.

No fear, thank God.

The truth was there in her natural moisture. He had barely touched her and already her body was readying itself for him, aroused just from her simple explorations. He had been surprised to find that watching the myriad of expressions cross her face as she touched and played with him was as satisfying as the actual act of sex itself would be. Or at least almost, he mentally corrected. Something had to be done about the torture his poor cock had been put through.

He drew in a deep breath, knowing he had made the right move in starting this by allowing her to be in control. If he had gone about it his usual way, which was to take control—dominate— right away, then she probably would have run off, terrified that he was going to be abusive just like her husband. Nick scowled fiercely.

There were ways to dominate, and then there were

ways to dominate.

****

Morgan could barely think. Sitting astride Nick, feeling him so hot and hard muscled beneath her and knowing that her touch was arousing him was exhilarating. She could spend the rest of the evening just running her hands all over him.

Guided by instinct she splayed her hands against his chest, moving them along his pectorals and over his flat brown nipples. Emboldened Morgan flicked her fingernails against them, watching in fascination as they hardened into tight little nubs, smaller than her own, but apparently just as sensitive. The way the fire's light shaded and highlighted different parts of his body was captivating to her, each flickering shadow playing along the smooth expanse of muscle and bone.

After smoothing her hands over his pounding heart and down his sternum she peeked at him from lowered lashes. Exhilaration fled. His eyes were glittering shards of ice and deep grooves bracketed the sides of his mouth.

"Nick." Her voice shook, tears threatened. "Why are you frowning? Did I do something wrong?" As usual. And now he was angry. Morgan took her hands off of him, ready to grab her clothes and run home to cry. Lips trembling she started to lift herself from him only to have him press her back down.

"Oh no," he pulled her down for a kiss, his mouth lingering over hers, smooth and seductive, "You're not going anywhere. We're not even close to being finished here." He lifted his hips, nudging his denim covered cock against her. "I'm frowning because I want you so much it's painful."

Maybe it was true, Morgan thought. He was certainly hard enough, and had been that way most of the night, yet hadn't done anything to relieve himself. Maybe her ineptitude hadn't ruined the evening.

"Morgan, sweetheart… "his breathing was ragged, his voice deep, gritty and raw. She could see a thin line of sweat beading on his forehead, "there's more to me than just my chest and neck."

She glanced down and then back up. Hazel and Indigo gazes collided. A snake of fear wound into her throat but then she saw the naked longing on his face, defined by the tautness of his jaw, the cords of straining muscle in his neck…and she knew she couldn't let him suffer any more. He had already given her so much pleasure, more than in her whole lifetime.

She was sitting on his abdomen, slightly below his bellybutton, her dress hiked to the juncture of her thighs with only her panties guarding her from his naked skin. Drawing a deep breath she lifted herself to her knees. Denim jeans scraped her inner thighs and stomach as she moved, the raspy texture firing her nerve endings, until she was past his crotch and sitting on his denim covered thighs.

She could feel the heat of his eyes and knew he watched her, waiting to see what she would do now. The weight of his anticipation was palpable and she knew she wanted to do this. Overriding any fear was her desire to please him.

Hands trembling she reached for his fly, fingers hovering over the button and zipper of his jeans. Drawing in a deep shaky breath she tried the button at his waistband first, struggling to pull the metal piece free. With each frustrating tug her knuckles brushed against the line of coarse hair on his abdomen.

"It's all right," he soothed, his hands joining hers to pop the waistband free. "Now unzip me…don't be afraid." He smiled and smoothed her hair out of her way, "I'm not giving you more than you're ready for, I just want to make a little room."

Slowly Morgan lowered the zipper, revealing black cotton briefs and, beneath them, the thick rigid shape of his erection. Nick rose up onto his elbows, the heavy muscles in his arms, shoulders and stomach bunching and flexing. A male animal in his prime. Her mouth went dry while the place between her legs got wetter, hotter.

His midnight eyes glittered devilishly, challengingly in the shifting light, making her blood run hot with anticipation.

"That's much better. Now…put one of your legs between mine," he suggested, "Ride my thigh."

He bent one leg up and moved the other out to the side to give her room to sit. Blushing she did as he said. Bracing her hands on his thigh she maneuvered one leg over his and mounted him. Heavy denim rubbed the crotch of her panties, creating a strange heat inside her. He clenched and unclenched his thigh muscles, the motion moving her against him. Her lips parted, her eyelids grew heavy and unconsciously she mimicked him, sliding her hips subtly back and forth.

"Tell me how it feels, Morgan."

"Oh…that feels…" She moaned, closed her eyes and let her head fall back as he moved his thigh higher against her, the light friction between herself and him making her breathless and desperate. She leaned back, panting. "Nick! I…I don't kn—"

"Easy," he calmed her, his hands coming on her hips, helping her move a little faster, "relax and just enjoy. Do what feels good."

She shivered. The flames in her body growing hotter and higher, licking towards the orgasmic bliss he had brought her to the other night. Her body tightened, her skin burned and between her legs clenched, empty and aching, throbbing in rhythm to his movements. She sobbed, knowing only Nick had the power to give her the release she was seeking.

"Nick! Please."

"Mmm," was his response just before his mouth closed over her nipple, wetting and tugging at the lace of her bra. He flicked the hard peak against the roof of his mouth, nipped it with his teeth and the slight pain amidst so much pleasure was almost enough to throw her over the edge.

"Oh…God." Her mouth opened, trying to bring more air into her constricted lungs and automatically her hips moved faster, rougher against the abrasive denim. Shocking pleasure, ragged sensations moved through her body, into her womb. She could feel the wetness of her panties and some dim frame of mind knew that she was probably staining his jeans. She didn't care; all she cared about was that wonderful release he had given her before.

Strong hands closed hard on her waist, slowing her movements. She struggled against them, whimpering and sobbing, grinding against him in frustration as her body shook with need. You're a slut. I married a slut and sluts don't deserve to feel any pleasure. No, not Richard…this was Nick. Nick, who held her, stroked her and was whispering in her ear.

"Nick!" She pleaded, half sobbing.

"Shhh sweetheart." Nick stroked her hair, smoothing the damp, tangled strands away from her face. "Not yet." He muttered hoarsely. "You're not coming until my cocks inside you."

Nick heard her sharp intake of breath and before giving her a chance to think, or worry, slid his hands between her thighs and cupped her buttocks, pulling her up his body until she was spread directly over his face. Unbalanced Morgan pitched forward, catching herself by planting her palms on the floor above his head. Nick took advantage of her ass in the air and grabbed her panties, shredding them until they fell to the floor, leaving her delicately glistening core naked and vulnerable above him.

His control broke. Consumed by lust he raised his head and covered her with his mouth, slipping his tongue through the plump lips. She jerked and cried out, the sound sharp and broken. Her dew covered his mouth, tasting sweet against his tongue. She was wet, weeping with the desire to have him inside her. Nick groaned, imagining his cock sliding inside her tight wet warmth and tightened his hold, preventing her from pulling away, pressing her down onto to his face while working his tongue and lips forcefully over her throbbing flesh.

Chapter 28

Hearing her cries Nick moved his hands forward and spread her labia with his thumbs, opening her slick pink flesh to him. His forearms held her satiny thighs open, keeping her off balance enough for him to do his work. Gently he licked at her opening, savoring the spicy scent of her sex and swirling his tongue around and around until she was shuddering and gasping above him, unconsciously pushing her hips back and forth in time with his slow strokes.

Fire crackled and hissed in the hearth. A thin sheen of sweat covered both their skins.

Holding her firmly he raised his head slightly and took her throbbing clit into his mouth, sucking hard. Her shocked scream rang through the room; she bucked against him, writhing on his face as he alternated between long slow pulls and light, teasing sucks. Slow, patient and skillful he pushed her towards the edge, holding her ruthlessly.

She shuddered, grinding against him and sobbing breathlessly. "Nick…s-stop. I-I can't…"

Her silky wetness coated his mouth and chin, his cock was a raging length of steel in his pants, ready and willing to ride her into oblivion, but the magic word 'stop' rang like a death knell in his ears. Gritting his jaw and feeling like a convict who had been denied his last meal, Nick pulled his mouth away from her.

Her eyes flew open, golden bright and glazed with unfulfilled need. "Nick?" She trembled, jerking against him. "Please…"

"You said 'stop', sweetheart."

Her hazy eyes widened as though shocked, "No, that's not what I mea—" she closed her eyes, bit her lip, then whispered, "Please. It won't stop. My body…" she rotated herself against him and he sucked in a deep, harsh breath, "it's throbbing."

Nick breathed a sigh of relief and cupped her buttocks, stroking her quivering flesh with his thumbs. "Well," he murmured, before pulling her close and putting his mouth on her again, "let's see if I can make it stop." She cried out while rotating her hips on him and he felt her body begin to tense as her orgasm came closer and closer. Wanting to be sure that she would be wet enough to take him soon he pushed a thumb inside her passage, hissing a curse as it was enveloped by her fist-tight scorching heat. Delicate little pulsations squeezed his thumb, sucking it deeper and signaling that the end was near for her.

No way, not without me inside you.

Carefully he pulled his thumb from her slick passage. She made a small keening sound and he kissed her inner thigh reassuringly, licking and nibbling her skin, distracting her while he reached down and carefully unfastened his jeans. He grimaced in relief as the heavy, aching length of his cock was finally freed.

She was arching above him, panting in short breaths as his lips found her swollen clit. He swirled the tip of his tongue around the hard knot of flesh, lightly this time so that she wouldn't come. Sharp cries were bursting from Morgan's throat and Nick gritted his teeth, sucking at her as his cock hardened to painful proportions. Pre-cum leaked from the tip, coating the sides of his shaft. He yanked his head from her, cursing savagely, unable to wait any longer.

"Morgan, sweetheart," he reached up and caught hold of her waist, urging her to a sitting position on his chest. Using one hand he smoothed her sweat soaked hair out of her face and stroked the curve of her flushed cheekbone. Glazed eyes stared back at him.

"Please Nick," her voice caught and she squirmed against him, seeking that which he held just out of her reach, "please; I can't wait...it-it hurts."

His cock twitched sympathetically, releasing another creamy droplet.

"Easy Morgan." He soothed, stroking her and praying that his patience and control would last a little longer. "I want you to slide back until you feel my cock against you." He felt her tremble and knew some of her anxiety had broken through the heated fog she was in. "No, don't be afraid. Just get used to it, its there for your pleasure, not to cause pain."

Eyes wide and apprehensive she hesitantly slid down his body until the head of his cock bumped between her buttocks. She froze while Nick's whole body clenched at the contact. He fought to remain patient, trying to think of anything besides how good her satiny skin felt pressed against his agonized flesh.

He propped himself back up onto his elbows for a better view. Against his brawn she looked so tiny and fragile, reminding him again of how easy it would be to hurt her.

And yet she trusted him enough to be here with him like this, even though she knew she was completely vulnerable. His heart squeezed painfully tight in his chest.

He smiled at her encouragingly. She was sitting on him, unmoving, his cock stabbing her back, her gorgeous mass of dark hair hanging over her shoulders and flowing down her back to settle on his thighs. Her full bottom lip was caught between her teeth, her eyes half lowered as she studied his chest and flexing stomach muscles, seemingly fascinated.

Somehow she managed to look like a luscious sex goddess and innocent virgin at the same time. Nick grinned, this…this was how he had fantasized about her, sitting astride him like Lady Godiva, about to go for a sweet, wild ride…except…he frowned at her cream-colored sundress.

It definitely had to come off.

"Take off the dress, Morgan." He kept his voice neutral, neither pleading, nor commanding, not wanting to frighten her. "Let me see how beautiful you are, sweetheart."

****

They stared at each other. The leashed desire blazing in his deep blue eyes overwhelmed her, almost as much as the feel of his hard, amazingly hot penis pressing against her. The combination of heat and the contrary roughness of denim between her thighs kept her frozen in place above him. Nick reached for her and slid his hands up her bare thighs to her hips, taking the hem of her skirt higher and higher until warm air tickled the dark mound of her sex.

Her blood pulsed, slow and heavy in her veins with each caress of his fingers. She moaned, closed her eyes and let her head fall back.

"Come on, baby." He crooned softly, sliding his hands to her waist and slowly baring her to his hot gaze. "Look at me. Look at what you do to me."

Morgan roused herself and opened her eyes, watching him. His eyes went to the V of her spread legs, fastening on the dark hair that protected the folds of her sex. Color bloomed on his harsh cheekbones and his eyes glittered intensely.

"You're glistening...right here." He slipped a hand between her thighs and cupped her, sliding his middle finger into her. Morgan quivered, biting her lip as her inner muscles clasped at his finger, drawing it in. Beyond her control her body moved, thrusting in time with his slow, deliberate stroking. "God, Morgan...you're so wet, so ready for me...My ultimate fantasy woman."

Carefully he withdrew his finger from her but kept stroking her opening, rimming the tender flesh with her own moisture, drawing her body tighter and tighter. Morgan couldn't speak, could barely draw breath as he reduced her to a shivering, gasping, desperately physical being.

"Shit. Take the dress off, baby."

Driven by the stark urgency in his husky words her shaking hands found the hemline of her skirt. She hesitated for a long moment before raising her arms and pulling the dress completely off, leaving her sitting on Nick wearing only her lacy pink bra.

"Oh...wow...look at you." His voice was mesmerizing, low and raspy, filled with male appreciation and desire.

Morgan felt a fierce feminine power surge inside of her, banishing any thoughts of shame or of covering herself. Emboldened by the pure lust on his face and the worshipful touches of his hands she reached behind her and unhooked her bra, letting her breasts spill out, heavy and full, nipples hard and wanting.

Nick's growl was one of pure masculine torment. His pupils dilated to almost black. He took her wrists, "Reach behind you…feel me. Feel what you do to me. I'm powerless in your hands."

She did as he said, feeling the heavy length of his penis. She stroked him from base to tip, trying to close her hand around him but failing. The tip was slick and she rubbed the moisture around, loving his hoarse sounds of pleasure. Her gaze roamed over his face, drinking in the obvious signs that she was pleasing him. Sweat beaded his forehead, tracing tiny paths into his hairline. His eyes were shut tight, dark skin pulled taut against his cheekbones, tendons standing out in his strong neck. His breathing was harsh and loud in the quiet room, the muscles in his chest and abs quivering with his obvious efforts to retain control. Morgan knew he was completely able to take her. He had more than enough strength to pick her up and slam her down onto his rigid cock, ending his agony, but without a doubt she knew that he would lay there, suffering until she was completely comfortable with his body.

Until she decided the time was right for her.

Lifting herself up onto her knees she gripped his cock with her hand and tentatively began to ease down onto him. The first hard inch parted her and she stopped, gasping at the slight burn.

"Fuck, you're so tight." He cursed raggedly.

Even though she could feel her own wetness easing his way he was much bigger than Richard had been, and his was cock stretching her, bordering on pain. She felt swollen, already filled by him and he wasn't yet completely inside. Morgan felt the dark edge of fear begin to worm its way into her brain and forced herself to focus on Nick. To remember that this was natural, that she wanted it—him— she sunk down another inch and his hands coming up to clench her waist, stopping her downward motion.

"Easy Morgan…easy baby. It's alright," he soothed when she whimpered and bit her lip, wincing at the burning assault. "Let your muscles relax."

"I swear…I'm trying."

"Touch yourself," he whispered, "I'll hold you up."

Morgan could feel the heat that suffused her face, her body as a wave of embarrassment washed over her. She opened her mouth but nothing came out. She had touched herself before, but never with any luck, and never in front of anyone. Attempting it while Nick watched…she shook her head. "No, it-it will be fine…" She punctuated her words by wiggling and bearing down on his cock again.

"Oh Jesus…" Arching his head back Nick groaned, heavy biceps bunching as his hands tightened on her waist hard enough to leave bruises. A sheen of sweat coated his chest and he cursed again, raw and ragged. "Shit. Stop, Morgan." He gulped in a big breath, fingers easing on her sides. "I don't want you to hurt yourself." As he spoke he rotated his hips beneath her, tiny, subtle movements that pressed his cock against her sensitive inner tissues, reigniting her flames. She twisted her hips, bracing her palms hard on his chest, mimicking his short thrusts. "That's it, baby," he encouraged as her head fell back, "Move with me. That's right."

Morgan felt his hands leave her side. One slid around to cup her buttocks and help her move while the other trailed down her thigh. She jerked, blood pumping in a heavy rhythm when he paused briefly to caress her clit. Tension coiled, winding through her body but then his fingers left her again.

Nick took one of her hands, raised it from his chest to his lips and sucked one of her fingers into the hot recesses of his mouth.

"Oh…God…" His tongue stroked her finger, swirling around the tip, flicking lightly and then with more force. Morgan felt her nipples swell to painful little peaks, as if remembering when his mouth had done the same to them.

The sucking slowed and he released her finger from his mouth. It glistened wetly in the dim light. Watching her out of hooded eyes darkened to midnight he guided her hand between them and pressed her finger to the tiny nub hidden in the secret folds of her body. He moved her finger around and around, slick caresses that had her back arching and her thigh muscles stiffen. He encouraged her, whispering softly about how beautiful she was, how responsive, and as he worked her clit with her finger any embarrassment, she felt drifted far away. She stroked, eyes closed, fingertip moving firmly on her smooth flesh. Vaguely she realized that Nick had taken his hand away, that she was now sitting astride him—naked— with half of his cock inside her body…pleasuring herself.

In front of him. For him.

A gush of wetness answered her erotic thought, easing her tight passage and allowing his cock to slide deeper within her. Half of him was now inside her now and she moaned at the sensation, digging her nails into his chest.

"That's better," he said, his voice rough and hoarse, "Keep touching yourself…Soon you'll have all of me."

She opened her eyes to see him watching what she was doing, his eyes focused between her legs. The expression on his face was one of fierce sexual excitement, animalistic…and it would have scared her at any other time. But now, now she wanted as much as he could give her.

Morgan closed her eyes, arching her back as the need to have him inside her overrode any sense of discomfort. Morgan's finger moved faster, she undulated above him, gasping as the sensations, the tightening and coiling within her body, in her vagina where his cock throbbed, flooded together, twisting and turning, colliding together.

She exploded. A violent pulsing seized and invaded her whole body. She planted herself down onto Nick, taking all of him—hard.

They both cried out.

Morgan's head fell back and she couldn't stop a keening wail from escaping her as the never-ending pulsations took over her body, sucking at his cock now deep inside her. Dimly she was aware of Nick's heaving breaths, of his muscles quivering beneath her. Veins stood out on his body, running the length of his ropey muscles, giving life to the chain tattoo. The tension inside him was palpable and Morgan realized he was waiting, waiting on her to tell him she was ready for more.

"Take me Nick," she gasped, frantic with the

wildness blooming between them, "hard as you want, just like you said you would the other night. Fill me up. I won't break."

"Fucking hell, sweetheart," he rasped, "I wanted to go easy the first time."

"No," She moaned, writhing on top of him, "I want you, nothing but you." She ground her hips down as hard as she could, breathless and shivering, taking every bit of him. "Now, Nick. Please."

His hands gripped her hips with bruising force, fingers digging into her skin as he took her at her word and let go. He pounded up into her, each heavy thrust jerking little cries out of her throat. He let go of her waist, adjusting her thighs wider on his hips so that her weight drove her down. Reaching down he found her clit and rubbed firmly. Inside her the coiling tension began again, rising higher and hotter with each ruthless pass of his finger, making her wetter as he shoved hard into her, twice, three times, again and again, the tendons in his neck standing out as he clenched his jaw. Each deep jolting contact hit nerve endings deep within, driving her body feverishly towards release.

Like red-hot lightening the fury was upon her. She screamed as her body clamped down, squeezing his cock in a vise-like fist.

Nick came with a loud shout, pulsing hotly inside her, his semen marking her as his in the most basic, primitive way. Panting like she had run ten miles Morgan collapsed onto his sweaty chest, whimpering and shaking as stray little convulsions continued throughout her. His penis rested inside her, not as full, but still an obvious presence and she knew that tomorrow she would be very sore.

Sore…but not torn and bleeding like afterwards with Richard.

She moved slightly, wincing at the various aches throughout her body. She could still feel the imprint of Nick's powerful hands and knew that she would have marks from that. But unlike being bruised from Richard beating her, these bruises had occurred while Nick showed her what real lovemaking was supposed to be. And now she knew the difference.

Nick heaved a big sigh and then his arms came back around her, gently pulling her up until her head was resting against his throat. She winced, feeling his penis slip free of her body.

"You OK?" His voice rumbled deep and contented from his throat, vibrating against her cheek. "That was…more intense than I had planned. Did I hurt you?"

She nodded and felt his beard stubble scrape against her skin, "I'm fine."

"I want honesty Morgan. I didn't scare you at all?"

"I was nervous, at first…and maybe a little scared when we…when you…" she buried her nose in his collarbone, "you know."

"I'm going to guess the 'you know' is when I put my cock inside you." He stroked her cheek, "I should have gone slower, not let things get out of hand. I didn't want you to associate us and what we were doing with him." He growled the last word.

His big body had tensed against her and she knew he was thinking about her comparing him to Richard. "I didn't. Really, Nick." She assured him, "The only time he came to mind was after. And that was only briefly."

"And? What did you think about him?"

The fire crackled and hissed in the hearth, drying

the sweat from their naked bodies. Long moments passed while Morgan lay on Nick's chest listening to his heart thumping, trying to decide the best way to answer him.

She sighed, knowing that his question wasn't based on jealously, but on concern for her. "I was thinking that even though you are bigger and stronger than Richard, and you could hurt me just as easily—more so—if you wanted too, that you had just shown me the true difference between making love and…and what I…what I endured, with him."

There was a moment of thick silence between them which Nick broke.

"Come here," his palms slid around her waist, urging her up higher on his chest, "I think there's been enough talking."

****

Hours later Morgan lay awake; propped up on her elbows and watching the dying firelight playing across Nick's sleeping face. After making love to her again, much slower this time, he had gotten up and grabbed a few pillows off the sofa along with a lightweight quilt and made a bed for them near the fireplace. He had cuddled her, keeping her pressed close against him while they talked; him telling her more stories about the horses, and her telling him about her artwork. He had asked all kinds of questions about Lisa, the studio and the shows Morgan had coming up. Morgan blushed, remembering how enthusiastic she had been while talking about herself, but Richard had never expressed an interest in her art, had in fact made her stop painting completely. But Nick had seemed so honestly interested.

Eventually exhaustion had taken over and they had both dozed off, but Morgan had been awakened by a log slipping and crackling loudly in the fire. Since then she had stayed awake, watching him, aware of the lingering aches in her body and amazed at what had occurred between them in such a short time. His breathing was deep and even, his face peaceful, the severe lines gone, making him look several years younger, less fierce, but no less handsome.

Smiling she leaned over him and pressed a kiss to his mouth, then snuggled against his side, not wanting to be separated from him for even a moment, awash in the pleasure of just touching him. And to think she had foolishly tried to keep him out of her life. She hadn't known love could be like this.

Morgan caught her breath, staring down at Nick, heart pounding in her throat as the words rang loudly through her mind. He slept on, completely oblivious to what she had just admitted. But she couldn't it, any more than she could deny her body food or water.

"Nick?" She pressed her hand to his jaw, loving the feel of his beard stubble abrading her palm. Knowing he was deeply asleep, that she was safe, she put her mouth near his ear and whispered, "I love you."

Chapter 29

The sound of the door banging and heavy boots crossing the hardwood floor brought Morgan awake the next morning.

"Yo, Nick," Jake's voice called from the kitchen area, a mere ten feet from the room where she lay naked against Nick's side. "You up yet? It's almost eight."

"Oh, God…Nick," frantically she pushed on Nick's arm, "Nick wake up! Your brother's here!"

Nick shifted beside her and groaned, then sat up, running a hand over his head in irritation. Boots sounded in the hall. Nick leaned over, reaching for the sofa and grabbed two pillows, handing them to her. Immediately she plastered them to her front. "Jake," he shouted, "don't you even think about stepping one foot in here."

The booted footfalls hesitated and then stopped. "Uh…okay. What's going on?"

"Morgan's here." Nick glanced over at her where she sat partially behind him and smiled, reaching out and stroking her knee where it peeked out from the bulky pillows.

Jake started walking again, "Oh hey, that's great. Let me just—,"

"Damn it Jake!" Nick cursed, "I said stay the hell away from here if you know what's good for you." He ran a hand through his hair again and Morgan was beginning to recognize it as a habit. "This isn't exactly a great time for a brotherly visit."

"Oh…uh…hell. I'm sorry. I'll just-uh…I'll see you at the barn then."

They listened to his rapidly fading steps and then the door slamming. Nick heaved a sigh and said, "Hell, Jake'll be traumatized for the rest of the day."

Morgan stifled a giggle, then shifted beneath the covering of pillows, shyly aware of her nudity—and his. Most certainly his, she thought while her eyes roamed the broad expanse of his back, following the firm, hard line of muscles along his ribcage before his head swung back around to her, catching her unabashed perusal. Indigo eyes glowed hotly at her from half-lowered lids. She swallowed tightly, recognizing the meaning in that dark glow.

"I…I really should go," she said, clutching the pillows and beginning to scoot away from him. Her gaze bounced around the room, searching for her clothes. "I know you have stuff to do."

Nick looked at her, eyes roaming down her body, then casually leaned over and wrapped his hand around the calf of her uninjured leg, just below her knee. Before Morgan could try and jerk away from him she was being gently, yet inexorably pulled back towards him. She stared at him, wide-eyed while he ripped the pillows from her grasp and tumbled her backwards to the floor.

"Is your leg ok?" He asked solicitously. "Do you need me to rub it?"

Morgan shook her head, "I'm—it's ok."

He stared at her, judging her honesty she guessed. Apparently satisfied that she was telling the truth his naked weight came heavily down on top of her, between her thighs, startling a gasp from her. He propped himself up on one elbow and looked down at her consideringly. "You think you're just gonna get up and leave after last night?"

He shifted his hips, settling himself more comfortably against her and Morgan felt the hot, heavy prod of his penis at her entrance. Her hands came up to clutch at his shoulders, whether to push him away or pull him close she wasn't sure. He put one fingertip under chin, urging her to face him. Cheeks burning Morgan met his dark eyes. They were tender, filled with the wealth of knowledge of everything they had done last night. His mouth quirked and she willed herself not to melt into the floor from embarrassment.

"That's no way to start the morning, sweetheart." His head lowered and he kissed her, tenderly at first on the mouth, coaxing, persuading until their tongues met and caressed softly, then harder, and more aggressive. His hands stroked up her ribs, calloused fingertips tickling her sensitive skin, cupping her breast, plying the peak with his fingertips until it was aching and painfully hard.

Gasping she pulled his head down to her breast, "Please Nick."

He took her nipple into his mouth, pulling strongly with his lips and raking it tenderly with his teeth, then licking away the slight sting. She arched against him, begging for more.

"This is the best breakfast I've ever had." He muttered into her skin, kissing his way to her other breast.

She giggled, but the sound was cut short when his

hand began sliding down, gliding low over her belly, fingertips brushing her and then resting on her mound. Morgan held her breath, awash in a myriad of sensation while he probed her gently. She flinched, her body sore, but made move or sound to stop him, part of her remembering how angry Richard had gotten when she complained and the other part of her just not wanting to spoil the morning. Nick groaned, the sound low and guttural, and pressed his face into her neck. "You're already wet."

His finger dipped shallowly in and rotated against her inner walls. Morgan bit her lip, then moaned into his shoulder and mimicked the slow motion with her hips. He did it again, encouraging her with soft whispers. Sweat broke out on her body as he increased the depth and motion until she was breathless, throbbing, arching against him, trying desperately to keep his finger from leaving her aching body.

Nick whispered something low and unintelligible. His finger slid out, then came back to her, only this time the feeling was fuller, the sensation of discomfort heavier within her body and she realized he had added another finger. Now two stretched her already sore passage. Harsh reality threaded through her hazy mind. If his fingers were already causing such discomfort how in the world was she going to handle his penis? And there it was, pressing hard and ready against her thigh.

Morgan bit her lip, holding back a whimper and wincing as he pushed his fingers back and forth inside her. Morgan knew that Nick would not hurt her if she said to stop, but part of her did not want to ruin the morning by telling him 'no' and then have that tension wavering between them. Especially not after their beautiful night together.

She turned her head away, desperate for her body to feel the same depth of pleasure she had experienced before he had introduced the second finger. Suddenly she became aware that the pushing inside her body had stopped and that Nick was watching her with fierce intensity. He withdrew his fingers and cupped her jaw, turning her head to look at him.

"Morgan, sweetheart. If you're sore and I was hurting you you should have told me." A slight frown played across his dark face as he smoothed a lock of hair over her shoulder. "Now I feel like a jackass for enjoying what was causing you pain."

Morgan bit her lip, tears trembling on her lashes. She blinked them away. "I'm sorry, please don't feel bad. But Richard always got mad—"

A muscle in his darkly stubbled jaw started ticking. His eyes flicked to her scarred cheek.

"Hush," he commanded softly but firmly. "I'm not him, and I don't want you to ever let me hurt you. I'm a big guy Morgan and you're very small. If you're too sore to make love this morning it's not going to make me mad. It just means that I'll have the pleasure of running you a hot bath and letting you soak while I go out and deal with Jake's damaged sensibilities. Okay?"

She nodded and he kissed her sweetly, lingeringly on the lips. Seeming entirely at ease with his total nudity and unconcerned about the impressive erection still straining against his navel, Nick stood up, then bent down and picked her up, cradling her high against his muscled chest. The crisp line of hair on his abdomen brushed against her hip, reminding her of how very naked they both were. Morgan knew he would never drop her but still looped one arm around his neck. The other she used as a maidenly shield across her breasts. Nick noticed and raised one eyebrow, giving her a boyishly lopsided grin.

"No one will disturb you up here so don't feel like you have to rush," he said as he mounted the stairs with her locked against him, "I'll probably still be at the barn when you're done. Just come and find me."

He carried her past several doors and into what she assumed was the master bedroom. Nicks' room…with Nick's big king-sized bed on the far side. The covers were still turned down from the last time he slept in it. Erotic images flooded her mind about what could happen between those sheets and she felt her blood heat. Against her arm her nipples were stiffened, poking and prodding her skin as if to remind her that they were there and seeking attention.

"Next time." Nick whispered, nuzzling her ear.

****

His bathroom was huge and stark white, with the only color coming from the grey slate tiles on the floor and the navy-blue towels hanging on the towel bars. An old-fashioned claw-foot tub sat beneath a large window and a separate glass enclosed stand-up shower was situated in the corner.

She didn't get to bathe alone.

Once Nick had run the water and deposited her in the tub he had muttered 'to hell with dealing with Jake' and climbed in behind her leaving very little room to move, which meant she had had no choice but to sit directly on top of him.

Morgan leaned back against Nick's wet chest, sighing with delight as the hot water eased the soreness between her legs. "Ohhh…that feels so good. I've never bathed with a man before. I figured you for a shower guy."

"Usually I am, that's why I had the shower installed, but this is a special occasion. Does your leg hurt?"

She nodded, "Yes, it's beginning to ache, but the hot water should keep it from cramping." Nick ran his hands under the water along the length of her thigh, squeezing and kneading the sore muscles as he went. When she hummed her appreciation he soaped up a washcloth and began running it over her tummy and breasts, paying careful attention to each spot he passed. Her nipples were hard points and squeaky clean by the time he finished with them. The washcloth disappeared, his bare soapy hands smoothed over her skin, down her stomach to slide beneath the water, down her inner thighs and then back up to the juncture between her legs.

"Ummm…Nick." She moaned, shifting back against him as his fingers slipped around the soft folds of her tender flesh, made slick by the bath water and her escalating excitement. There was nowhere she couldn't feel him. His thick penis bumped against her back, riding her spine. His arm around her waist caged her to him as his fingers probed delicately, the chain tattoo wrapping his bicep flexing with each small movement of his hand.

"I thought—" She broke off, gasping as his fingers hit a spot that sent small sparks of electricity zinging through her.

"It's alright. Just let me wash you, sweetheart." His voice was seductively soft against her ear, "I promise, nothing more than that."

Each gentle stroke told her differently and soon she was squirming against him in earnest, arching her hips up with little panting breaths. "Please...oh...I-I think I'm c-clean now." She clutched his forearm when he ignored her. "Nick, you-you promised!"

The top of his dark head came into her peripheral vision and he nipped her neck, "Shhh...just let me comfort you, that's all I want Morgan." The tip of his middle finger circled her wet flesh, sliding down the slit of her body, then stroking upwards to tease her stiffened clit. "You're so beautiful, all wet and slick and shimmering. With your hair pinned high up I can see all of you...every inch."

Morgan closed her eyes and let her head fall back against his shoulder while his deep voice filled every recess of her body and mind. Her nose brushed his stubbled jaw and she turned her head, pressing her mouth against the skin of his throat, stifling her moans against him.

"Your breasts are flushed and deep rose from the water; your nipples are glossy red berries... My God, it's mouthwatering...the most tantalizing sight I've ever seen." He kissed her neck, binding her with his rough, sensual talk. His finger flicked her woman's bud relentlessly, "You make me so weak it's scary." Her body rose and fell as he heaved a deep contented sounding sigh.

"God Nick...please..." Her hips arched, sloshing water over the rim of the tub. Morgan leaned forward beneath the water and grabbed his hand, intending to pull it away. "I—I can't take much more!"

"Yes you can." He ignored her frantic efforts to

pull his hand away and finally gave up, flopping breathlessly back against his chest. "That's right, relax back against me...you're getting close now sweet." Her stomach and thighs quivered. Tension filled her muscles as she strained against Nick's moving hand, sobbing, clawing at him. While rubbing her clit he pressed his free hand to her opening and pushed one finger slowly inside. His voice, low and gravelly, sounded near her ear. "I can feel all those little muscles starting to flutter, like butterfly wings kissing my finger...there..." he moved his finger slightly deeper, back and forth, "that's right baby, relax and let yourself come. I don't want anything from you right now but to make you come."

One more push from his fingers and her body tightened, every nerve drawing taut, then exploding as release coursed through her. Heart pounding, she jerked against him while her inner muscles squeezed and sucked at his fingers, holding him firmly inside her. Mindlessly she cried out, not caring who heard or that water was sloshing all over, soaking the floor. Dazed she fell back, resting against him, limp with exhaustion and satisfaction. Behind her she felt Nick tense, then curse. His hand left her clit and he quickly wrapped his arm around her stomach, holding her locked firmly against him. "Oh fuck..." He groaned, burying his mouth against her temple. His penis pulsed strongly against her back and she knew he had come as well. "God Morgan," he paused, sucking in deep gusts of air, "I swear there's nothing in this world more beautiful than watching you come."

Her heart caught on a beat, love for him exploded inside of her, filling her up until there was no room for anything else but him. The heartfelt tenderness of his words, so poetic and out of place coming from a man who looked so hard-edged and dangerous brought tears to her eyes. They flowed over, down her body to melt into the bathwater while his fingers brought her body to a shatteringly sweet orgasm.

Morgan lay against him, limp and breathless. "Oh…oh wow,' she panted, "Nick I'm wiped out. I don't think I have enough strength to even get out of the tub now."

"That's what I'm here for—giving orgasms and helping with baths. Sit up, let me get out and grab some towels, then I'll get you out."

Morgan tilted her head on his shoulder, looking up at him. There was a twinkle in his blue eyes as he met her gaze and he looked very pleased with himself.He shifted, leaning forward with her and she felt his chest muscles ripple against her back. Bracing his hands on either side of the tub he lifted himself out.

Oh…wow. Her brain skittered and then a double-take, trying to process a completely naked and dripping wet Nick. He turned to grab a towel and her eyes skimmed over his heavily muscled back, seeing what she hadn't had a chance to see before. The chain tattoo didn't only wrap his forearm, but whipped up around his shoulder to trail down one side of his back and over his buttock, which was as tight and hard and as dark as the rest of him. And then he turned again, offering her an unobstructed sideview that made her almost choke. Good…Lord…no wonder she was beyond sore this morning. Even at rest his penis was a thing of awe.

Talk about an ad for a women's magazine…

She glanced back up at his face to find him

watching her with a smirk on his face and eyes filled with amusement. "Get a good look? Want me to turn slowly and flex?" He lifted his tattooed arm and flexed his bicep, making the muscle knot. The image was supremely male, slightly intimidating and for a moment an inner swelling of caution darkened her mind. Unaware of her momentary relapse Nick grinned and winked at her and almost as if by magic her mental slip backwards was gone. Richard was gone. In their place was Nick. Big, tattooed, rough and all male…her Nick.

Morgan watched him as he dried off, letting her eyes follow wherever the towel led. Slowly it ventured over his chest, then made a leisurely glide down his sternum. A slow controlled sweep brought it over his ripped abs before heading for the line of dark hair that arrowed down his navel. As Morgan's eyes lowered along with the towel she realized another part of him was rising, thickening and lengthening. Choking on a startled breath her eyes shot up to his face. He grinned and laughter lightened his dark normally intense eyes.

"You keep looking at me like that babe and you're never going to be able to walk again."

Chapter 30

Leaving the warm house and warm woman upstairs was one of the hardest things he had ever done but Nick shrugged into his jacket and headed out the back door. Jake would have had the horses all fed by now but Nick knew his brother would have questions. Besides if Morgan were feeling anything near to what he himself was feeling right now he was pretty sure that she could use a few minutes to alone.

Last night and this morning had been...beyond his fantasies. Electric. Mind-blowing.

Sex—no, making love— to Morgan had left him feeling like his life before her had been empty. A shell of what it could be. Just him going through the motions and living a half-life. And now...now he couldn't see a future without her. Nick stopped halfway to the barn and stood there, drinking in the frost-bitten morning air. Letting the crispness sting his nostrils and clear his head. Clear head, clear thoughts.

Damn...he could have done without the clear thoughts part.

She was so sweet. So perfect. So deserving of something right. Even moreso now that he had sampled her body. And the simple truth was that no matter how many times he wrapped himself in Morgan's warmth, no matter how many times he indulged himself and blacked out the rest of the world with her, the simple disastrous truth was that he was still a murdering ex-convict.

****

About forty-five minutes after Nick left her alone to dress and refresh her makeup Morgan had gathered enough courage to leave the security of the house and face him in the bright light of day. She just hoped she wouldn't melt into an embarrassed little puddle in front of him and Jake. Jake…her cheeks burned as she thought of Jake almost walking in on them in the living room this morning. Oh God…he knew that she and Nick hadn't even made it upstairs to the bedroom.

She stepped outside onto the back porch, glad that her leg was only mildly achy and that her limp would not be too bad today. The bath and massages from Nick had helped with that.

It was a chilly morning with dew still making a sparkling blanket over the ground. Horses of all different colors grazed contentedly in the pastures surrounding the house. She inhaled deeply, taking in the view from the house, breathing in the freshness of the farm, the peacefulness of such beauty. Her mind wandered back to the story Nick had told her about his childhood and Buckshot. Through sadness and with determination he had been able make this beautiful place—his dream— a reality. A sudden, fierce gladness about that infused her.

Knowing she had dawdled long enough she stepped off the porch and made her way towards the barn. A very swaybacked Appaloosa in the closest field caught her eye and she pictured Nick as a child, dark haired and already exceedingly handsome, riding the horse bareback, free as the wind, laughing and happy.

The barn's oversized double doors were open so Morgan ventured partially inside, straining to hear any noise that would alert her to Nick or Jake's whereabouts. Several stalls were standing open but all she heard were soft the nickers of curious horses. Morgan walked over to the open tack room and peeked in, only to be disappointed. She had hoped that maybe Nick might be in there cleaning something and she could face him in private before seeing his brother again. But except for an endless array of gleaming tack it too was empty. Something brushed against her ankles as she turned to leave. A black cat, its motor revving loudly, was winding its slinky body between her legs, rubbing itself against her ankles. Always having been an animal lover Richard's disdain of anything alive and furry had forced her to live for years without the joy of a pet. An absurd burst of elation gushed through her and suddenly she wanted nothing more than to stroke that furry little body. To feel it's coat beneath her palms, alive, warm, and purring.

She squatted down and wiggled her fingers at it, grinning as the cat flipped onto its backside and did a series of twists with its paws in the air, trying to look as cute as possible. Its motor cranked up even louder, as if to make sure it had her attention.

"You must be Boo." She said, rubbing its exposed belly. "Your dad and I saw you out hunting last night." Her fingers slid through the silky black coat, enjoying the massaging sensation of the cats' purrs beneath her fingertips. "I heard you have a little family somewh—" She stopped; her attention caught by a tense male voice approaching the barn.

"—told you you were full of shit, Nick. That

excuse gets real old, real quick."

Nick's deep baritone caressed her ears. "I can't lose Morgan, Jake. Damnit, I love her."

Morgan caught her breath, her blood slowing in her veins as the words sank into all the pores of her body. Her brain was the last thing to grasp them. *I love her.* Morgan had thought, dreamed, of a lot of things since meeting Nick, but hadn't let herself dare to hope for so much, so fast. She wasn't even sure she was ready to hear that particular declaration, and she hadn't—not officially yet since he had only said it to Jake—but, oh wow, even hearing it unofficially felt very, very good.

Giving the purring cat one last rub Morgan took a deep, shaky breath and rose to her feet, wiping her damp palms against her shirt front. If she had enough nerve to do everything she had done last night and this morning with Nick then she had enough nerve to face him right now. Jake or no Jake.

Jake was talking again, sounding slightly frustrated so she started towards the barn entrance intending to let them know she was there. Boo followed beside her, tails twitching importantly.

Nick's next words froze her in her tracks.

"Morgan needs someone more like you." He said. "Sweet. Easy-going. The romantic type." A tense silence followed. Morgan, confusion churning in her gut, strained to hear any reply, hoping that Nick was just fooling around with Jake. Surely he couldn't be trying to…surely he couldn't mean…

"I'm only saying what's best for her, Jake."

Feeling increasingly sick she edged to the open doorway, staying plastered to the wall and concealing shadows until both brothers were in her line of vision.

Nick had his back to her, holding a young horse while Jake was mounted on a blue roan Quarter Horse. Boo paused beside her, watching her with gleaming greenish yellow eyes.

"Sweet? The romantic type?" Jake gave a sharp bark of laughter. "I am so sick of hearing that shit goddamnit!" He threw his arms out to the side in a gesture of surrender, startling a snort from the horse Nick was holding. The lines of his lean, handsome face hardened and in one graceful movement he swung down from the roan. "Fine," he said and threw his horses' reins at Nick, "if that's what you think is best why don't I go up to the house right now while she's all rosy and blissed out from a night with you and see if I can get lucky? Hell, maybe she'll have been thinking of you and already be soft and wet."

Nausea churning in her gut she watched Jake give his Nick a hard smile, then moved as if to brush past him towards the house. "Oh yeah," he continued, "the more I think of it the better its sounding. That way I won't have to waste much time on foreplay or swee— oomph!"

Morgan saw Nick's back muscles bunch and then his arm moved in a lightning-fast jab. She covered her mouth with her hand, smothering a horrified gasp as Jake went flying, landing on his back a few feet away.

****

Nick let his fist fly, knuckles connecting with Jake's jaw. At the last moment he had pulled the full force of the punch, but still the blow was enough to knock his brother off his feet. Instant, sickening regret seeped into Nick's stomach. The horses he had been holding jerked backwards, yanking the reins out of his hand and took off into the barn. Nick didn't give them a second glance, knowing they would each go to their stall. Jake sprawled in the dirt, holding his jaw and glaring up at him. "Jesus Jake, I'm sorry. I didn't mean—"

"Shut up." Jake sat up, massaging his jaw and wincing. "Shut. The fuck. Up. The only reason I'm staying down here is so I don't knock your thick head off your shoulders." Jake glared at him, daring him to open his mouth. Wisely Nick kept it shut. "I deserved it for saying what I did, but I said it to piss you off and make you realize what a stupid shit you're being." Jake's palm slapped the ground, frustration evident in every line of his body. "Jesus Nick, you've never acted like such a damn fool before. She looks at me"—Jake shoved a finger into his chest— "like a friend or brother. She looks at you like—oh…shit."

Jake's gaze focused on something over Nick's left shoulder and frowning at the sudden shift in his brother's attention Nick turned. Looking small and lost, framed by the huge gaping doorway was Morgan, her face stricken and pale, ghost white against the shadowed interior. Boo sat at her feet, her tail curled possessively around Morgan's ankle.

"Morgan." He read the scene through her eyes, heard the scene through her ears and his gut clenched in certain fear. He took several steps towards her, stopping when her arm lifted as if to hold him off. "Morgan, baby…it's not what you—"

"I'm-I'm sorry." Her mouth worked, opening and closing, "I-I didn't mean to—" Her chin trembled and she clamped her lips together, staring at him, betrayal clear in the watery gold depths. Voice shaking with suppressed tears she said, "I heard—" Her eyes flicked behind him to Jake, then back to him. She clamped a forearm against her stomach as if feeling sick. "I-I need to go. I need to go home."

Her voice, ghostly and weak, made the hairs on the back of his neck prickle. He closed several more feet between them, shaking his head, "No sweetheart. You need to stay here, where we can talk."

She shook her head and began edging along the wall of the barn, away from him, giving Nick flashbacks of another time, another place.

"Please baby, don't do this." He pleaded, knowing he was seconds away from losing her. "What you heard is not what you're thinking it is!"

"Oh? I didn't hear you tell Jake to go have sex with me?"

"Fucking hell!" He shouted, needing to break through whatever mental block she was erecting. "No, goddamnit, that's not what you heard!" His traitorous brain churned up a scene from last night, but superimposed Jake with her instead of himself. It was more than he could bear and stay sane. "You know damn well I didn't say that. Like I'd ever let another man touch you."

She inched along the barn, easing closer and closer to the edge and, Nick thought, freedom. Escape. "You don't own me Nick." Her brows drew low while her chin nudged upwards, showing a little of the spirit he had come to enjoy. "You don't 'let' me anything."

"Yeah, well that may be, but you're sure as hell not leaving here until we talk about this."

"Listen to him, Morgan." Apparently Jake had recovered from the blow and was now standing behind him, "What you heard us—me—saying was stupid, and I apologize. If you knew—"

"Oh I know," she cut him off with a hysterical sounding laugh, "I know. I know I just heard the man I…" she hesitated, chin quivering. Nick wanted to gather her up, kiss her until she was clinging to him. Do whatever he had to do until she swore she'd never leave him. "I know I heard you say…" her voice trembled and she clutched her hands together, "you said you l-loved me, Nick…and in the next breath I hear you saying that I'd be better off with Jake. How could you say that? Especially after last night?"

Those big golden eyes looked so tormented that if he had had a dagger in his hand he would have cut out his tongue with it. Not that that would solve this steaming shitpile of a mess he had made.

Thoughts scattered, his answer wouldn't come and he hesitated a moment too long. Apparently Morgan took this as some ominous sign because she choked off a sob, pushed violently off the side of the barn and made a break for the clearing between it and house.

"Morgan! Goddamn it!"

Nick slammed a fist against the wall and took off after her, knowing it was foolish to chase her—especially with her past—but the gripping, clawing need to make her understand, to not let her get away again, overrode his calm. Tore away all of his common sense.

He easily overtook her and caught her before she even got near the house. She stumbled on her bad leg and he caught her from behind, lifting her, struggling, high against his chest. Her feet dangled off the ground and she slammed her heel into his shin, right below his kneecap. He cursed, raw and succinct, the blinding pain almost dropping him to his knees. But he also had an insane urge to grin. She hadn't held back anything back with the hit, which meant her usual bout of fear and anxiety, her usual cower reflex hadn't triggered…yet.

"No, no! Nick!" Her body bowed against his hold, long hair whipping back and forth, and he knew she was gearing up to ram the back of her head into his chin. "Let…me…go!"

"Hit me, Morgan." He put his mouth close to her ear, resisting the urge to kiss the fragile shell. "Do whatever you feel like. You know I'm not gonna hurt you, no matter what."

She lunged, grunted, panting and wiggling against his unbreakable hold. But her fragile strength was already wearing down, no match for his. Her head lolled back against his shoulder and he saw her eyes close. "You've already hurt me."

He knew she didn't mean physically. "I know you think that, sweetheart. But which was worse—hearing me say that I love you," he paused to let those words sink in, "or the other part?" He gazed down at her face where it rested on his shoulder. "Which scared you more? Which made you run?"

A frowned marred her brow. "Both—the last. I don't—" she shook her head as though confused. "Put me down, please. I won't be violent."

He let her slide down his body, knowing she would feel his condition, but there was nothing he could do about it. Her wiggling had been a major turn on.

He realized his mistake the minute he set her free. She whirled on him and planted one small, balled fist in the center of his chest. "You bastard! How dare you?"

It didn't hurt, he barely felt it, but the pure unexpectedness of the action got an 'ummph' out of him. Which seemed to satisfy her because she shoved him again, backing up him several steps and coming after him. "How dare you!" She stomped her foot and Nick's eyebrows rose as he studied the heightened color in her delicate, furious little face. Maybe last night had released more than her sexual hang-ups. "You're trying to put the blame for this,"—she made jerky gesture between herself and him— "on me! When it was you saying you wanted your brother to have me!"

Nick held his hands up in surrender, "I know what you heard. Fuck knows if I could redo that whole scene I would. And I know what Jake said, but he was full of shit and didn't mean it! Christ Morgan, you saw me knock him on his ass for it!"

"Last night," she went on as if he hadn't said a word, "last night was the most wonderful thing that I've ever experienced! But then," her eyes teared and she paused, sniffling and wiping at her nose with her hand, "then I came out here today and heard you saying you l-loved me. And that turned into the most wonderful thing because I…I…" her bottom lip quivered and she swung around, giving him her back. Her silky hair swung, tempting his touch and he gathered a thick lock in his hand, letting the strands flow through his fingers the same way they had last night.

"You what, Morgan?" He knew, deep in his gut he already knew because Morgan simply wasn't the type of woman to sleep with a man, to trust a man with that part of her, without that one last little factor. "Tell me sweetheart. I can handle it."

"Because…I-I love you too." She muttered.

Nick let out a shout of laughter while a wild surge of energy thrummed through his body. She loved him. "Well hell. Don't sound so miserable about it sweetheart."

Her eyes shot golden daggers at him over her shoulder. "Well, I should feel miserable! Because then you turned into an-an," she sputtered and flung a hand up in the air, "asshole, and you ruin what could have been something beautiful and romantic." She hunched her shoulders, collapsing in on herself, and finished in a small, tight voice. "It made me feel like I did when I realized what my marriage was going to be like."

Shit. Nick closed his eyes and let his head fall back. "Oh no, baby, no." he groaned, "I never want to make you feel that way." He moved closer to her, crowding her with his bulk, and turned her around in his arms. "No, don't struggle." He held her loosely, easily, caging her against his chest with one arm wrapped around her back. He cupped his hand under her chin and forced her to meet his gaze. "I said Jake would be better for you because there are… things you don't know Morgan, things about me and my past. It's part of why you heard me say what I did and how Jake responded to it."

"So tell me what that is." Her eyes and voice pleaded with him. A few wisps of hair had caught on her cheek and he swept them behind her ear. He let his fingers linger, tips stroking and caressing. "Please." She whispered. "You say you love me, so if I'm not supposed to be upset about what I heard, then tell me what I need to know."

Nick let out a long shuddering breath and shook his head, hating the cowardice that ate him up inside. "I love you Morgan, but I-I just can't…not yet."

She pulled out of his arms and backed away. Trails of silvery tears streaked her pale cheeks. "I'm sorry Nick," she said in a shaky voice, "but I've lived a life of lies and secrets before. I won't do it again."

****

Nick stared at the empty spot where Morgan had stood, letting his eyes trace the imprint of her shoes until the image was implanted in his brain. His cowardice had cost him, no doubt. More than he ever thought it would. He sighed, wanting to run and chase her down again. To demand she accept him but let him keep the truth to himself.

"I've lived a life of lies and secrets before. I won't do it again." Being sucker punched in the gut would have been less unexpected, not to mention hurt a whole lot less.

He rubbed a fist against his eye, surprised to feel wetness coat his knuckles. Hell, he couldn't blame her. That existence wasn't fair to either of them, but most especially her. And to think everyone thought ex-cons were tough. Hah. Not when a woman was involved. Wearily he scrubbed a hand down his face, wondering how things had turned to shit so quickly.

A hand clamped down hard on his shoulder. Nick looked over to see Jakes concerned green eyes staring at him.

He rolled his eyes, "Get the pity off your face, Jake. I don't need it."

"Why the hell are you standing here?" Jake shoved him in the shoulder, "You need to go after her, Nick. Right now. Get off the fucking woe-is-me machine, grow some balls and tell her the truth goddamnit!" Jake treated him to another shove, this one harder than the last. "If you don't Nick,"—Jake leaned in until they were nose to nose— "you will lose that woman forever. And damned if she'll never trust another man."

"I don't want her to trust another man." He growled, and then winced at the selfishness of the statement.

"So quit letting a shitty label dictate your life." Jake said. "You know what you have to do, convict. Make a choice, either go after her and win her back, or just stand there, pissing into the wind and lose her forever."

His truck keys were in the house so Nick started in that direction, then remembered the blow Jake had taken. He cleared his throat and turned back to Jake. "About earlier," he said, "I'm, uh…sorry I hit you."

Jake huffed a laugh, then winced and gingerly poked at his jawbone, "Yeah, well, I was partway expecting it given the shit I was saying. Can't believe I'd forgotten how hard you hit though. Now"—he clapped Nick on the back in an 'all is forgiven' way— "goon, before you lose your woman. I don't want to even consider what being around you will be like if that happens, so do us both a favor and don't fuck this up."

Chapter 31

The cold clammy sickness in Nick's gut threatened to swallow his nerve. Gone was the calm, cool demeanor he was famous for, replaced by a monster known as desperation.

He loved her. She loved him. Damnit…those factors alone had to be enough. What the hell was being in love good for if it failed to solve this problem?

In the middle of a turn the steering wheel slipped loosely beneath his slick palms, forcing him to brace it with his knee while he wiped the sweat on his jeans. Several times his foot had risen off the gas pedal; slowing the huge truck down to almost a crawl until the engine faltered and almost died. But then her sweet voice would sound in his head saying the words he had wanted—craved—but never expected so soon.

I love you too.

His determination renewed, shoving aside the clawing sensation of impending doom. Morgan loved him. She had trusted him with her body, had trusted him to show her how making love should be, had trusted him not to hurt her. A woman like her did not express her love lightly. God knows he hoped he could convince her she hadn't made a mistake, that he was worthy of her love, no matter what he had done in the past. No matter what fucking label he had to live with.

Nick's booted foot pressed down on the accelerator

and the truck jerked, tires squealing as rubber gripped the pavement. The thick sheltering woods outside his windows once again became a greenish-brown blur as he guided the truck along the road toward her house.

She wasn't there when he banged on the door ten minutes later. To be sure she wasn't just avoiding him he picked the lock on the back door and let himself in. He walked through the kitchen and down the hallway, searching for any sign that she was home. Her bedroom was at the very end of the hall and he poked his head in the open door. A myriad of scents tickled his nostrils. The subtle clean smell of body lotion and another, more exotic perfumed smell—Cashmere Mist, he suddenly remembered her saying and couldn't stop from imagining her slathering those creams and perfumes all over her body after a hot bath. His eyes strayed to the rumpled bed and instantly his brain flash-backed, highlighting in bright lights the night he had worshipped her with his tongue, tasted her secret flesh and drank in her spicy sweetness. She had gifted him with her first orgasm.

While he had given her her first taste of pleasure.

An ache formed low in the pit of his belly. Nick breathed deeply in and out several times, but the ache stayed, clenched tight as a fist, reminding him of all he had to lose.

Damn.

Heading down the hallway he stopped at the only closed door. A quick twist of the knob and it fell open. The faint aroma of paint thinner hit him first, then the bright streams of daylight coming in the bare window showcased paintings in various stages of completion. They hung on the walls or sat on homemade easels around the room. Mostly landscape's with a few seascapes here and there.

He walked farther into the room, absorbing this inner sanctum of talent. A collection on one wall appeared to be devoted to wild animals and Nick found himself staring into the curious, yet wary eyes of a zebra, forever caught on the edge of flight.

One large painting in the corner caught his eye. It was covered by a white sheet. Curiosity peaked he went over and carefully lifted the protective sheet. Nick stared at the image of himself looking intense and arrogant, sitting on a dark horse riding down the middle of a street, the distant Montana Mountains creating a breathtaking backdrop. A grin broke out over his face, so wide and ridiculous that it strained the muscles in his jawbones. The harsh sensation of impending doom lessened as he stared in wonder at the meticulous painting and gazed into the blue inkiness of his own eyes, picturing her bent over the painting, carefully holding her paintbrush, stroking and blending the colors of his face and body until perfect. Her talent and love of her art was obvious and he couldn't help the sweep of pride that ran through him.

Using extra care he replaced the sheet over the canvas and left the room, quietly shutting the door behind him. He exited the same way he had entered, being sure to lock the door behind him, and then headed out across her field. When he reached the broken down fence separating her yard from the woods he hesitated as doubts assailed him once again, rolling in queasy circles around the pit of his belly. He could get back in his truck and go, she would never know he had been there searching for her. Never know he had seen the painting, never know any of it—his past…his shame…no, she would just think he had let her go. That her 'been there done that' reasoning had satisfied him and he had seen the light.

And, like Jake had said, she would be destroyed again, left thinking he didn't care about her, didn't love her like he said he did.

There was no way he could live with that.

Taking courage from her immortalized tribute to him Nick relaxed his mind, letting the tension flow out of his brain, down his veins to his fingertips and then out of his body, knowing exactly where he was going to find her.

****

The stream flowed lazily along. The glistening, clear water breaking over rocks and fallen limbs, tickling her toes with its wetly trailing fingers. The tears had long since dried on her cheeks, leaving her skin faintly itchy, but for some reason she refused to rinse her face in the gently flowing stream, somehow feeling that doing so would corrupt its clear beauty. So the tears had dried and now she itched. A fitting, yet annoying reminder of the choice she had given Nick-tell her everything, or let her go. Apparently letting her go had been the easier of the two.

She would have to move again. There was no way she could live here, exist here, while the years passed, chipping away at her heart and soul, knowing that Nick was only a walk-through-the-woods away, riding his horses, cleaning stalls, working shirtless in the hot summer heat…entertaining new women.

Telling them he loved them…

Fresh tears welled, ignored her attempts to blink

them away and overflowed down her cheeks, taking the last of the itchiness with them.

She sensed his approach before she heard him. Her skin tightened, tingled the way it did whenever he touched her, alerting her to his presence. That essence of raw power preceding him, sending out shockwaves that touched her hair, her skin, her body, before he even made himself known. A subtle prickling along her spine varied her breaths, making them shallow and uneven. Against her will other parts of her responded too, becoming soft, moist…and ready…

Damn him, she thought angrily. Her body was attuned to his now, just like an animal who senses their mate. He had put his mark on her body, her mind, and her soul. She should have been smarter than that; better able to prevent it from occurring, but the thrumming in her body wouldn't cease, not even when her mind replayed over his jerkiness earlier.

He had made his choice. She just had to convince herself of hers.

His heavy footfalls stopped right behind her, so close that his shadow, distorted by the sheltering canopy of trees, fell across her back and head. An exasperated sounding noise came from above her. "You're sitting next to a pile of rocks and leaves Morgan. Prime nesting material. Didn't I tell you to be careful of snakes?"

The muscles around her mouth shook. She laced her fingers together and squeezed, pressing her bones together. Determinedly she tightened her lips and kept her head down, watching the water twirl around her toes, numb to the coldness. "You came all the way out here to tell me that?" I will not cry. "Thanks for your concern, but I checked."

His sigh was long and loud., sounding as if it had traveled from very deep within him. "Damnit, don't be like that." His booted feet moved into her peripheral vision as he squatted down beside her, forearms braced on his knees, strong, dark hands hanging limply. She hoped he wouldn't touch her because if her did she didn't think she had the strength to remain remote. "I'm sorry about earlier Morgan, if I could take back what I said I would. Again, I apologize. It wasn't fair to you and it really wasn't even about you."

Morgan dipped her head until several thick locks of hair fell over her shoulder to block him from view. Her hair had always been a perfect hiding mechanism. "Quit playing with me Nick. You made your choice earlier."

"Damnit," one balled fist slapped against his thigh causing her to jump and flinch. He must have seen the movement because the next instant one hand was sweeping her hair away while the other cupped her jaw, his grip warm and firm, forcing her to meet his eyes. "Morgan…" His eyes were bright, liquid blue. He shook his head and looked at the stream, then closed his eyes. "I didn't choose anything over you earlier. I love you and noth—" He broke off and sighed, chest and shoulder muscles rising and falling with the motion. His eyes met hers again, invading and deeply searching. His mouth opened, then closed.

A long moment of silence reigned during which Morgan could actually see him struggling, could see his inner fight and the torment in his eyes as he stared at her. He was hurting, whatever this secret was it was hurting him, and she hated it. If it was this hard for him to get it out, then maybe it didn't really matter. They could work on whatever it was and maybe knowing that he loved her was enough.

"I'm an ex-convict, Morgan." His voice was dead. Flat. No emotion or inflection whatsoever. "I spent six years in prison for killing my father when I was seventeen. I murdered him, in cold blood."

Morgan choked on a breath, blood turning to ice in her veins. She tried to breathe, to suck in the necessary life-giving air but her throat was tight, strangling her. Blackness edged her vision. Panic…Dimly she was aware of Nick pounding on her back, speaking directly to her face. Murderer…oh God…

His hand clamped onto the nape of her neck. She gasped, a ruthless gust of air shoved itself down her throat and into her lungs, gasping, coughing, and choking she tried to scramble away from him, but his hand clamped hard around her upper arm, stopping her struggles.

Trapped next to him she froze, every muscle in her body gone stiff, wary. Her chest hurt, raw inside from her panic attack. Nick had killed-murdered, his own father? Oh…God help her. She was sitting here alone, miles from help, with a murderer. He had killed his father with the same hands that had touched her, caressed her everywhere, inside and out…and she had enjoyed it.

She had laid moaning and writhing under his touch, under hands that had killed. Her mind flashed back to Richard, focusing on his fists right after one of his beatings. He would stand over her, gloating while his knuckles shone wet and shiny, covered in her blood. Fresh and thick, it would run sluggishly over his hands and down his wrists. Had Nick stood over his father afterwards, bloodied and gloating while he watched him die?

A small, mouse-like noise escaped her tight throat and she tried once again to scramble away.

Unbreakable fingers tightened on her arm. "Please don't be afraid of me Morgan. I'm not like your husband. I'd cut off my own arm before hurting you. No matter what you're thinking right now, deep inside you know that the absolute truth."

She couldn't look at him. "I thought that of Richard…" her voice went whisper-soft, "and look how wrong my instincts were."

"Please don't say that, Morgan." His voice, usually so strong, bordering on arrogant, was weak with vulnerability and desperation. Shame. Something she would have never associated with a man like Nick Evanoff.

'I hated my father…had out differences…last straw…gambling debt…' His earlier words ran through her mind, and suddenly some of the fear left her, leaving her with a burning desire to understand. He had already told her a brief bit of his childhood. Maybe there was more, much more. Based on her own life experiences Morgan knew she had no room to judge him until she knew the truth.

She drew in a deep, shuddering breath and pulled her feet from the water, tucking them underneath her Indian fashion. His hand was still on her arm and she gave a little tug until, hesitantly and one by one, his fingers were removed. "I won't run away, but you have to make me understand Nick. Because right now all I can see is you covered with your father's blood and I can't—" she stopped, shaking her head miserably. "I can't merge that Nick with the one I know. The one I fell in love with."

Finally she looked at him. His handsome face looked haggard and strained, as if telling her his dirty little secret had sucked all of the arrogance out of him. All of his pride was gone. But his eyes, those beautiful, midnight blue eyes were what had upset her the most. They were staring at her with a hopeless desperation that she recognized all too well, having seen it plenty of times in the mirror, when no one but her had known of her own private hell. It was a lonely, bleak place to be. A darkness when everything else around you was bright and sunny. Looking into Nick's eyes she knew without a doubt that, like her, he had known a similar darkness and, also like her, had lived with it all these years.

It was this knowledge that kept her feet still, that kept her from lunging up and running back to her house where she would lock the door and pack her bags. People had judged her all through her marriage, Richard had fooled them with his cloak of saintly deeds and social graces. It had been she who had been sneered at and deemed the cause of their marriage problems. No one had given her the opportunity to explain...no one had wanted to listen.

She would not do that to Nick.

Morgan cleared her throat and nodded towards his arm. Those same arms that had held her so tenderly and made her feel so safe, but had also committed a brutal murder. She had caressed those rippling, bunching muscles, felt them flex and move beneath her fingers as he drove her towards ecstasy. Those same muscles had bulged ad flexed when dealing a death blow.

She swallowed tightly past the pain in her chest

and forced herself to focus on the here and now. "The chain tattoo...it symbolizes your time in prison, doesn't it?"

"Yes."

"Why didn't you tell me this before?"

He rubbed his eyes with his hands, and then dropped them to his sides. "I tried, damn it. But every time I started to I chickened out." His voice dropped to an agonized whisper, "All I could think about was losing you, and what you had already been through with your husband. I figured the last thing you needed was to know you were cozying up to an ex-con."

She could see his point, if he had told her before she had really gotten to know him, she most certainly would have run screaming in fear. Probably all the way back to Chicago where she would have turned back into a timid little mouse, hiding away from everyone and everything, never knowing the pleasure that could be found in a man's arms. But she also would have stayed safe, not winding up in the arms of a convicted murderer. A murderer who she had fallen in love with and who was now begging her for understanding.

"Please..." she whispered a little sickly, torn between the emotions warring in her head and her heart, "tell me what happened. Why you did it...Please, I need to understand why you would...why you would kill your own father."

Nick had gotten up and walked a few steps away, probably guessing that she needed some space. He always seemed to know what she needed even before she realized it. She sat still and watched him as he leaned against a tree and passed a shaky hand over his hair, then crossed his arms over his chest. The look he threw her was frantic, as if nothing mattered more than her believing him.

"My dad was not a dad to be proud of. The only good thing about him was his way with horses, which I happened to inherit." He flashed her a brief, very grim smile. "But he got fired from the stable he worked at as a trainer because he was caught drinking in one of the stalls. After that everything went even more downhill, he could never keep a job more than a month and he only got meaner and more belligerent. My mother worked two jobs trying to support us and I did my best to shelter Jake. Somehow, like our mother, he managed to stay sweet and did great in school. Straight 'A's all the way through."

"But then dad found a new pastime—besides beating the shit out of us I mean—and that was gambling." Morgan's heart began to pound, knocking against her ribcage as her sense of foreboding grew. "He loved to gamble, but each time he lost." Nick stopped and took a deep breath. Unconsciously Morgan began to hold hers. "Each time he lost, which was often, he would come home and knock me around. Sometimes he went after Jake even though Jake was a lot younger than me…and he always…" Nick paused, looking at her with eyes so filled with pain that Morgan had to stop herself from jumping up and going to him. "Always went after our mother. She was so beautiful and sweet, much like you." He gave her a soft, sad smile and Morgan felt he eyes grow wet.

"Oh Nick."

"He slashed her with kitchen knives, beat her with a blet buckle until she went blind in one eye…and yet somehow she stayed a sweet, loving wife and mother.

Always loving him and making excuses. For years and years he abused her, treated her like a walking pile of shit." Nick ran a hand down the tree trunk, tearing off pieces of bark as he went. "I could handle him coming after me, even as a kid I was pretty big, but when he went after our mother, I went off on him. Many times the whole house would be wrecked because of our fights. I can't count the number of times the police were called out to take him away, only to have one of his drinking buddies bail him out again and again." A muscle in his jaw bunched, throbbing just under the surface of his dark skin. "And the living hell that was our existence would start all over again. Our house was a rented trailer with paper-thin walls. Each time he got out of jail he would go after my mother first. I could hear him with her…in their room. The loud slaps, the sound of things breaking…her crying and begging him to stop…"

Morgan stared at him, horrified, unaware that she had taken several steps towards him. "Oh…Nick. I'm so—"

"Don't," he said quietly, "I need this to be out. I don't want anything else between us. No more misunderstandings. So please, don't say anything until I'm finished."

He waited until she nodded. "Each night I would hear him forcing her, raping her. And there wasn't a fucking thing I could do about it."

He stopped and took a big breath, turning away from her, but not before Morgan caught the glimpse of tears in his eyes. "Some people believe a man can't rape his own wife, that it's right and goes with being married…but they obviously haven't been in thee other room, listening to it…" His broad body tensed, then began to shake. A low, guttural groan filled the silent clearing and as Morgan watched, frozen sick with helplessness at the visions and memories his story conjured, Nick gripped the trunk of the tree with both hands and dropped his forehead against the rough bark.

This was not Nick the successful horseman; this was Nick the young kid who had had no way out of a desperate situation other than to kill his own father. He might have been punished and served his time, but he was still hurting, even after all these years. Morgan's brain jerked back to awareness and she closed the last remaining steps between them, throwing her arms around him. He jerked like she had poked him with an electric prod, his big body tensing for a few long moments, and then he turned in her embrace. She snuggled her face against him, breathing in his familiar scent and listening to his pounding heart.

After a long moment his arms went around her, locking her tightly against him. "Go on," her voice was muffled in his shirtfront and she angled her head slightly away from him, "tell me the rest…I'm not going anywhere."

His hand smoothed over her head, playing lightly with the long mahogany strands, apparently lost in thought. Morgan rested he cheek against his chest and just waited, giving him time to gather his thoughts.

"I love your hair," he said finally, stroking his fingers down it, "the first time I saw you, right here, you were sitting by the river with the moonlight highlighting your face and hair."

Morgan smiled, "And to think I thought I had found the perfect private spot."

"You did. I just happened to come with it." The weight of his chin landed on the top of her head. His beard stubble had grown so much that she could feel the prickles through the thickness of her hair, massaging her scalp as he spoke. "You looked like an angel, and right then I knew you were the woman I wanted." His voice lowered, growing deeper, huskier.

"I think that's when I fell in love with you, even though I didn't know it or recognize it at the time."

Tears burned at the back of her throat, choking off her voice and the response she knew he was waiting for.

So she showed him instead.

Sliding her palms up his chest to his shoulders she entangled her fingers around his neck and urged his head down to hers for a kiss. It was deep, sweet and infinitely tender. His lips moved against hers, coaxing and endlessly patient, while his tongue met and parried, dragging a soul deep response from her.

He had killed his father, been locked up in prison for it. Yet in a short amount of time, with only gentle touches, patience and kind words, he had driven away the nightmarish memories of her previous life.

No matter what, she loved him.

Chapter 32

Nick settled back against the tree and Morgan leaned into him, letting him take her weight against his chest. She didn't know what to do with her hands so she wrapped them loosely around his neck and rested her head just below his shoulder. His powerful body shuddered once and then he wrapped his arms tight around her waist.

Morgan stroked his neck, trying to soothe away the invisible beasts that plagued him.

"I don't want you afraid of me Morgan." His voice rumbled against the top of her head. "Not ever."

"You've shown me enough times that I don't have to be," she murmured. "The horses show me that I don't have to be."

"The rest may change your mind."

"I know what I feel Nick," she insisted, leaning back to look up at him.

"But I—"

"Shhh," she pressed her lips against his and after a moment's hesitation he was guiding her into a slow, searching kiss that left her feeling weak, boneless. "Just tell me, Nick. It can't be any worse than I'm already picturing in my mind."

He stared down at her, blue eyes hollow and tired, drilling into hers. Then he blew out a long breath and dropped his head back against the tree, rolling it back and forth. "It's damned ugly Morgan. I hate that you have to know, but I'm not going to keep it from you, no matter how much I want to." Morgan's heart constricted, doing a tight little 'thump, thump' against her chest. Nick's hands tensed on her back. Then he stroked up the length of her spine and slowly down again. He did this several times, almost as if he were trying to calm or prepare her the way he would a horse.

Morgan braced herself for whatever horrible words were going to come out of his mouth.

"Anyway," he began, "his drinking escalated and so did the fits of rage he would go into. We dreaded hearing him come through the door. Hell," he gave a short laugh, but Morgan found no trace of humor at all, "we hated seeing the clock hit noon because we knew he would be coming in, demanding that my mother fix his goddamned meal." Nick paused and took a deep breath. Morgan stroked his neck encouragingly, picturing his bully of a father stomping into the house and yelling for food.

"So," he continued, "in order to stay out of the house I got a job at a local convenience store when I was seventeen. I worked as many hours as I could, just to stay away from home. Then one night I came home early and everything was quiet. So quiet it was spooky. I was used to the TV blaring with dad parked in front of it, or hearing mom crying in the bedroom, or them shouting…but that night there was…nothing." His voice had deepened, becoming more forceful and determined. Morgan's skin prickled, her heart pounding in her chest. Dread, fear of what he would reveal filled her throat, stinging like battery acid. Like an animal sensing an impending storm she knew what was coming.

"Thank God Jake was spending that weekend at a friends. I don't know what he would have done…how it would have affected him…I—uh…I walked into the house, went to each room looking for someone…and when I opened the door to my parent's room I saw the end of my mother's shoe on the floor, peeking out from behind the door."

"Oh Nick," she whispered, burying her face against his neck, "I'm so sorry…so, so sorry."

Against her ear she heard his throat work, swallowing wetly, again and again.

"I still remember the long creaking sound that door made when I pushed it…Wider and wider it opened until I saw my father standing over my mother, holding a baseball bat."

His voice cracked and Morgan clutched him to her, gripping fistfuls of his shirt in her fingers. Pain for what he had gone through—then and now—rippled through her body, making her heart crack wide open and bleed for him. Tears gathered on her lower lids, hovering there until she blinked. Sniffling she pressed one wet cheek against his shirt.

"It was a long time ago sweetheart," he said while using his thumb to brush the tears off her other cheek.

She sniffled, "I know…But your mother sounded s-so, so s-sweet…" she squeaked. Unable to continue she pressed her face against his warm hand while the lump in her throat grew to the size of a baseball.

"Are you sure you want to hear the rest?"

She nodded and after a moment he sighed and cleared his throat. "Dad…he-uh…well, she was already dead. He had smashed her skull in…numerous times.

Blood…" a fine tremor shook his frame, "mom's blood…was everywhere. Even on him. I ran to a neighbor's house and called the police, but when they came dad had disappeared."

Morgan stared at him, horror-struck, picturing his mother as he had seen her—not just dead on the floor, but viciously bludgeoned, over and over again until nothing was left of the mother he had loved.

No wonder he had hated his father enough to kill him.

"Oh…Nick." She breathed. "I'm so sorry I made you relive this…I pushed you and pushed you for the truth but—" she stopped, the words trembling on her lips.

"Hush, Morgan. It's alright." He pressed his lips to the top of her head, "Like I said, it was a long time ago and you deserved to know. The rest…" He shrugged, waiting on her answer, she guessed.

"Please," she kissed the pulse dancing at the base of his throat, "finish it."

"Child services stepped in and sent Jake to live with our aunt. Since I was seventeen they weren't too concerned with me, but I spent a few months in some shitty group home, filled with anger and rebelling against everyone." His voice dropped lower, each word becoming more savage. "Then I learned that my father was out on bond! I couldn't believe it. What a fucking crock."

Morgan felt his hands clench into fists on her back, heard the deep shaky draw of breath in his chest and snuggled closer against him, petting and soothing him with her touch. "Go on," she whispered.

"Christ, Morgan…after what that bastard had done

they let him out on a five thousand dollar bond. So what else could I do? I went looking for him, filled with a rage so hot it practically leaked out of my pores, I knew all his hangouts, knew everywhere he would feel welcomed and forgiven, which was just about every bar or strip club within five blocks of our house."

In her minds eye Morgan saw him. A rough youth, big and handsome, on the verge of manhood but filled with such rage that he sought out his father in these dark, sleazy places…all for the sole purpose of revenge.

Morgan found it hard to connect that rough youth with the soft-hearted, successful man who was now holding her against him like a second skin.

His nose nuzzled the baby-fine hair at her temple. "Anyway…late one night I saw him coming out of the Starlight Lounge. The bastard was laughing and had his arm around one of the strippers. He was drunk of course, and he had the nerve to smile at me…I lost it." Nick spit out each word with biting clarity. "I saw red. Everything in my line of vision was red. I beat the hell out of him, picturing mom's bloodied face every time I landed a punch. Nothing could have stopped me. I remember the stripper screaming and I told her to shut up and get the fuck away. Dad was lying, actually half-sitting, against the wall where I'd left him…and there was a broken beer bottle on the ground…I gutted him with that beer bottle Morgan. And I left him there to die."

Her mind whirled with the visual of Nick gutting his father. Nausea rose, acrid and burning. She swallowed it down, not wanting him to see how much it bothered her. "You were hurting Nick. A hole had been carved into your heart. You didn't know what else to do."

"Hell, wish you had been there when I was sentenced. I could have used your support." His huffed laugh sounded more like a sob, "But you're right; I didn't know what else to do. All I knew was that this murderer who was my father had taken my mother away from me, and was now laughing and carrying on with his life like it had never happened." His big body tensed beneath her stroking palms. "Like she never existed."

"It's obvious you loved her very much." Morgan said softly. "I wish I could have known her."

He swept his hands through her hair, lifting it until it veiled out behind her and then letting it drift through his fingers like fine silk. "Yeah, mom would have liked you. You two would have had a lot in common."

He didn't say abusive husbands, but he didn't have to. Morgan knew exactly what he meant.

"When the police found me later that night I was sitting on the front steps of our house, waiting. I didn't fight. I didn't lie and say I hadn't done it. I was glad I had done it because there was no way that bastard deserved to live. I was eighteen and I spent six years in that hellhole prison. It could have been much longer, but luckily the police knew our family history and how violent dad had always been. There were also neighbor's testimonies on my behalf. The judge felt that me witnessing my mother's murder was partly punishment enough. The six years was just to make sure I would never forget what prison was like, and hopefully never go back."

"And you haven't Nick." Morgan's heart ached for him, for the childhood he had lost. For the birthdays and Christmases he had spent in prison. "You learned from it and became a good man, exactly as the judge meant you to. Exactly like I know your mother would have wanted you to."

Nick's brittle laugh, short and sharp, surprised her. "The hell of it is is that if the police had done their jobs each and every time we called them, then maybe, just fucking maybe, my mother would still be here to see the man I became."

She looked up at him, at his dark head resting against the trunk of the tree. Her eyes traced the strong line of his neck up to his powerful jawline. Everything about him was strong, powerful…beautiful. She pictured him locked behind bars, imprisoned for years, tried and convicted for committing an act of revenge against his mother's killer.

His mother's fate could have easily been hers too.

"I still love you, Nick."

He flinched against her, and his voice was flat when he spoke. "Think about it Morgan. I'm a killer, an ex-con. That label never goes away."

"Are you trying to convince me not to love you? Because it's not working." She pressed a kiss to the underside of his jaw. "You're no killer, and I don't care about labels."

"I'm bad for you," he stated firmly, gazing up at the canopy of trees, "bad for your future."

Morgan let out an exasperated sigh and brought his hand up to her scarred cheek, pressing his palm against it. "If Richard hadn't been killed then this—" she pressed his palm firmly against her deformed skin, "and worse, would have been my future. So you're not scaring me. I've had bad, Nick. I've had the devil himself. I know what bad is…and you're not it." She turned her head and pressed her lips against his palm. "I love you. I want you. You and only you."

He brushed his hand through the hair at her temple and urged her head up. "You're crazy," he said gently, and then he smiled at her, a blindingly beautiful, very rare smile. "And I'll spend the rest of my life showing you how much I love you."

****

The next morning Morgan awoke in Nick's big bed, alone. She stretched, wincing as her sore muscles protested. He had made love to her frantically at first, and then more tenderly as the night wore on, not stopping until early morning. It had been wonderful, and she now knew what being thoroughly well-loved felt like.

A strange noise from the foot of the bed drew her attention and she shimmied across the sheets to hang her head over the edge. A bouquet of wildflowers and a brown cardboard box, loosely closed, sat on the floor. Frowning Morgan reached out and flipped up the lid flaps. A tiny black and white kitten peeked up at her, huge greenish yellow eyes blinking sleepily. A purely un-adult-like jolt of giddiness shot through her, making the pit of her stomach quiver with excitement.

Richard, not wanting to deal with fur and messes, had never let her have a pet. Morgan knew the kitten must have come from Boo's litter and that Nick had picked it out for her. A vision of the tiny kitten perched securely in Nick's big hand had her heart turning over and over in her chest.

The kitten mewled again and smiling Morgan reached into the box, picked it up and kissed its nose.

304

Its rumbling motor started up immediately, sounding too loud for its little body.

"Well hello to you too, sweetie." Cuddling the kitten next to her Morgan reached down on the floor again and picked up the flowers. A note was attached to the stems.

'The flowers are from me, picked by hand. I couldn't let Jake keep showing me up when it comes to romance. I hope you like the kitten; her siblings kept beating her up. I figured you had better take care of her.

I love you sweetheart…Nick.'

Smiling through tears and clutching the kitten to her chest Morgan read the note over and over again, wondering what she had finally done right to deserve so much.

Chapter 33

Two years later…

Morgan reined her snow-white mare, Majestad, to a halt near the edge of the creek and glanced around the copse, loving it just as much now as when she first discovered it. The moon was full and high overhead, making the water twinkle like diamonds. She smiled, breathing deeply of the brisk night air, hardly believing that two short years ago she had been a broken shell of a woman, licking her wounds and seeking nothing but solitude in the vastness of Montana. Sure she still had nightmares and sometimes jumped at loud noises, but Nick's patience—in the bedroom and out—had gradually acted as a balm to her frazzled nerves. Every single day he touched her, kissed her, held her in his arms or made her laugh—whatever it took to make sure she knew how cherished she was. Every morning she woke up feeling cherished, the languor of each night with Nick still thrumming lazily in her veins.

So now, when her life with Richard would reenact itself in her dreams she had Nick to turn to, and nothing drove away the nightmares better than Nick's warm body against her, his strong arms wrapped around her, and his hands stroking her panic away.

It was Christmas Eve and the full-blooded Andalusian mare had been her gift from him, along with a specially made saddle designed to cushion her leg and hip, thereby taking the strain off her joints. Morgan grinned and stretched in the saddle, testing her leg. A warm flush climbed from her neck to her cheeks as she remembered how she had told him she would thank him later.

Majestad shifted restlessly beneath her, her delicate ears flicking back and forth, following the sounds of the illusive nightlife. The mare was one of the few horses Nick had purchased that ad not had a horrific life and had not been a rescue. She had been imported from Spain to a ranch out in California and he had found her on the ranch's website. In order not to arouse her suspicion Nick had had Jake fly out in his stead to see the mare in person. Two weeks later the mare was delivered to Evanoff Farm, all unbeknownst to Morgan.

Until today.

"It's later."

Morgan gasped and glanced wide-eyed over her shoulder. Nick sat bareback astride Lucky under the low limb of a tree, his face concealed by the shadows, but with his large, dark body highlighted by touches of moonlight. His eyes glittered, the weight of his gaze falling on her and she shivered, reacting to the pure, unadulterated magnetism of him. Long, sinewy muscles, showcased in light and shadow, rippled as he guided the horse slightly closer.

A small, involuntary sound of need tore from her throat. She knew firsthand what that body felt like—hard steel and imposing power, and the magic it could create within her…she grew wet just thinking about it. The gelding snorted, nostrils flaring, arching his thick neck and shaking his long white mane in a breathtaking display of supremacy. The horse had recovered remarkably well in the couple of years Nick had had him, but was still scarred and only allowed Nick to handle him. Majestad answered the gelding's snort, nickering low in her throat and Morgan tightened her hands on the leather reins, turning the mare to face them.

She raised a brow at Nick. "Your horse is scaring my mare."

Nick snorted, sounding almost like the gelding. Amusement tinged his voice. "Trust me, sweetheart, that's not fear she's showing him, gelding he may be."

He rode closer, muscles shifting with the movement of his horse, becoming larger and more commanding the nearer he got, until he was knee to knee with her. Morgan's heart thudded in her throat as her gaze locked with his. His hot blue eyes flared brighter. In a sudden move he palmed the back of her head, tangling his fingers roughly through her long silky hair and urging her face up to his.

She didn't even pretend to resist when he leaned down and pressed a hard kiss on her moist lips.

"It's later," he whispered again. He trailed his mouth down the side of her jaw, her neck, licking and nibbling.

Her breath hissed out of her. "Oh God, Nick…what are you doing to me?" Her eyes closed, a soft moan escaping as she tilted her head to the side to give him better access.

"You remember what you told me you would be doing to me later?"

"Hmmm…" It was so hard to think when he touched her like this. His teeth nipped her earlobe. She shuddered, goosebumps springing to life up and down her arms. "Maybe," she gasped.

"Maybe huh?" He sucked her neck hard, almost to the point of pain, making her squeal with a mix of surprise and pleasure, then released the abused flesh to lightly lick and soothe. "I think that's a lie. Tell me again what you want to do to me," he persisted. "Tell me and then show me."

He grasped her small chin, rubbing her pouty lower lip with his thumb, knowing she still struggled with shyness and uncertainty at times. Heavy-lidded gold eyes gazed up at him, passion clouding their beautiful depths. In two years she still hadn't figured out that he wasn't good enough for her, but hey, he'd decided long ago not to fight the issue. All he could figure was that somewhere along the way of life he must have done something really good, and his reward was sitting right here in front of him.

Never had he felt more complete. His woman.

Morgan smiled, Cheshire cat-like and rubbed her hand up his thigh, sliding her small fingers between the horse and his leg, almost reaching the point where his cock nestled, hard and aching. Then, while giving him a smile of pure bullshit innocence, her fingers traveled back down, teasing and burning him through his jeans.

He gritted his teeth while his cock swelled even more.

"I think…" she said in a husky, seductive drawl, "I think that we need to continue this off of the horses."

He grabbed her hand and placed it firmly over his groin, cupping his hand over her fingers so she couldn't pull away. "Baby, I still have a lot to teach you if you think we can't continue right here." He smiled into her huge, now somewhat apprehensive eyes, knowing if he pressed for it she would willingly allow a little more…kink into their loveplay. "But not tonight."

Reaching past her he took hold of her reins and turned Lucky, leading her to a grove of trees about fifty feet from the stream. He dismounted; ground-tied the gelding and came around to her. Morgan leaned down to him, long hair falling forward like a cloak, and wrapped her arms around his neck. He grasped her around the waist, easily lifting her off Majestad. A light slap sent the mare off to graze near the gelding.

"He won't hurt her?" Morgan's worried gaze followed her beautiful dainty mare.

Nick shifted her in his arms, lifting her higher against his chest as he walked towards the secluding cluster of trees. "No, sweetheart. Lucky's a pussycat when it comes to females, and besides, I think your mare's more than capable of handling him." He ducked his head, laughingly avoiding her swatting hand.

"My Majestad is innocent," she proclaimed.

Nick grinned down at her, "Yeah, about as innocent as you are."

Arms full of soft warm woman, Nick walked deeper into the trees, confidently following a leaf strewn trail barely discernable in the darkness. Morgan snuggled her head under his chin, planting light nibbling kisses on his throat. Nick groaned and shifted her more comfortably against him, each step rubbing his raging hard-on against the stiff fabric of his jeans. Finally he saw the mammoth-sized tree that had inspired him over six months ago and gestured with his chin for her to look over her shoulder. "Look."

Morgan turned and her mouth dropped open in

stunned awe. Nestled and hidden amongst several large trees was a small cottage that could have been lifted straight out of Lord of the Rings. Made of thick redwood and grey stone, the tiny structure boasted a Spanish style arched doorway and shiny multi-paned windows. A black wrought-iron bird bath stood off to the side and across from it was a small, two-person covered gazebo.

Nick kissed her temple, then whispered, "Merry Christmas, sweetheart. Again."

"Oh…Nick…" she breathed. "It's, it's…sooo beautiful!"

Everywhere she looked she found special little touches; a deer feeder at the edge of the wood line, baskets filed with trailing vines hanging from the gazebo, a stone bench situated near the gentle creek. Wonderingly she looked at Nick. "I've been here before, I know I have, and this—" she made an all encompassing gesture with her hand, "none of this was here. I know it!"

Nick didn't answer, just carried her over to the gazebo where he sat down with her still snuggled in his arms.

"Nick?"

He avoided her gaze until she cupped his beard roughened jaw and forced him to look at her. She stroked, petting him gently. He seemed uncertain, embarrassed even, and it unnerved her a little. "When…Why did you do all this?"

He coughed a little and cleared his throat, "Because I love you." It was said almost helplessly. "Because you mean everything to me and I didn't want you to regret ant of it."

"Regret any of what?"

He stroked her hair and they both watched as the satiny mass slid smoothly along his calloused fingertips. "Being here...with me. I know how much you loved your cottage and that you hated giving it up, even though you didn't show it."

"I loved it yes, but not more than I love you. And it needed so much work." She rubbed her fingers along his shadowed jawline, still unable to believe he had done this for her. "I wanted to be with you, Nick, here on the farm, more than I wanted to fix up a lonely house."

She wrapped her arms around his neck and lifted her face. His mouth met hers, tongues tangling in a deep, slow kiss filled with sensual promise.

He was the first to pull away and, panting slightly said, "Enough of that, let me finish."

She nodded encouragingly and relaxed in his lap.

His chest rose and fell on a deep breath. "So I thought, what could I do for this beautiful woman who gave up her solitude and home just to be with me? And then the answer came, just like that!" He snapped his fingers, and then grew serious again. "I would give it back to you. So I built the cottage," he waved his hand towards it, "just big enough for you, so you could come here when you needed privacy or just to get away." He paused and even in the darkness Morgan could see a flush deepening across his high cheekbones. "There's uh...books. Romances, horror...just like you like. And uh...of course painting material...canvases, brushes, tarps, everything and more that you—umph!"

Morgan slammed her lips over his, shoving her tongue into his mouth and wildly kissing him until they were both breathless, bodies heaving with the exertion of their kiss. Beneath her greedy, roaming fingers his back and shoulder muscles clenched like iron. Warmth infused her body, seeping into her pores as she strained to get nearer to him, almost climbing his body in her need. His erection pressed hard against her, insistently prodding her hip through her thin riding jeans.

Nick, growling low in his throat for her to hold on to his neck, slid an arm beneath her legs and stood up, carrying her quickly across the small clearing to the door of the cottage.

Keeping her body against him with only one arm he shoved the door open. Morgan had a brief glimpse of a snug interior before he violently kicked the door shut, blocking out the bright moonlight and securing them inside. Their ragged breathing was loud in the silent little house.

He loosened his hold on her and with agonizing slowness she slid down his body, biting her lip when she felt his obvious arousal pressing hard against her belly. Her stomach fluttered in response and when her feet touched the floor she took two steps back.

He followed, prowling after her, muscular rms hanging loosely by his sides. "Like I said earlier," he paused and a quick grin lit his dark features. "It's later."

Chapter 34

Morgan swallowed, backing away as he stalked her. His muscles flexed with pantherish grace, rippling with each deliberate move he made. He smiled and his teeth flashed white in the dim room, a big, hungry male intent on her as his prey. White hot anticipation rose up. Her heart pounded, racing triple time in her chest. She was so soaked between her thighs she could feel the moisture seeping through the thin material of her jeans. Her nipples were tight pinpoints of pain and the only thing that would bring relief was his mouth on them, tugging, sucking, licking...biting.

She dragged in a shuddering breath. One more step and she backed up against something soft. Startled she yelped, lost her balance and fell backwards onto the futon.

She felt Nick standing over her and opened her eyes. Dark, heavy-lidded pools of lust regarded her from way above. A strangled moan caught in her throat as he came down on her slowly, letting his heavy body crush her into the yielding mattress. His legs situated themselves between hers; his cock nestled snugly against her core. She trembled, arched against him and ran her fingers along his back, pulling his shirt up as she went. Nick growled low in his throat and kissed her neck, her shoulder, nibbling his way across her collarbones. Her fingers dug into the thick muscles of his shoulders. Wave after wave of tension consumed her, roiling in painful knots low in her belly. She whimpered, shifting restlessly beneath him.

"I take it this means you like my gift?" Nick asked, nuzzling the sensitive area below her ear.

"Nick...s-stop teasing me!" She clutched the back of his head, shuddering as his hands insinuated themselves between their bodies and moved up the insides of her thighs, stopping just short of where she ached to have him. "I need you," she gasped, raising her hips against him. "Now."

Nick cursed, raising his upper body slightly off of hers and yanking his shirt off. Morgan sighed in delighted pleasure as two-hundred and forty pounds of pure male muscle came back down on her and began working open the buttons on her cotton shirt.

"Fuck this," he growled, and then with one tug he ripped her shirt open. Buttons popped and flew, landing with little pinging sounds on the hardwood floor.

"Nick!" Morgan squealed in outrage, grabbing at his hands. "What am I supposed to wear home?"

He eluded her flailing hands and, grinning said, "My shirt, what else?"

Her surprise and outrage quickly changed to stunned pleasure as he caught both her wrists in one hand and with the other shoved her white riding bra up to her throat. His hot, wet mouth latched onto a pouting, throbbing nipple. His tongue flicked her rigid flesh, rhythmically pressing her nipple up against the roof of his mouth. Each strong tug sent an answering hunger straight to her clenching womb.

"This is the way I like you," he muttered, his breath rushing past her damp nipple, "hair splayed out like a dark cloak…God…you're so soft, velvety…and so sweet. I could spend days here just licking you." He released his grip on her wrist and resumed exploring the turgid peak with just the tip of his tongue, caressing round and round, then licking up like an ice-cream cone.

"Really? All day?" Morgan giggled lightly, running her hands up the middle of his back and into his hair. "Then Sultan would kick the barn down because you never came to feed him."

"Jake would handle things." He grinned wickedly at her, "Now lose the bra."

He waited while she wiggled and found the back clasp, then took the bra from her and threw it on the floor. Still inherently shy Morgan resisted the urge to cover her exposed breasts and lay back against the comforter. She blushed, staring up into Nick's gleaming dark eyes as his gaze ran hungrily over her breasts. He shifted his body to the side. Nimble fingers went to work on her jeans, opening them and shoving them down her ankles. Morgan helped by bending her knees up so he could yank her boots off and then kicked her jeans the rest of the way off. Her plain cotton panties went with them. Nick groaned, leaning down to kiss her quivering belly. His fingers stroked down her stomach, past her belly button to the narrow line of her dark pubic hair. "You're so beautiful, Morgan. And you're mine." His lips traveled over her skin, his blazing blue eyes met hers across the length of her belly. "Spread your hair out like a fan and put your arms over your head. Grab the headboard," he ordered. "And don't let go."

Slowly she complied, reaching up behind her and

trailing her hair across the bed, then wrapping her fingers around the smooth wooden bars of the futon's headboard. The position arched her back, yet pressed her buttocks into the mattress. Nick nudged her thighs apart and moved into position between them, then sat back on his heels, eyes gleaming hot, burning her naked skin. Morgan closed her eyes, but the image of him sitting above her, enjoying her helpless nudity still burned behind her eyelids. Her fingers clenched reflexively on the headboard.

In a deep, silky voice he said, "Don't move…and don't let go." His fingers slid past the silky hair into the wet folds between, probing, rubbing…creating sinful magic deep in her core. Each caress winding her body higher, tighter. A choked sob escaped her and he shushed her. "Relax…just feel."

Slowly and gently his fingers probed, first one deep inside, stretching her, then another. She clenched around him, muscles tightening against the invasion. Slowly he withdrew, easing his fingers from the tight grip of her tiny, clasping muscles. Using the tip of one soaked finger he stroked around her distended clitoris. Morgan whimpered and bit her lip, fighting each relentless sensation as again and again he stroked, making her cry and writhe against him. Twisting his hand he eased his thumb inside of her while keeping up the agonizing rhythm, letting her get close and then backing off.

She sobbed in frustration, sweating and arching her hips against him as grinding, helpless pleasure surged in her body, only to slowly fade away. Morgan clutched his sweat slicked biceps, spreading her thighs wider in blatant invitation. "Nick…please."

"Not yet, sweetheart." He leaned over her again and licked a path up her sternum and over the plump underside of her breast. His lips clamped onto a stiff little nipple, pulling hard, relentlessly, making her scream softly as each tug wound a heavier response between her thighs. She bucked against him, throwing her head back onto the cushion as her body wept, dampening the comforter beneath her hips.

"Please, Nick. I'm so ready." The plea was whisper soft. Using her ankles around his hips as leverage she lifted herself to him, wiggled her ass in a way she knew made him crazy and was rewarded with his hissing curse.

"Jesus, baby. You're driving me insane."

Nick jerked himself away from her and off the futon. Moonlight from the window caught his bronzed face, shadowing the rough planes and tight lines, making him look savage and dangerous in the dim light as he yanked with short, vicious tugs at the buttons and buckles on his clothes.

Morgan stretched and sighed, noting the way his gaze followed her deliberately sensuous, slithering motion. She smiled at him—her dark warrior—ready to conquer. The heavy erection he was unveiling a formidable weapon. Muscles in his chest and arms bunched and tightened, the thick chain tattoos winding down each bicep flexing with every move. Even though Morgan knew he would never hurt one hair on her head she couldn't help the flutter of feminine anxiety that shook her.

Nick must have noticed because he paused, looking at her. "Ok?"

She nodded, relaxing again and holding her arms

out to him as he stepped between her legs, spreading her wide and locking her ankles around his lean hips. Braced on his hands above her he said, "Nuh-uh baby," and shook his head slowly. "Put your hands back where they were." He waited while she did as he said, then took his cock in his hand, fisting it and stroking up and down, watching her with narrowed eyes.

Using his hand he guided the head of his cock and pressed firmly against her, running the thick shaft up and down her labia, circling her clit with the broad head until she was thrashing and whimpering, mindless with a need that only he could fulfill.

Positioning himself he pressed into her, only an inch or so, and Morgan felt her body grip him, pulling at his cock with greedy muscles. His jaw was clenched; tendons in his neck standing out as he slowly pulled himself out. She whimpered, planting her heels against the small of his back to try and stop his retreat. Nick cursed and kissed her roughly, and forged back in. Demanding entrance with his body, thrusting and retreating, using his rigid cock to open her tight little sheath. He licked his thumb and found her clit, rubbing hard against the stiff flesh. Her hips jerked upwards and she cried out, taking his cock deeper. She felt her wetness coat him, slickening both him and her sheath, easing his movements while he continued the torment.

"That's it, baby. Take it. Come for me…" One more hard rub and she did, exploding, screaming out as he surged heavily into her clenching body, all the way until he hit the entrance to her womb and could go no further. She felt his balls slap against her ass.

Nick rested against her, catching his breath, face shoved into the side of her neck. He inhaled, nostrils filling with the scent of sweat, sex, and her natural delicate musk. He could feel the blood pumping heavily in the veins of her throat and began to move, deep and thick within her, dragging his hard length almost all the way out, only to forge steadily back in. Thrust and retreat, his cock plunged again and again. Faster, harder, deeper…He heard her breathless cries, watched as the force of his thrusting moved her back and forth on the futon, trying to counter the power behind his slow purposeful thrusts.

His orgasm bore down on him, crashing into his balls and jerking through his penis. He slammed into her—once, twice, three times, shouting hoarsely— mindlessly, shooting off like a firecracker.

Somehow above the ringing in his ears Nick was aware of Morgan beneath him, shuddering and clutching him with her arms and legs, soothing him with her fingers as tears trailed wetly down her cheeks.

Breathing like a thoroughbred that had just run the derby, he cursed beneath his breath. "I'm sorry, sweetheart." He tunneled his hands into her sweat-soaked hair and pressed his damp forehead to hers. "I meant for tonight to be slow. Gentle." He pressed a soft kiss to her lips, then rubbed the tip of her nose with his. "A Christmas special."

She smiled, softly stroking his stubble-roughened cheek. "Nick," she paused, and her eyes darkened. Her mouth opened and closed. Nick felt her chest rise on a deep breath, as if she were gathering courage.

Frowning, Nick prodded her, "What sweetheart? Did I hurt you?" Alarmed he braced himself and pushed off of her, cursing himself for not being more considerate and slow. Damnit, he could have—

"No!" Frantic hands grabbed him, cutting across his self-accusations and hugging him back down. "No. You didn't hurt me."

"Then what baby? End the suspense." He grinned at her, "You're kinda scaring me."

Her swallow was audible in the quiet room. Nick stroked her hair back from her face and waited, sensing that this was something big. Just...what the hell was it?

"I was going to say...that is..." her mouth twisted and a bright shimmer of tears made her eyes glow. "I wanted to say that...that...the only thing that would make this Christmas more special, was if you..."

He cupped her face, holding her eyes with his and whispered, "Was if what Morgan?"

"If you...if you would be my...h-husband."

His eyes widened and what felt like a ridiculously huge grin took charge of his face.

"Sweetheart," he said slowly, pressing his lips feather-light to hers, "you know just what to say to a man."

A word about the author...

I was born in Germany but live in the US. My mother and grandparents raised me and I had a lovely childhood of art, riding and showing horses, caring for all kinds of animals, writing books, poetry and short stories, reading and trips to the library and museums. My mother was my best friend and encouraged all of my many creative endeavors. I now try to live my life with a focus on honoring her memory and how she raised me.

Thank you for purchasing
this publication of The Wild Rose Press, Inc.

For questions or more information
contact us at
info@thewildrosepress.com.

The Wild Rose Press, Inc.
www.thewildrosepress.com